YOU
BELONG
HERE NOW

YOU BELONG HERE NOW

A Novel

Dianna Rostad

wm

WILLIAM MORROW

An Imprint of HarperCollins*Publishers*

P.S.™ is a trademark of HarperCollins Publishers.

HarperCollins books may be purchased for educational, business, or sales promotional use. For information, please email the Special Markets Department at SPsales@harpercollins.com.

FIRST EDITION

Designed by Diahann Sturge

Dedication illustration © ONYXprj / Shutterstock, Inc.
Chapter opener illustration © nutriaaa / Shutterstock, Inc.

Library of Congress Cataloging-in-Publication Data has been applied for.

ISBN 978-0-06-302789-3

21 22 23 24 25   LSC   10 9 8 7 6 5 4 3 2 1

For Jessica:
A brave girl
with more grit and integrity
than could fill these pages
1988–2018

I am only a fox to you like a hundred thousand foxes. But if you *tame* me, we will need one another. You will be unique in the world to me. I will be unique in the world to you . . .

—Antoine de Saint-Exupéry, *The Little Prince*

AUTHOR'S NOTE

FROM 1853 THROUGH THE EARLY 1900S, THE CHILDREN'S AID SOCIety in New York rescued over 120,000 orphans living on the city streets in the aftermath of war, Spanish flu, and immigration. The orphan train carried them out to the rich soils of farms and ranches. Lucky ones found hope in kind families, and some were callously taken on as young laborers. While fiction, the three young people you will meet here are meant to stand for the many lives too often unrecorded and unknown to history.

YOU
BELONG
HERE NOW

CHAPTER 1

NARA SEARCHED THE TRAIN STATION, PISSED AND WORN OUT. HER boots stopped at the edge of the wooden platform. A person could sit on a suitcase and see from one side of this valley to the other. To fend off the morning sun, she put a hand to her brow. She didn't have to walk the scrub, for not a soul stirred out there. Nara walked in front of a board the county kept for postings, people wanting this or that. An indifferent wind usually tossed them to the grass, so that flapping paper sure caught her eye.

WANTED: HOMES FOR ORPHAN CHILDREN
BULL MOUNTAIN, MONTANA—Saturday April 29, 1925

These children are of various ages, having been thrown friendless upon the world. They are well disciplined and come from various orphanages. Persons taking these children must be recommended by the local committee and treat the children in every way as a member of the family, sending them to school, church, and clothing them. The following well-known citizens have agreed to act as a local committee to aid the Society:

ELLA CONNELLY and JUDY STEVENSON

The name Ella Connelly jumped out like a foot-long grass-hopper.

"Of all the damn people." Nara ripped the post off the board.

Even if that reckless woman weren't the adoption coordinator, children aren't workin' animals. Not that Nara knew much about kids, for she never wanted them herself. The only thing she could raise up had hooves. She tossed the paper into swaying blades of grass where it would dissolve in the rain, then leaned against the door of the telegraph office. Papa's deep, barking voice echoed from inside.

As the telegrapher, Mary saw everyone coming or going, so if you wanted to know what happened anywhere in Montana, or maybe you just lost a white feather in a blizzard, Mary was your gal. But even she couldn't conjure up a new foreman in all this emptiness.

When Nara had marched that louse off their ranch with a boot to his butt, she had no idea Papa would be so ticked. He hustled her down to the train station to search for anyone loitering or desperate for a job. But you have to want this life like no other.

Nara huffed, and dunked her cold hands into the pockets of her dungarees. As she stood there, she imagined cattle wandering off their range through holes in the fence. "Waste of a day," she grumbled, itching to get back to work.

The door to the office squeaked open and Papa stormed by. Gray whiskers on his upper lip bristled. "Last time I trust you to run things while I'm gone."

"What are you gonna do when you're too old to move? I'm all you've got."

She followed him to their wagon, and they rode home in silence. The wind hissed past her ears. For days she'd been running their operation on her own. To punish her for firing the foreman, Papa had instructed their only other ranch hand to take a few days off, letting Nara do all the work. Each night at dinner, she did her best to look fresh and spry, though she was beat. He'd lower his paper on occasion, squint at her to observe the effect of his "lesson," but she'd just smile at him. He'd grunt in return and that paper would go back up around his stubborn head.

The wagon rolled into their ranch yard, sending the chickens scattering, and before Papa could stop the horses, she jumped down. Her boots dug into the ground as she stalked to the stalls to rig up her bucky board cart. She'd just as soon handle prickly wire and slivery pine posts than follow him inside for breakfast and more of his gripe. She yanked bridles and such off the wall and chucked them in the cart.

Her mare waited in its stall, snorting and stamping its feet, wondering if they were gonna get to work. "Hey, girl." Nara laid her head on its withers, breathing in that grassy horse tang, more familiar than her own smell. "We've got work to do." The mare's muzzle tickled her empty hand looking for its regular carrot or apple. "I'll make it up to you tomorrow."

She walked her mare out of the stable and noticed Mama had placed a Stanley bottle and pail of food in the horse cart. Her stomach growled seeing the big helping of last night's pie in the pail. Nara turned and waved to the shadow in the kitchen window of their ranch house.

NARA SPENT THE rest of the day on the range, her fingers numb from cutting and pulling wire. But her insides hadn't worked out the resentment, so she drove her cart, bumping over cow trails stomped to powdery earth from the years her family had raised cattle on the scrubby land.

The sun lay low in the western sky, using its late-afternoon shadows to play tricks on her eyes as she searched the boundaries of their land for more breaks. "Whoa!"

Nara's heart clenched. Her face twisted in misery for the gruesome sight before her.

A tiny wild horse struggled with all its might to free itself from the barbed-wire fence. Every time the filly tried to break away, that devil's rope would clutch her silvery blue coat like it could pull it clean off her bones. Blood dripped from its bitty hooves and darkened the thirsty earth.

Nara searched the horizon for the band of wild mustangs that left their youngest to the cruelty of this fence. It seemed a shame, for the foal was a rare blue roan. The grass around the fence had been stomped and chewed to the ground surrounding the little filly. The band had lingered a little while before taking off. Nara jumped down from her cart and placed one hand on her rifle pack, then hung her head. She imagined the mama horse stood with her newborn until that last moment when the swishing tails and flying manes of her brethren began to disappear into the hills. Only then would she have abandoned her own. Self-preservation is a strong instinct.

A shot echoed in the valley, and a bullet grazed the metal fence with a spark. The little mustang spooked and twisted with violence to free itself from the barbed wire.

"Ivar! Don't you dare!" Nara hollered.

Ivar pointed the barrel of his rifle to the sky and nudged up his hat, shaking his head as if she were a few eggs shy of a basket. With one keen eye on her callous neighbor, she rummaged around in the back of her cart for nippers, glad she'd been out mending posts. Cutting an animal away from a fence with just a Buck knife was a bloody mess. She jogged over rough ground to protect the mustang from the next bullet.

"Nara, what're you gonna do? The band's moved on."

Of the many times she'd wrestled one of her calves from the devil's rope, she'd always come away with a bruise or two. She stepped toward the mustang. "Shh . . . I'm not gonna hurt you."

Its ears shot back in a show of strength, a velvety muzzle let out a high-pitched cry for its mama, tired little hooves stamped the ground. Blood matted its silky new coat. This little thing couldn't be more than a month old.

"I know you've got spirit, girl. You don't have to prove anything to me."

Ivar cocked his rifle from over the fence. "Let me shoot it. That mustang's gonna kick the crap outta you."

"Ivar Magnusson, you shoot this little filly and you'll ride outta here with more holes in your butt than an anthill!"

Nara moved swiftly to pin the foal against the fence, but that wild horse wouldn't be still. Bucking its all, the mustang swung its head around and popped Nara in the face, knocking her hat to the ground. "Shitfires," she hissed, keeping ahold.

Ivar kept his rifle trained for the moment she couldn't manage the mustang anymore, but quitting wasn't her way. She trapped the horse with her shoulder. The nippers clenched the first barb so close to the foal's skin, she gritted her teeth for the pain she'd inflict. The metal snapped, freeing the foal's back half.

The horse bucked around and knocked Nara on her hind end. The second barb pulled on its tender skin, flesh bowing out.

She jumped up. "Damn you, Ivar! Are you gonna just sit there?"

With all her weight, she trapped the bloody foal against the fence before it ripped off half its hide. Nara's stomach tightened as she strained to get the nippers around the second barb. Ivar jumped the fence that divided their properties and trapped the foal with a strength she would never possess.

"God's green earth," he swore under his breath.

Cold metal broke under her nippers, the foal's front legs gave out, and it pitched forward to the ground. Nara grasped its four shaky legs and laid it on its good side. The fight had drained from its frightened eyes dried over from thirst, and it writhed around with less conviction. "Don't give up, little girl."

"Pretty cut up. Shooting it would be a kindness. She's gonna end up chicken feed anyway, but before 'en she'll eat your grass down."

"She'll heal up. Get me some rope." She pointed with her jaw toward her cart.

He dusted himself off and went for the rope. "Nara, you are one peculiar woman. You oughta save your strength for your cattle."

She searched the endless flat-topped buttes in the distance, looking for any speck of the mustangs, but the sun had begun to singe the hills in colors of fire, extinguishing itself like the embers of a hot cigarette. Nothing much moved north, either, except green grass flowing down the hills in waves. The wind held its breath for a moment and then gusted, throwing hair in her eyes, blurring the surrounding mountains.

Ivar returned with a shake of his head and knelt close, a faint scent of dirty hair and sweat on him. Eyes the color of silver always made him seem a little chilly. On the rare moment when he smiled, he looked like his younger brother who left Montana years ago. He helped her load the foal into her cart, tipped his hat, and rode off.

She drove the cart gently, while her eyes roamed the familiar folds of her family's ranch. Sagebrush cleaved to the sandy soil and ponderosa pines huddled together in the chalky mountains that surrounded their vast range. Papa usually had a little something laid aside whenever anyone went belly-up, and over the years he'd built up quite a reputation as the largest stock operation in the county. You couldn't see from one end to the other on the Stewart Ranch.

But even so, it wouldn't take Nara long to find the mustangs. Like every creature, they had their own daily rituals and rhythms. At sunrise, birds skimmed for fish in the deep, rippling currents of the creek. When the sun blazed overhead, creatures of every kind, feathered, furry, and slithering, escaped to rocky nooks, scaly branches, and grassy patches of shade. By afternoon, she might hear the clopping of a bighorn ram as it tottered over the tops of the hills on its way to the Yellowstone River where it would take a cool drink. The cattle spent their afternoon beneath the pine trees and then walked for the troughs as the sun tilted west. From the porch after supper, she could see pointy ears roaming the western hills. By dark, those wolves would be howling out their morbid song, celebrating a meal. Her aching body in bed, the screech of an owl would pierce the brisk night air, calling out for its mate to the starry sky. As a child she had tried to stay awake long enough so she could go to the hills and wait for the mythical creature called the sidehill gouger to emerge in the dead of night with his lopsided legs, making those distinctive tracks on the sides of the hills as he chased down errant children who dared to rove the hills alone.

But the wild horses roamed free and never stayed in one place too long, except one. The mustangs gathered in a shallow valley after sunset. When her cart could take her no closer, she got down and released the foal onto shivering fetlocks. The will to live must beat fiercely in every heart, for that filly ran across the field with all its might, stumbling just once. The band saw the foal coming and encircled it, snuffling it over to see if it belonged to them. Nara watched them for a while, and they watched her right back, ears pricked. One by one, they dipped their muzzles to the sweet buffalo grass, yanking and tearing at the earth, demanding their place on it.

SHE HEADED BACK home, her bumping cart jarring her butt good. The last of the light slipped away, and a dark blanket settled over the mountains. The wind had grown bold, breathing cold air through her jacket as if she wore nothing but her skin. She walked through the yard, ready for supper, but Jim, their only ranch hand, waved her over.

Most of the Cheyenne in Yellowstone County wore their hair in two long braids with an old-fashioned hat, but Jim wore close-cropped hair, a Stetson, dungarees, and long-sleeve shirts with a collar like every other cowpuncher. He held out a metal trap, its sharp teeth smeared in blood, and then dropped it in the dirt with a thunk. "Found another trap. Lamed a calf. I had to shoot it."

Nara shook her head. "I wonder how many he laid before I fired him."

"No telling."

"I'm sorry Papa hired that idiot over your head. If I have anything to say about it, it won't happen again."

His hair shone in the starlight and his chest filled with air as he contemplated her words. "Our fathers are still angry. Another generation will bleed it out."

Her father had grown up during the Battle of the Little Bighorn when Custer and his men had been slaughtered. But Custer had been hunting down Jim's people, trailing them as they moved their encampments with women and children. The animosity of that skirmish remained in the soil, angry blood of the fallen, bubbling up from time to time.

Jim pulled a rumpled pack of cigarettes out of the chest pocket of his shirt, shook one out, and offered it to Nara. Her trembling finger took the white roll, and he watched as she put it between her lips. He fiddled around in his pocket and brought out a shiny metal lighter. His flicking thumb produced a flame that lit up his face and filled the air with the flammable smell of butane. His eyes were so dark she couldn't see inside him, but if she dared look too long, they'd flare up like that lighter, torrid and flustering. She puffed her cigarette to life and turned away. He lit his own cigarette, and they stood in the darkness of their own discrete worlds, connected by smoke and dust whipped up by the relentless north wind.

* * *

The kitchen window held a view into Mama's small world. Nara could always find her head bobbing around in it. As much as Nara appreciated the stability of her mother's presence, she would never want to take up that motherly role, for the kitchen felt like a dim prison, and a woman can't raise kids and cattle at the same time. Simple as that.

Nara sat down on the porch and took off her boots the way she had every day of her life for the past thirty-odd years and set them right next to Papa's. She opened the screen door, and Papa lowered his newspaper. His gray eyebrows rose in silent greeting. He was communicating again. Mama must have intervened and starched his shorts. Papa wiggled in his chair and grimaced. Mama eyed this with satisfaction and winked. Nara had to cover her mouth to stop her laughing.

Her young cousin Minnie sat in the rocking chair eyeing the latest Sears & Roebuck catalog. It was like a Bible in their house. Smooshed-up pages, it could always be found somewhere lying open.

Mama called over her shoulder, "Minnie, come on over here and help."

Nara hovered over the coal stove in the corner that kept their house warm. With her hands and bottom to the heat, she watched Mama flour up veal cutlets and lay them in a crackling pan. The sizzle smoked up the air, making her stomach growl. Once her bottom was good and warm, Nara sat at the table, glad to take a load off.

From behind his paper, Papa said, "You fix up those fences between us and the Magnussons?"

"Sure did."

He put his paper down. "How many breaks?"

"Seven."

"Seven? It's Ivar. Like father, like son. If you see his bull over on our side, you make sure it goes back a steer. You hear?"

Papa went on muttering and cussing under his breath. Mama set a cup of coffee down in front of Nara and asked, "Where'd you get that bruise on your jaw?"

"Foal was caught on the fence."

Mama twisted up her mouth. "I could use your help in the kitchen more."

"Mama, you know full well I have too much to do with the cattle, and isn't that why we have Minnie here?"

Her cousin looked up from the catalog to roll her Kewpie-doll eyes. Nara's uncle had left the girl with them a couple of years ago when her mother died. He was a doctor in Billings and didn't know how to raise a young girl, and since Mama had lost her "favorite" daughter, he thought she could use the company, but, as Mama confessed to Nara the other day, "That girl is moody, doesn't seem to hear a word I say, like I'm not even here."

Papa put his paper down and said, "You don't need to be out tending cattle. That's why I employ *men*. You're gonna get wrinkled workin' in the sun all day. No man'll want you then."

"I don't even know why you bother. One of the traps your foreman set lamed a calf. The very thing you hired him to tend, so what good was he? Especially if he couldn't get along with Jim."

"That Indian needs to learn his place."

"Jim is the finest hand we've ever had, and you know it."

"Can't make him foreman. Ain't nobody gonna take orders from him."

"They will if they want their pay. Besides, I think the reservation is the first place we ought to look for another hand. Jim'll know somebody."

Papa leaned forward and pointed his finger, about to give her an earful, but Mama leaned between them with plates in her hands. Food was her way of shushing things over, and if that didn't work, she'd swat your butt with that dish towel she always kept hanging over her shoulder. For a woman who proudly claimed she didn't spank her kids, she knew the art of a whipping better than anybody.

Mama gave them both two good, long glances, then walked over to the sink and said, "That family up in Roundup, their son's returned from the city. Says he's thinking about staying."

"That's just what he's saying while he's back home," Nara said.

"Minnie, are you gonna help with supper or not?" Mama called out.

"Coming."

Minnie turned to Nara with a conspiratorial smile, though they were anything but kindred spirits. Minnie was a girlie girl. She had plucked her eyebrows down to thin lines like that rodeo queen Vera McGinnis, who was more showgirl than cowgirl.

Mama put a plate down before Nara and said, "I heard there is an orphan train coming through with kids."

Nara looked up into her mama's face. "Just what are you proposing?"

Mama tilted her head and walked back over to the stove. Papa lowered his paper. "I heard about those orphans from out East. Mary told me a man down in Wyoming took one in. The boy killed the entire family in their sleep and skipped out with their savings from the kitchen tin. Nobody's seen hide nor hair of him since."

CHAPTER 2

CHARLES TOOK A SEAT TOWARD THE BACK OF THE TRAIN AND SAT low. People out on the platform bustled about, hefting bags. Station attendants pointed everyone to their correct trains. A cop walked around swatting his palm with a baton, coming closer. He said something to the attendant by the door, who then stepped into the carriage, eyes searching. Charles ducked below his seat. Shoes of all sizes and types scuffed down the aisle. Charles searched with dread for a pair of shiny boots. Some kids laughed in the rows toward the front. A woman's fleshy feet waddled by, straining the seams of her Mary Janes. She grunted, and along came her suitcase. Someone crinkled wax paper, and the smell of a chicken sandwich wafted by, making his stomach growl louder than it should. The attendant shouted something from the front, but someone started coughing, so Charles couldn't make it out. He held his breath.

The door closed with a gratifying thunk, but it wasn't until he felt the train beneath him jerk forward that he let out his last breath of New York air.

The wheels clattered faster and faster, so Charles figured he could finally sit up straight. The other kids looked at him funny, but he didn't care. He felt grateful to be on that train. Buildings began to disappear like worries. Houses and shops faded away as if someone had taken a brush and painted over them, turning everything green and blue.

In the train car about twenty children sat around in the same suits and dresses. None of them were exactly cherubs, for they came from the same gutters as him. A tiny girl sat in front of him. Her hair was so blond it glowed like a halo. He figured girls worked in the kitchens out West, but she was no bigger than a bucket and sure didn't look like she could carry one.

The freckly Irish boy from the train platform sat across the aisle. Charles had snuck into the boarding line for the train and then stared the boy down. Nothing worse than a snitch. The smaller boy spent his time either smiling at nothing or studying a dog-eared dictionary. At first Charles thought the boy might be a numbskull, but after watching him a little longer, he figured nothing had ever happened to knock the grin off the boy's face. Charles didn't know how to deal with him, so he grimaced at him a few times, and the Irish kid put his happy face somewhere else.

As the day progressed, green hills emerged from outside his window. Charles laid his head against the cool glass. It was the last thing he remembered until someone jostled his shoulder.

"Charles."

No answer.

"Charles!"

He rubbed his tender face to rouse himself, forgetting about the shiner and sore jaw. He looked about and thought perhaps they'd made their first stop. The adoption agent, Mr. Morgan, stood over Charles. The stubble of the man's black beard lay just beneath his skin.

"Follow me," he said curtly.

Charles looked out the window. The train had stopped in the middle of nowhere.

"Get up. Right now."

With a pounding heart, Charles followed the adoption agent, Mr. Morgan. He was a thick man, almost a complete square with his wide shoulders.

He urged Charles down the steps and onto the gravelly area where the train connected to the tracks. Charles hesitated, and the adoption agent waved him down with impatience. At least he'd gotten a ways out of the city, though how far, he didn't know. His boots crunched into the tiny rocks as he took the last big step down. A group of railroad men had gathered, watching a man perched on top of the train car. He wrestled with something on the rooftop.

"Charles here had been sleeping like a railroad tie when I woke him," Mr. Morgan quipped to the group of men as if he held Charles in some kind of esteem.

Back at Grand Central Station, Charles had been discovered in the line of kids to board. Mr. Morgan had insisted they alert the police. But a nice lady, who was clearly in charge, had contemplated Charles's beat-up face with gentle eyes. She told Mr. Morgan there had been an addition at the last minute. She hadn't said the lie comfortably, but she wrote his name on the roster nonetheless. Mr. Morgan had stood fuming. No man appreciates a lady giving him orders.

Mr. Morgan shoved Charles forward toward the railroad men. "This young man might be big enough for the task."

With blackened fingers on their chins, the men sized him up. A man with an official-looking hat spoke up. "I'm the engineer on this line. We've got a real dynamiter over here, son."

The engineer took Charles to the back of a car and explained nobody had the strength to release the brake, which had gotten stuck. "The wheels on this car have been puttin' out sparks. Might set a fire." The engineer pointed up a ladder. "Up there on top of the car is a wheel. Try and move it to the left."

Being so big, people often asked him to do these kinds of things. Charles crawled up the ladder and found the wheel, relieved he wasn't going to be thrown off. He wrapped his hands around the metal wheel and wrenched on it with all his might, but it didn't budge. He tried again, and when it wouldn't move, he felt a little deflated. He shook his head at the men on the ground. Their faces fell in disappointment.

The engineer called up, "One more time, give it all ya got."

Charles wrapped both hands around the wheel and put every bit of his weight into it, shaking and straining until at last the wheel moved and the brake released.

The railroad fellas gave him some hoots and shouts. Charles crawled down from the ladder proud but a little embarrassed from the attention. Faces crowded up into the windows to see what happened. He thought he saw a few smiles, or at least relief.

* * *

Steel wheels filled their traveling car with a swift, grinding noise. Charles squinted out the window at grassy hills rushing past. The landscape had changed from when they'd first left New York, and yet the people who came out to adopt them were the same no matter where they stopped. Overalls, sunburned skin, and dirt in their wrinkles. The train had been to several stations already, and thirteen of the kids were gone. The rest lay about with tired, hollow faces. Some tried to hide their bawling, but the telltale sniffling and red eyes gave them away. A big girl sat nearby. She had buckteeth and crossed eyes that were puffy from shame. She'd almost been adopted yesterday, but the man had pulled his wife away and said, "That girl's so ugly, she'd have to sleep in the barn." The girl had covered her face with her hands and gone back inside the train.

It wasn't easy being picked over day by day, rejected as others left to their new lives, but Charles wasn't about to cry. Though he still couldn't understand why he hadn't been picked yet. Mr. Morgan had asked him to smile or keep his head down to hide the bruises on his face.

The tiny blond girl was still on the train. She sat in the seat across from Charles, getting closer to him by degrees, but he wasn't encouraging her. Her golden white hair had been chopped short in places. She'd probably had bugs. There was more dress than girl sitting there. Even so, that big dress couldn't hide the burns on her wrists. She caught him staring at them and pulled her sleeves down.

Charles paid her no mind and picked up a book another passenger had left behind. *The Lone Star Ranger.* As the train snaked farther west, he thought maybe his pop was up there somewhere whispering in angels' ears. Charles curled up against the window and gingerly laid his face on the cold glass. He pulled the leather cording from underneath his borrowed shirt and grasped his metal horseshoe in a hand that felt broken.

Charles fell asleep until the little girl got up. She probably needed to use the privy again, can't hold her water. He pulled out his book, looking for the correct page, when he heard her cry out. He turned to see a boy, his hair parted straight down the middle and smoothed down with so much grease that he was a walking fire hazard. For an orphan, he sure was portly around the middle. He'd been bugging her since they'd left. Each time it got worse.

Hands on her hips, she said to the boy, "You tripped me on purpose."

The boy snickered and stood up, towering over her now. "Did not. Ya tripped over that dress. It's too big for you, Opal." He said her name in a nasally voice.

The Irish boy named Patrick watched, shifting around, and then finally got up. Charles wanted to see what the freckly boy was made of.

"Leave the lass alone." His voice quavered.

"Why don't ya make me, spud nigger?" The bully shoved the smaller boy down onto the train floor.

Charles turned his head forward, not wanting to get involved. A scuffle ensued behind him with a wallop into a gut, and labored breathing. That didn't bother Charles, he'd seen worse, but a sharp yelp from the tiny blond girl made him look back. The bully had twisted the skin on her arm, giving her a red burn over her white scars. Charles rose and stepped over the Irish boy, who struggled for breath, leaned over Opal's white head, and pushed the bully back down in his seat. Charles glared at the jerk until he stopped laughing and put his eyes elsewhere.

She rubbed her red arm and uttered her thanks so soft he barely heard it.

Charles grunted and turned to go back to his book, but the adoption agent opened the door to their car. "Next stop. Get cleaned up."

They filed out to the platform and lined up like animals. The country folks began to hover all around them, prodding and poking, looking behind ears. They would always start with the smallest, Opal, but they didn't linger long. After they passed her by, her face would pinch up in confusion and follow them until they set on another child. Her little white head would drop like they'd broken her neck. None of these people needed a doll. A companion was all she could ever be. But a girl her age wouldn't understand that.

After the country folks picked over the girls, they would move to the boys. Patrick always managed to stand next to him. Charles thought he was about thirteen, fourteen. He carried the lilt of his Irish family. The sun lit up his reddish gold hair and exposed a tender pink scalp just beneath. On the first stop, a man had passed by the boy and spit on his feet. His sky-blue eyes shone over, but the boy raised his chin, refusing to look down at that spittle on his shoes. Charles figured he'd get picked before an Irish boy ever did, so he didn't mind standing next to him.

A couple stepped up onto the platform. Charles liked the look of them, as they didn't appear worn out and had on clean clothes. They stopped near Opal. The man leaned in close to Opal and she tilted back. Patrick watched this all carefully, then began to fidget. He glanced over at Mr. Morgan, who stood talking to prospective parents, then Patrick began to sidle down the line. The jerk who'd been bugging Opal narrowed his eyes on the smaller boy but said nothing when Charles made a slashing gesture across his neck.

Patrick crept sideways until he was next to Opal. The man knelt on one knee. His wife tugged on his arm. "We don't need no girl."

The man said something to his wife that Charles couldn't hear, but then Patrick said, loud and clear, "Sir, you'll want ta know, my sister soils herself fairly bad."

Opal's head shot up, her cross little brows in a temper.

The man wrinkled up his nose and stood. His wife pulled him away. "I ain't cleaning up crappy drawers."

Mr. Morgan caught Patrick and came strutting over. "What are you doing? Trying to get the jump on the other boys? Get back to your place."

When Patrick returned, Charles leaned down and whispered, "You should mind your own beeswax. I heard the lady at the station tell Mr. Morgan that little girl had to get adopted, and not to bring her back, on account of her mother."

Patrick said behind his hand, "But ya didn't see the way the man was eyein' the lass."

Charles shook his head. "Out of the frying pan and into the fire," he grumbled.

It wasn't much of a town, from what he could see. A small crowd of country folks stood under a shady tree in their weathered skin and thin floral dresses, waiting their turn to look over the wares.

One of the men climbed the steps and stopped near Patrick. "How do ya do, sir?"

The man grimaced, then moved in front of Charles, whose stomach rumbled. The crowd had arrived before any of the children could eat the sandwiches and bruised fruit Mr. Morgan managed to scare up at each stop. The shorter man began his close inspection of Charles. Sun reflected in his murky eyes. He had the honest smell of earth on him. Charles softened his face, as he'd been encouraged. He wanted off that train and judged the man before him to be as good as any in this part of the country. Eventually this train would run out of track.

"What's your name, boy?"

Charles didn't much like being called "boy," seeing how he looked over the top of the man's thinning hairline.

"Charles."

"Mmm." The man grabbed his jaw, rubbing his whiskers, and then looked around at the other kids lined up in a row.

"I'm strong."

The man's gaze settled on Charles's swollen eye. "You certainly look it, but do you think you can follow orders?"

"Yes, sir."

"You're pretty tall. How old are you?"

"Sixteen, sir."

The farmer widened his eyes and nodded like he didn't be-lieve Charles, then looked to the adoption agent, who stood in the shade of the train car. The farmer walked toward Mr. Morgan, and they talked for several minutes. Patrick fondled his old dictionary and smiled up at Charles. "Looks like ya got yourself a new da."

The farmer and adoption agent came over and stood before Charles and Patrick.

The farmer pointed at Patrick. "This one doesn't look like he can work hard. None of these Irish can."

Charles gritted his teeth and kept his face shut.

"Now, this one looks like a strong young man, but that shiner on his face has me thinkin' he'll be more trouble than he's worth. And from the stubble on that jaw, I won't have but six months' of work out of him, and then I'll have to pay him, right?"

Charles held his breath while they exchanged words.

"When he turns eighteen—he's sixteen," the agent said.

The farmer shook his head. "Looks older than that."

The adoption agent pointed to his roster. "It says right here he's sixteen."

If Mr. Morgan guessed the truth, his face betrayed nothing.

The farmer looked down the line of boys, then waved a hand in dismissal. "I know how it works. These older boys come out here lyin' about their age, get a little bit of hair on their chest, and then go work for better pay on the railroads or in the mines. I ain't no fool."

"But look how big and strong this young man is. You wouldn't want a younger, weaker boy."

The farmer turned to consider him again, so Charles stuck out his chest and flexed his forearms. Tired eyes roamed over every contour of his frame. "You're a biggun but you look half starved. You have a bad back, son?"

Charles stood up straight as ever. "No, sir."

"Well, I'll tell you sure enough. You work for the railroad and you'll have one."

"Don't care to work for the railroads, sir."

"Hmm. Not sure where I'd find work clothes to fit such a big boy." He walked all the way around Charles. "Etta, come over here and look at this boy."

His wife walked over wearing an apron splashed with whatever she'd been cooking. Stale kitchen grease drifted by on the breeze as she came near. Just thinking about home cooking made Charles's mouth water, but she must have made up her mind about him already, for she pulled on her husband's hand and whispered in his ear. She pointed down the row of boys to the jerk who'd been picking on Opal.

Mr. Morgan pursed his lips. "I have other papers to get signed."

The farmer gave him one last, long look and then walked off, too. Charles dipped his head. If that man wouldn't take him on, Charles didn't know who would.

More folks stepped onto the platform to look them over. A

man held his wife's hand. She passed by Charles and her eyes found his battered face. She cringed, and Charles turned away. None of these people could see any good in him. If they'd known him before, they'd be right.

Even though Opal stood at the front of the line, none of the folks stopped to look at her for long, except one lady whose face lit up as she tried to communicate with the girl. Opal peered up at the lady, might have even smiled, but the lady's husband pushed her down the line toward the bigger girls. Opal stepped out of line as if she intended to follow them. Her eyes tilted downward as she watched them talk to the cross-eyed girl, then take her off to Mr. Morgan for adoption. Charles figured Opal would go back to New York and her lousy mother.

A lady in overalls stopped in front of Charles and insisted he open his mouth. He'd seen her itch at her greasy head with her fingers. He opened his mouth a tiny bit but not enough for her to put a finger in.

Her brows wrinkled up as she tried to see inside his mouth. "Open up," she said.

When she became frustrated with his poor showing, there came that dirty finger, and Charles pulled away. Somehow the lady got off-kilter and fell back. She landed on her butt with a thud, shock on her face and everyone else's. Mr. Morgan ran to her aid.

"I didn't push her."

As she got up with the help of Mr. Morgan's arm, she pointed her finger at him. "You did too!"

Mr. Morgan glared at Charles. Patrick stepped into the fray and said, "I'm sorry ya fell, but I saw yer foot catch on that warped board just there." He pointed to a board sticking up.

"I'm very sorry, ma'am. I can escort you down the steps," Mr. Morgan said, trying to take her away.

She spluttered. "How dare you. I was pushed." She pointed her finger at Charles again.

"No disrespect, but Charles's arms were at his side when ya fell. Saw it with me own eyes."

"Thank you, Patrick." Mr. Morgan glowered at them both. "Ma'am, please allow me to help you off the platform."

He managed to get her to leave, but she poisoned minds as she told her story to the crowd below. Suspicious, flittering eyes landed all around Charles like stinging insects. He turned his back on them.

Most of the other kids were taken, and Mr. Morgan busied himself with the paperwork. Anyone not chosen had to remain on the platform and try to smile, even though being passed over made them feel worthless. Mr. Morgan had said, "Someone might change their mind if you stand out here." Nobody ever did. Charles, Patrick, and Opal huddled together, couldn't look each other in the eye, but they stayed close for the safety of each other's shadow.

Charles felt something wet hit his back. He turned, eyes wild for the fight, teeth bared. "Whadya think ya doin'?" He wiped the tomato off his back.

The gang of kids below called out, "Train riders!"

Charles stalked to the edge of the platform. "Ya want me to come down there?"

They ran off like scared mice into the tall grass, looking back and laughing.

The last of the country folks cleared away, taking the rest of the orphans with them. Patrick and Opal didn't have to say anything, for Charles could see the desolation in their worried faces that matched his own. Mr. Morgan came over to them. His finger stabbed the air in front of Charles's face. "I don't know what happened out here, but see that it doesn't again. The last stop is Bull Mountain, Montana. Since you're all that remains, I'm certain you'll find nice families there. *If* you behave."

Mr. Morgan then turned to Opal. "It might help if you'd speak when the people come to see you."

Opal looked toward the crowd leaving and winced like she might run after them. To God only knew what end.

Mr. Morgan set his hand on Patrick's shoulder as if it could soften the blow. "Try not to say anything until they've committed. Just nod your head. Understand?"

Patrick gave no answer. Charles could see from the proud set of Patrick's jaw that he had no intention of keeping his mouth shut. Might be a little steel beneath that easy smile.

* * *

Steel wheels rolled and clicked over the tracks as they crossed over flatlands bordered by rivers and dotted with lakes. Travelers at various stops began to fill up the seats around them as they traveled in the direction of the sun, chasing it across the land. But they never caught up. The sun disappeared behind mountains with flat, rocky tops. Charles wondered what lay farther west, and if he could ever find a place in this rugged landscape. It felt right to him, calm and remote.

"You from New York?" Patrick asked.

"Hell's Kitchen. You grow up in Ireland?"

"We had hills and streams in Cork. Everything is green in Ireland. I didn't like New York. I wish me family never left home."

"What happened to your folks?"

"Me mother and older brother died of Spanish flu. Auntie took care of me for a while, but she hasn't got any money. She thought the Children's Aid Society would be able ta help me."

"Ya didn't wanna go back to Ireland?"

"Me gran-da worked at stables where they race the horses. He could have shown me the ropes, but I couldn't afford the ticket back home."

"Sounds like a great place. Why'd your parents leave?"

"Ma wanted to start a new life. Me aunt had come over already. There wasn't anything left there for her after my da died in the war."

Charles bent his head to his lap. "My pop died in the war, too. We never did hear how it happened. He just disappeared somewhere in a place called Belgium."

"My pa's horse was shot from underneath him. It fell over on him and crushed him. That's what the fella told us that come to say he died."

Being just two boys who could neither understand nor change the past, their conversation naturally died out.

Charles picked up *The Lone Star Ranger*, while Patrick began to thumb through his dictionary. Different as they were, they each had their dreams. Charles looked over at the pages in Patrick's dictionary. The boy underlined the words with his finger as he silently mouthed the meanings and pronunciations. It seemed like anyone different out here was looked upon with a wary eye. Charles decided to start talking respectable, fit in better, lose the New York accent. It would make it harder to track him down.

The train slowly shaded over into darkness and conversation came in whispers, but even so, in a full train car there will always be a racket. People make noise. Charles laid his head on his jacket wedged against the window and put his hand over his ear. The car had gone completely dark, the windows black, except for the shadows of trees blurring by.

One by one, everyone nodded off. Their heads rolling about looking for comfort. Opal was turned away, so Charles couldn't tell if she was asleep or not. The two ladies beside her rested their heads together, sleeping. Opal's little hand reached over and pulled a pin out of one of the ladies' hats and pocketed it without disturbing so much as a hair. Her face returned to the dark window.

The wheels had slowed to make a turn. The sounds softened. Shadows outside began to pass by a little slower. Charles tapped Patrick. His head had fallen back as he buzzed away with a young man's snore. Charles poked his shoulder and whispered in his ear, "Patrick."

Orange lashes flapped as the boy began to take in their surroundings. He grabbed his neck, rubbing it like he hadn't slept on it right, then peered outside the window.

Charles whispered, "Listen. I don't think anyone is gonna want us tomorrow."

Patrick's chest caved in as he released whatever hope he'd been holding on to. "I fear it, too."

Charles learned early on you need someone to see what's coming when your back is turned, and though the boy didn't look like he could fight, he sure looked dependable enough. "We don't have to go back to New York. There's another way."

Patrick leaned in and said low, "I know what yer thinkin'. Ya remind me of my older brother. He was always in trouble. God rest his soul."

"Look, I can't go back. I'm jumpin' off this train as soon as it slows down again."

Patrick leaned forward, eyes wide.

"There's work out here. Honest work for anyone who wants it."

"I've never been on me own. My aunt, she—"

"Won't take care of ya when you get back. I know that story, Patrick. Believe me. I had friends on the street with that story."

"How will we eat? Where will we sleep?"

"Don't worry about it. I've done it before. I'll figure it out."

Patrick sat back and looked straight ahead. Charles could see him mulling it over in his mind. "There's still one stop left," Patrick said.

"Do you honestly *want* to be taken in by those people? Besides, we're not too far from being pushed out on our own.

As soon as they have to pay us for our work, they'll throw us out."

Patrick breathed in real deep. Charles wasn't going to let the boy think he had any other options. He'd be worked to death and have a broken back by the time he was eighteen.

"What about her?" Patrick said.

They both looked over at Opal, who watched them intently.

"Too small," Charles said, trying to avoid her little dark blue eyes. "There's one stop left, and she'll be the only one. That'll give her the best chance she's got out here."

Opal kept on watching him with an earnestness to her face now, making him feel guilty, but he felt in his heart he was right. Patrick went quiet. Charles thought he might chicken out.

"How do we do it?"

Charles explained that the train went slow around the curves. He would tap Patrick's arm, they'd leave everything behind, and walk quietly to the back door where the cars joined.

"What if Mr. Morgan catches us?"

"He sleeps in the nicer car with the velvet padded seats. He'll be snoring from now till morning."

Patrick nodded, stuffed his ratty dictionary down the front of his shirt, and lay back, but Charles would have to stay awake. He concentrated on the train beneath him, but the gentle vibration under his feet nearly lulled him to sleep, so he picked up his book. He read for a bit, then his eyes began to feel heavy. The words disappeared now and again, and he'd jerk awake just before the book fell from his hands. He put the book down to watch the blurring shadows outside.

The train car staggered, then slowed. The shadows passing by took form. He tapped Patrick's shoulder. The boy rubbed his eyes, and then stood to go up the aisle first. Charles crept behind. As they passed by Opal's row, he stopped a moment. Her head lay against the glass. Better she didn't catch them leaving. No telling what she'd do. Her little chest rose and fell in a sleepy rhythm, her thumb beginning to slip from her mouth. It still had little red indents from her teeth. Charles moved on.

A man up ahead began to rouse from sleep, turning this way and that. Patrick stopped right before the man's arm swung out into the aisle. Patrick looked back at Charles, who then reached over and lightly touched the man's arm. The arm recoiled as if an itchy fly had landed. When the man's eyes began to blink, Charles shoved Patrick from behind and they hurried past. Charles held his finger to his lips, and they stood in the dark until the man stopped moving. Charles bid Patrick to wait for a time. After several minutes, he nodded for Patrick to go ahead. When he opened the small door, clunky-sounding wheels and shrieky wind whooshed inside where everyone slept. Charles urged Patrick out and turned to shut the door, but Opal stood right there.

She looked up at Charles with big eyes pleading, lashes flapping. He breathed out real hard and then pulled her outside, shutting the door swiftly but with a light touch on the hardware, lest anyone wake up. They crowded together on the metal platform, where the ground beneath them rushed by. Wind tore at his clothing like icy blades. "Whadya doin'?" he yelled to Opal in a whisper.

"I'm going where you're going."

"We can't take you with us."

"Why not?" Her eyes tilted downward.

"You're too small."

She folded her tiny arms. "Then I'll tell."

Patrick and Charles looked at one another. A full conversation couldn't be had with the wind and not wanting to wake anyone. Patrick nodded and then dove off the train without another word, leaving Charles to figure out how to deal with Opal. The boy landed awkwardly and rolled into the weeds below.

Opal looked up at him, determined. Charles grappled with all the problems and consequences of bringing a little pipsqueak of a girl with him, but in the end he figured there was nothing else to do but take the stubborn mite.

"Okay." He pointed to the grass rushing by below. "Now Jump!" he said in her ear.

She turned to do it but then braced her little body as if she wouldn't.

"I'll help ya get clear of the gravel. On count a three."

When he got to three, she still wouldn't be pushed.

The train began to speed up and Patrick still lay where he fell. Charles wondered if the boy hurt himself. "We gotta go now."

A light came on in the fancy cabin.

"I'm going with or without you."

She turned toward the cabin where Mr. Morgan slept, but held tight to the metal post.

Charles put his head to the wind and jumped from the train.

CHAPTER 3

NARA CAME OUT OF THE TELEGRAPH OFFICE AND SPOTTED AN-other posting for that orphan train. The date had been crossed out and changed to today. "Holy cow," she muttered, searching all around.

Three couples clutched each other and stared down empty tracks. Nara approached them by slow measures, feeling mighty uncomfortable being here herself, but her father's story about that family murdered in Wyoming had her curious. These train riders must look different. The people waiting here had come from another county. Not one familiar face peered back at her. One of the men paced about, and Nara asked him, "Why is the train late?"

"I don't know," he said. "They were supposed to have arrived days ago."

Another man said, "Probably had engine troubles."

She regarded these folks with disdain even as she attempted to build a picture in her mind of the kids on that train. At worst, they could be dangerous. At least a real pain in the ass. She wondered what happens to a young person to make them kill a whole family like that, and how would anyone recognize a kid capable of it.

One of the wives stood with her arms crossed over her chest, clutching herself. What she was all worked up over, Nara couldn't imagine. She walked off. Having children was something other women did. The kind who don't have cattle to tend. One thing was a certainty. If she was ever so foolish to get married and start a family, it would be the end of her dream. Her husband would have all the joy of working her family's operation and she'd be stuck inside wiping noses.

It wasn't hard to fight off all the "many suitors" out here but getting Papa to hand over the reins was difficult for the simple fact that she sat down to pee, and little else. But, woman or no, if she were in charge, she would try things that would make their cattle operation run smoother. Like fall calving or getting some irrigation water in from the Huntley Project that promised to bring water from the Yellowstone River to farms and ranches. Or maybe buy a modern automobile to get them in and out of town quicker. It would make all their lives a whole lot easier.

A whistle caught her ear from down the tracks, and she turned to look. The couples had moved as close to the tracks as possible, like they were competing for the best stock. The ladies fussed with their finest but faded skirts. Rugged hands grappled with dusty Stetsons. The station platform filled up with steam as the engine grunted and scraped to a halt. A fireman with blackened arms jumped down, probably to catch a breath of fresh air.

A man in a city suit and oil-slicked hair called out, "Hello, folks!"

She strode out of there with haste, telling herself Mama would have had supper on the table by now, but in truth, she wouldn't be caught dead near an orphan.

* * *

When Nara got back home, Mama stood at the sink washing and clinking the dishes and silverware in sudsy lemon water. "Your plate's in the oven, keepin' warm."

Papa sniffed the air. "Did you buy that fancy dish soap again?"

"I like the smell, and it's only three cents more," Mama said, unchastened.

He popped open the newspaper and began reading again. The regularity of the argument tickled Nara as much as Mama's backbone in this small matter, for she often buckled to Papa's iron will. Minnie stood by Mama helping with the dishes with a sulky demeanor that aggravated Nara. Minnie'd been quiet lately, probably still smarting from the extra chores she'd been doled out since they were short a hand.

"Minnie, did you feed the horses?" Nara asked.

The girl handed Mama a plate for drying, then went limp as if she were going to collapse.

"Is that a no?"

"I forgot. I'll run out and do it now." She went out the screen door and let it slam behind her.

The gravy steamed in Nara's face as she sat down to her plate. She wolfed down her chicken and mashed potatoes. When she reached over to slather some butter on a piece of bread, she noticed Mama rubbing the same plate, though it was long dry. "What's wrong?"

"Minnie's been talking about secretarial classes in Billings. She ought to go back home—not much help or company to me anyway." Her voice sounded off.

Papa looked up from stuffing his pipe and wrinkled his eyes up. "Another one, huh? Folks are wanting to live in the city now. Easy jobs. Easy lives. Or so they think."

Nara set down her unfinished bread and pushed back her chair, making a scraping noise on the floor. She handed her plate to Mama. "I'll go help her."

"If you hadn't fired my foreman, you wouldn't have to."

Nara had been ready to open the door, but she was damn sick of this worn-out conversation. "Do you think I *wanted* to fire him?"

"Listen, I don't want you to get your hopes up. Your brother's coming back. The city will wear on him soon enough."

"No." She shook her head. "He won't."

Mama came between them, dish towel in hand as if she had the power to raise the white flag. No woman out here did. Nara walked out onto the porch to lace up her boots. Back in the kitchen, she could hear her parents having their usual shushy argument about how each of them would have handled that differently. Her brother, John, wrote to her regularly about how slap-happy he was working as an artist in a "vibrant place." But John asked her to keep their correspondence a secret, so anytime Papa mentioned his son coming back, she had to pull her lip over her head to keep her mouth shut. Papa had lost his son to the city, his rightful male heir to his land and cattle operation. Where that left Nara was yearning to fill her brother's shoes, while fending off the maternal expectations of everyone in the damn county.

From the direction of the stalls, Nara heard a struggle. She rounded the corner to see scrawny Minnie fighting with the hay bales. Truth be told, Nara could easily picture Minnie in a dress behind a desk with a typewriter, too cute for real work. Nara was about to help the girl when she heard a horse stamping around in protest. Jim must have come back from town. Cleaning hooves or something. Chestnut was a notorious kicker, hated its hooves cleaned. She went into the stalls to help him when she heard a motorbike coming up the dirt road toward the house. Jim couldn't be on his motorbike *and* in that stall.

The door to the stall banged open.

A voice she'd never heard before disturbed the hay-smelling air. She grabbed an old branding iron and crept toward the stall. Jim's motorbike got louder outside in the yard. He usually parked in the stable by the tack, so he'd be here any moment. It gave Nara enough courage to peer around the corner and inside the stall. The broad backside of a tall man she'd never seen before—he tried to put a rope around Chestnut's neck. The horse threw its sable head this way and that, eluding each attempt.

"Who are you?"

The man swung around, wild-eyed. He had the face of a young boy, big as he was. But there was something feral in him. She stepped back, waiting for Jim's arrival.

"I'm going to ask you again. Who are you?"

He looked down, searching for words. "My name is . . . Charles, ma'am."

"Don't you 'ma'am' me! What are you doing in here—trying to steal a horse? Is that it?"

The boy just stared and retreated too near the back of the horse.

"Drop the rope and leave that horse before it kicks you square in the ass."

The rope fell to the floor as he put up his hands.

"I ain't no sheriff, kid. Whose boy are you?" He wore britches from another place entirely. "You don't look like you're from around here."

Not your typical horse thief, maybe lost, but he seemed awfully big for her to handle on her own, and when he stepped forward, she realized her mistake.

"Minnie! Jim!"

He held up his hands again and stepped back. "I'm from Canada. Just passing through."

Minnie stumbled over to the stalls. When she heard the stranger, she ran toward the house on skinny legs, calling out for help. Jim roared into the stalls on his bike, and her father ran up in his bare feet, rifle dangling from his hand. "What's going on? Wolves again?"

Nara took the boy by the arm and dragged him out from the stall. "I found this young man trying to rope Chestnut."

Her father's grizzled brows soared in astonishment. "Horse thieving? Young man, do you know the *penalty* for horse thieving?"

Mama came stumbling to the stable door, the bun on her head near to falling off. She had a rifle in her hands. "Just thought I'd come around and check."

"Sir, I was just real desperate. We're out here and we're lost . . ."

The big boy ranted on about this and that, and her father held up his hand to quiet the babble.

Nara walked over to her mama and put her hand on the barrel, pushing it down. "Mama, give me that thing before someone gets hurt."

She handed it over without another word. Nara cocked the gun, bringing everyone's eyes back to her. "Now, you've given us a lot of talk, but we still don't know why you're out here stealing horses. Where are your parents?"

She hadn't asked him a difficult question, but he gawped at her as if she'd actually shoot him. He slumped a bit, and his eyes became softer, more vulnerable.

"You heard me. Where are you from?"

Mama walked right past the barrel of the gun. "If my senses are right, he's probably starving." She grabbed him by the arm as if he weren't dangerous. "Come on in here. We've got some supper. You can tell us over a plate of something hot."

Nara lowered the rifle with a prayer to the heavens for patience. But now there wasn't anybody who crossed Mama when she got her hen feathers all puffed up like that, chick in hand. Not even Papa, who rubbed the back of his red, wrinkled neck and followed Mama inside. Nara and Jim fell in and walked after Papa like one long line of obedients.

They all assembled around the supper table, but nobody wanted to park their boots next to a horse thief, except Papa, who sat at the head of the table as if a neighbor had come by to shoot the shit. The boy ate with uncoordinated stabs of his fork. If she didn't know better, Nara would swear he'd just learned how to use the utensil. Between mouthfuls, he managed to get out some garbled words. "Thank you, ma'am," and "This really hits the spot."

Papa said, "I'm Robert Stewart, and this here is my ranch. My wife, you've met." He pointed to the food on the boy's plate.

The boy nodded briefly and kept on eating. It must have been days since he'd last eaten. He looked gaunt around his face, dehydrated maybe. Yellow and purple covered his eye and jaw. He'd been fighting. Nara shook her head at the risk they were taking, bringing him into the house. He emptied his plate, scraping his fork. Mama filled it again, and then a little more, until he grabbed his stomach. Papa had the sense to stand up and back away, as did the rest of them.

The boy held up his hand and burped. "I'm okay."

Nara had about enough of his chewing and everyone else acting like he was some guest of the family. "All right. You've had your fill. Papa, I think it's high time we got the sheriff out here."

Mama looked stricken, but that "harmless" boy got up and

moved for the door. Nara aimed her rifle on him, while Jim blocked the door. Minnie ran up the stairs.

Anyone would be a fool to believe this was his first run-in with the law. But Papa sat back in his chair and considered the boy for a good minute, narrowing his eyes on him. "Well, Nara, hang on. I don't think that'll be necessary."

Papa had a way of turning things to his advantage.

"If you'd just let me on my way, sir. My . . . little brother is waiting. He'll be worried." From the corner of his eye, he watched Nara's gun.

Mama stopped fiddling with the dishes and came forward. "There's another one?"

"We don't even know if what he's sayin' is the truth," Nara said.

Papa stood up. "Everybody calm down. If we get the sheriff, we all know what'll happen to this kid. Now, he looks desperate enough, but if he's man enough"—Papa looked him square in the eye—"then he'll work off his offense."

The boy's sharp eyes considered the door, but returned to all of them, then focused on the table where his plate and fork sat. "I will, sir."

"What if, instead of a 'little brother,' he has more just like him?" Nara said. "What then? I think we ought to get the sheriff, just to be safe—besides, where will he and this brother stay? We're getting in way over our heads."

Mama came forward. "He'll stay here, too."

Nara slumped and collapsed into a nearby chair. "Oh, Mama. And then what?"

Mama's heart had a big hole in it, and Nara felt sure it was on that basis alone Papa said, "We'll just take this one day at a time. For now, we better wrastle up that other boy. I imagine he's as hungry as you?"

Mama rattled around in the icebox, probably searching for something to heat up. Nara wondered if her parents realized how old they were. "You can't go taking in every stray you find."

Nara shot a look over to the man-boy, and thought for a moment she might have wounded him. But he was a fast learner. He looked to Papa for his fate.

"Jim, you and Nara get the horses ready, and a spare." Papa turned to the boy. "Do we have a deal, young man?"

CHAPTER 4

ALL CHARLES TOLD THE FAMILY WAS THAT HE LEFT PATRICK BY THREE great big rocks in the shade of a pine tree. The old guy nodded, mounted his horse, and took off at a trot, so he must have known exactly where those things were, for he never asked Charles for another direction as he led them on through the starry night.

They rode in single file. Crickets chirping and horse hooves in sandy dirt felt good to Charles's ears, though his butt slid around in the saddle more than it should, and he couldn't quite catch the rhythm of the horse walking underneath him. If he wanted to work punching cows, he'd have to get the hang of riding quick. When the situation became apparent that he'd be laboring on a ranch, having to work off his offense didn't seem like punishment, and the Stewarts seemed to believe his story, except Nara. When she had snuck up on him in the horse stall, he'd thought she was a man. She dressed like one. Stood like one, and he'd swear she deepened her voice to sound like one. She reminded him of the infamous stories about Sadie the Goat. The toughest female gangster in New York's Fourth Ward. She used to head-butt her victims until her ear was bitten off and stored in Gallus Mag's pickling jar.

It took about an hour to get to the place, and when they rode near the entrance to the rocks, Patrick stuck out his head. "I better go in there and let him know everything's okay. He won't come out of there any other way."

Her father nodded, but Nara grabbed her rifle and pointed it at him. "Don't try anything, kid."

Charles dismounted none too gracefully and slid between the stones with only moonlight to guide him. Sagebrush clawed at his arms as he squeezed his way through. "Patrick, Opal. It's okay."

He saw a couple of dark forms huddled together. Patrick whispered, "Who are all those people, Charles? Are we in trouble?"

"Don't worry. They're a family with a ranch just beyond the mountain."

Opal spoke up. "Did they catch you stealing the horses?"

For a quiet little thing, she sure knew how to get to the heart of the matter. "They did, but they're not mad or anything. They just want me to work it off. I told them I was from Canada and we didn't have any parents. You're my brother and sister as far as they know. Well, I didn't tell them about you, Opal. I was afraid they wouldn't want you."

"Why'd ya lie ta them?"

"Because, knucklehead, if they find out we're the missing orphans, we'll be sent back to New York."

"What will we do, then? Just live with them?" Patrick asked.

"I don't see why not, as long as we all earn our keep." Charles turned to Opal, who folded her arms across her chest and puckered up her mouth.

"Aren't you being picky, for someone starving to death."

She tilted up her little chin and looked the other way.

Patrick shrugged his shoulder a little. "Ya don't think they'll mind me being Irish?"

"Don't think so, and the older lady cooks good, too. Look, I'm going with them. You guys can come if you want. But keep to the story."

Opal said to his retreating back, "Fine. But I don't wanna be left alone with anyone. Only you two."

"Don't worry. We'll figure it out."

They all walked out together. When Nara saw Opal, she lowered her gun a bit.

"Let me do the talking," Charles said from the corner of his mouth.

The mannish woman got off her horse and strode toward them. Her shrewd eyes landed on and moved over Patrick and Opal like they were something she'd never seen before.

"This your brother? Who's she?"

"I forgot about my little sister here, Opal."

Nara looked at him sideways like no way in heck she believed him. "How long you kids been out here like this?" she asked Patrick.

"A wee bit over two days."

Charles sucked in his breath. "He's our cousin, but we think of him as a brother."

Nara shook her head and turned to her father. They commenced a conversation without words, just two flinty expressions.

He said, "Get 'em up in the saddle. It's cold out here. They'll be hungry."

The woman mounted her horse and held out her hands to pull Opal up in front of her like it was a chore she wouldn't relish. She barked out, "Patrick, can you ride?"

"Ya."

An Indian they called Jim, who dressed like a cowboy, led a horse over to Patrick. Charles figured Jim must work for the family. Out in the West, Charles assumed cowboys were cowboys and Indians were Indians. Jim was some of both.

Patrick took the horn and reins, lifting himself up as if he'd been riding his whole life. "I rode a fair bit when . . . when we lived on the farm."

Charles gave Patrick the eye, hoping he'd keep his mouth shut. He'd have to fill in the gaps of their story and quick, because if he didn't, Patrick would. They all rode out of there at a trot, Charles's butt banging against the saddle, while he fought to keep his feet in the tiny stirrups.

When they got back to the ranch, his whole body felt as if it had been run over by the iron horse they came west on. The nice lady who was called Mama came out of the house. Even in the dark, Charles could see her eyes go wide and smiling when they landed on Opal. "Well, goodness. What do we have here?"

Mama Stewart bent down and gently brushed Opal's white hair out of her face and said, "You poor little dear, out here in all this cold," and with seemingly no trouble at all, Mama tucked Opal under her arm and with the other reached out to Patrick. "And who are you, young man?" she said. "I'll bet you're both half starved. Come on in here where it's warm, and I'll get you something to eat."

Opal looked back just once as Mama led them off to the table where Charles hoped she would stuff them till they couldn't talk. His own stomach comfortably full, he now looked forward to whatever bed they'd give him. The closest would do, but Jim said, "You and me will brush down the horses and feed them."

Charles could have fallen over right there, but he found some manly reserve and straightened his back. "Lead the way."

To this, Jim grunted out a chuckle as if Charles hadn't gotten the joke. But he'd gotten it, all right. They would try to work him to death for taking a horse, but there wasn't anything or anyone who could beat him down.

In the barn, it became clear Jim intended to stand around, smoke, and supervise. Those broad shoulders revealed a life of hard labor, but the way he folded his arms and stuck out his chest, Charles didn't think Jim was ashamed of it. His face didn't resemble the Mohawk Indians who helped build the skyscrapers in New York. They had no fear of heights and walked the beams with great balance, unlike the other workers who regularly fell to their deaths.

"Where do your people come from?"

Jim pointed to the ground.

"I mean what tribe?"

"Cheyenne."

"Where is the rest of your family?"

Charles thought he saw pain in those eyes, but it disappeared before he could be sure.

"Haven't got one."

"Me, either," Charles murmured.

After Charles finished with the horses, the rest of the evening was taken up by getting beds ready out in the bunkhouse for him and Patrick, and a bed inside the house for Opal. At first she fought sleeping separately from them, but when they showed her the bunkhouse and Jim lying there in his bed, she tore out of there and back up onto the porch, where Mama took her under her arm with a big smile. There was a lady who could charm the truth out of someone.

The bunkhouse had two big bunk beds made with raw logs. Charles was surprised they didn't have more ranch hands and hoped that worked in his and Patrick's favor. He found a bottom bunk with a mattress that smelled a little musty as he shook it out. Patrick, being lighter, took the top bunk.

Nara walked over and picked up Patrick's ratty dictionary he had placed on his bare mattress. "Why do you have this?"

"I take pleasure in erudition."

"Believe me, there won't be anything of pleasure out here, and as for furthering your intellect, you can knock yourself out. Though I doubt you'll have any time for that."

She pitched the dictionary at him, and he caught it just before it pelted him in the stomach. Mama hustled into the bunkhouse with pillows and blankets stacked up so high, all you could see was the bun on her head. "Now, don't let Nara scare you, boys. She's more bark than bite."

After all the bedding got doled out and beds made up, Nara lingered. She squinted at him from under that ivory straw hat. "You may have my parents fooled, but I don't believe one word you say. How did you get those bruises on your face?"

It seemed funny she felt so strongly about his bruises when she had one of her own down her jaw, but he didn't think she'd appreciate him drawing similarities between them.

Nara scowled at him from underneath her Stetson. "Well?"

"I tripped over a rock and fell right on my face—ask Patrick."

Patrick hesitated for a second. "Ya, saw it with me own eyes."

Her gaze shifted over to Patrick and then to Charles, with doubt. Her finger poked Charles in the chest. "You try anything funny, and I will shoot you. Understand?" Then she looked to Patrick. "The minute you slip up, you're outta here."

With that she turned and left them to make their beds. They looked at each other with raised brows. "I'm not so sure about this," Patrick said.

Charles waved it off. "She'll warm up. We just have to keep our story straight and work hard."

The last days spun through his mind and wouldn't let him sleep. He stared at the wooden slats above. Opal slept inside the house somewhere. He'd have to talk to her the next time they had some privacy and instill in her the importance of keeping her mouth shut. They were from Canada. Whereabouts? He'd have to figure that out pretty quick. Their parents are dead. Patrick is their cousin. They had been heading to California. Period. End of story.

* * *

Charles woke to the two words he would later come to love.

"Get up." A knuckly fist jostled his shoulder, jiggling his head all over the pillow. "Get up."

"But it's still dark out."

Jim stood over him. His square face unreadable. "When the boss says get up, you get up."

Charles propped himself up on his elbows, remembering the stack of dusty books in the corner of the bunkhouse he'd spied last night. "I was up late reading one of those Zane Grey novels. He's the best writer of the West."

"For a boy from Canada you sure know a lot about Zane Grey." Jim's dark eyes glittered at Charles in interest.

Jim went over and pulled on his boots, which sat there looking like he wore them whether his feet stood in them or not. The squeaky door shut behind him. A pair of long scrawny legs dangled over the edge of the bunk above Charles's head.

"Your leg still smarting?"

"Fit as a fiddle." Patrick jumped down from his bed.

They got dressed in what they had from the train and found some boots lying around in the bunkhouse. Patrick's were too big, and Charles's pair were too small, but he didn't care. They were real cowboy boots. He stuffed the toes of Patrick's boots with some old socks they found wadded underneath a bunk.

Moonlight lay upon the ground in bright patches as the soles of their boots scuffed the gravelly dirt, the only sound to reach his ears beyond the whistling of brisk air. The place felt calm, mysterious, and free. A lantern glowed from inside the stables where Jim sat smoking, splayed over a red motorbike with obvious pride.

"That yer bike?" Patrick walked around it, touching the metal parts and investigating the engine.

"Yup."

"How long have ya had it?"

"A year, give or take."

"Does it run?" Patrick asked.

"Has some trouble starting on occasion, but mostly it runs good."

Patrick's eyes lit up. "I might be able ta help ya with that. I used to—"

Charles dug his elbow in Patrick's ribs and said, "We've got to feed these horses."

Jim ground his cigarette in the dirt floor and showed them how to feed the horses and check hooves. "When you're done, come to the main house for breakfast."

As soon as Jim left, Charles went over and grabbed Patrick by the shirt. "You've got to be careful what you tell them."

Patrick nodded and then went back to brushing down a small golden mare. "I don't feel right about lyin'."

"Who cares. If they find out we're from that orphan train, we'll be sent back like that." Charles snapped his fingers in Patrick's face.

Patrick jumped a bit. "I don't want ta go back. I like it out here better. They have horses."

"Then let me do all the talking."

Charles moved his brush over the horse's flank. The quiet scratch of the brush over prickly hair felt soft to his ears. He didn't know what to expect this morning from the family who owned the ranch. In the light of day things might look different to them. Or, worse, Opal might have slipped up and said something.

He and Patrick finished with the horses and left the stable. The horizon to the east bloomed bright blue with enough light to see the big ranch house. He sized up everything around him and figured these Stewarts must do all right. A black and white dog came running and sniffed them both down with suspicion. Patrick took ahold of its ears, rubbing and scratching. The dog leaned into Patrick's knee.

"Pet him," Patrick said.

Charles grumbled a little. "Don't care for dogs."

But the dog kept following, its tongue lolling like it didn't have a care in the world. The smell of bacon salted up the air, soft murmurings of a morning conversation drifted through the screen door. People not quite awake and at it yet. In New York people were as loud in the morning as they were at night.

He and Patrick walked up some steps to a covered porch where a few chairs sat, impressions of bottoms worn into the wooden seats. Next to the screen door stood a long line of muddy boots in every size. Charles looked at Patrick and they both sat down on the steps to take off their boots. Patrick grimaced at the sole of the boot he hadn't walked in long. "Everything is covered in dirt and dust here."

"You haven't seen real dirt. Dirt is the gunk that smells like death itself, builds up on the sides of the street. Nothing can clean it off. That under your boot is soil. Everything good on this earth is made from it or made clean by it."

The boy raised his brows and dropped his boots in line with the rest. Charles placed his right alongside. That long line of boots made him feel all right. Like he was part of something.

They walked across the porch to the screen door. Voices that had been mere whispers began to rise.

"When your brother returns, we'll figure it all out. Until then, they stay. We can use the extra help right now, Nara Jean."

Nara's gravelly voice was even manlier when she talked low. "Even if that kid isn't dangerous, who is going to take care of them? I'm *not* doin' it."

Charles cleared his throat and opened the door. Nara turned around. Without her hat on, he could almost tell she was a woman, but her skin was dark from the sun like a workingman's.

She pushed out her chair, crushed a hat over her dark, curly hair, and spat out, "Eat up, boys. It's going to be a looong day."

After they all had breakfast, Papa Stewart disappeared, and Nara returned to show the three of them around.

She shoved open the screen door. "Come on, then."

Mama called out from the sink, "Be nice to those kids, and send Opal back after the chickens. I could use a little help and someone to talk to."

Opal's face brightened, but the smile in her was too afraid

to come out. The three of them fell in behind Nara. Her heels struck the ground like she could beat even the earth into submission. They tried to keep up, but she might have had eyes in the back of her head, because anytime they fell behind more than two steps, she'd turn and yell, "Giddyup!"

Opal was spared, for the most part. Nara showed her the chickens and coop, how to water them, collect eggs, and so forth. Opal handled the little chicks with fascination, petting fluffy feathers with her little fingers. Nara snapped at her, "When you're done, go help Mama in the kitchen."

Opal blinked from the force of Nara's words, then walked toward the house. Charles caught her and put his finger over his lips for her to keep silent with Mama about where they were from, but Opal looked at Nara with resentment.

"You boys hustle it up!"

She started them on what she called "barn chores," mucking stalls, oiling bridles, and scrubbing bits. Charles nodded, pretending to know what to do. After all, if they had lived up in Canada, he should know how to do this stuff. He went to the easiest chore, which should have been cleaning out stalls. As he scuffed around in the hay, the pungent smell of grassy horse manure floated up in the air. Nara studied him carefully before she finally said, "Is that how you were taught?"

She grabbed the pitchfork from him. "You've got to scoop up and throw the straw against the wall. See how the manure rolls down and separates from the straw? Maybe you had more straw up in Canada, but we can't replace all this bedding every time."

Charles took back the tool, grateful she wasn't onto him.

"Patrick, why don't you start on those bridles, while he finishes up these stalls? And make sure you get them good and clean before you put on the beeswax, you hear?"

Patrick smiled and said, "Yes, ma'am."

"We talked about all that 'ma'am' stuff at breakfast. You can address Mama like that, but you call me Nara."

After they were done in the barn, she had them scrubbing out cattle troughs. When Charles thought for sure she couldn't have another one of those big metal stinky things lying around anywhere, she'd always find one. They dumped the mucky water out and Patrick reached in with the scouring rag they'd been given. He pulled out slime that was a good foot long, like one big booger.

"Aagh." Patrick keeled over the edge and gagged.

He threw up chunks of breakfast all over the grass. Charles tried not to look, because once he did, it would be all over for him. From then on, they worked with one hand in the trough and their whole head out and turned away. By the time they were done scrubbing the slime out of ten of those big things, they were soaked to the skin and sour-smelling.

"We reek." Patrick wrinkled up his nose.

Nara came back to check on them and held out two sandwiches. They both looked at each other and grimaced. Patrick wiped his hand on the grass and took a sandwich from her.

She leaned up against a fence post. "You two all right? Maybe Mama has some extra aprons. You can join Opal in the kitchen."

Charles gritted his teeth. "We're fine."

She nodded like he was being a smart-ass and she had just the thing for that. She never showed them one thing about punching cows. Just weeds out in the kitchen garden, old stumps that needed digging, and only when the sky went completely dark did she let up.

"Go get cleaned up. Suppertime."

They stopped to wash up under the pump. Charles's shoulder burned, almost too tired to bring the water up. Him and Patrick wrestled off their muddy boots and stepped inside the house. He inhaled the home-cooking smells, but Mama wasn't serving up dinner. She was sitting with Opal on the couch asking her questions, pointing to those burns on Opal's wrists and forearms. Mama waved Nara over. She came and stood over Opal, intimidating her without realizing it. Opal sat with her head down, sullen. But silent.

"Charles, come over here and tell Mama how your little sister got these burns," Nara said.

In Hell's Kitchen getting out of trouble was all about talking fast. He dug around for an excuse for Opal's arms.

Mama stared at him. "You're the oldest. You must remember? She won't let me help her dress or bathe. Are there more scars we can't see?"

Charles grasped for anything to say, but Nara squinted at him. Too damn smart for her own good. She shook her head at him like he'd been the one to hurt Opal.

"Patrick, what do you know about these burns?"

The boy's cheeks splotched red and he turned away.

Nara crossed her arms. "We need to contact someone about these kids. Something's going on and not one of them is telling the truth."

CHAPTER 5

NARA TURNED IN HER CHAIR TO LOOK OUT TOWARD THE BARN, where high noon erased the shadows. She sipped at a cup of coffee gone bitter, but she could use the pep for later. Mama had gently indicated that Minnie should go back to Billings and take those secretarial courses. Minnie packed up so quick there was barely time for a proper goodbye. Nara had taken her to the station this morning and put her on a train, watching it chug-chug the happy girl back home. To a life of finger-pecking on a typewriter, wearing dresses, and city life. Whatever that meant. Nara had done her best but reckoned either you like it out here or you don't. Women out here can't be seen as pretty girls, or they'll get stuck inside washing other people's underpants.

During Nara's lifetime she'd seen a lot of people leave the countryside for the cities and an easier way of life. Her brother hadn't been invested in raising livestock. John could just sit and stare at the mountains for hours. He wasn't like other men. He saw patterns and colors most other people missed. He couldn't help it if he preferred his paints and canvases to rounding up cattle, chasing down errant bulls, or mending fences.

Nara heard a commotion upstairs. Furniture sliding, bumping, and scraping. She blew on her steaming coffee and gazed toward the ceiling, wondering what in the devil Mama was up to. Rather than figuring out the truth about these kids, she was hell-bent on acting like they were staying. Mama'd gone to the trouble of taking a train into Billings several days back and had come home late, grinning with excitement. Her heart would break when the kids moved on.

Mama had said Opal behaved warily around the stove. Must have been how she got those burns. Not one thing about their story passed the sniff test. A farm in Canada? Opal didn't look like she'd ever seen a cow, let alone milked one. Someone in town must have known something about these kids.

The other morning, she'd gotten the little girl up real early to help with the milking. Nara liked the quiet of it. The only sound in the barn was the hiss of milk on the steel pail and the occasional groan from the cows. The two of them walked to the barn with only the gentle light from a lantern swaying in Nara's hand. Before dawn was the most relaxing. A whole new day lay ahead, but she could start off slow and easy. Opal stopped at the barn door and just stared at the cow. The cow had swung its head around, and that was when Opal bolted. Nara had to chase after the bitty thing to calm her down. She found her on the front steps of the porch, her chest rising and falling as if she'd just seen a grizzly bear. And like every other interaction

Nara had with her, Opal was quiet. You had to read her like you would your animals.

Nara had sat with her for a time, and after the girl's breathing slowed, she asked her, "Haven't you ever milked a cow before? That old cow isn't gonna hurt you."

Opal fondled the clasp on the bib of her overalls. "It'll step on me."

"Only if you lie down underneath it."

Opal gawked at Nara as if she'd said the craziest thing. Nara almost chuckled, but then pulled a stern face. "Come on, kid. Day's a-wasting."

But now the little girl was upstairs helping Mama with whatever project she had going on up there. Curious now, Nara got up from the table and went up the stairs. They were in John's old room, untouched since he was a boy. The college pennant he'd sent away for would be hanging on the wall across from his bed. He must have lain in bed every night dreaming of the day he could leave. Maybe that was Papa's mistake right there, letting him buy that pennant and forming an ambition to leave for college. She walked into the wrong room, for the windows gaped open, and brand-new pink, frilly, silly curtains played with the wind. She stopped in her tracks.

"Mama, what the . . ."

The pennant was gone. Her brother was gone, and everything had been girlied up. There was a new brush-and-comb set that lay on Minnie's old vanity with the round mirror. The other furniture had been painted white, and a new bedspread lay over the spot where her brother used to kick up his heels in the afternoon.

"We're just fixing this up for Opal."

"You didn't change this when Minnie slept here. You can't do this. This isn't permanent."

Even Opal looking down at her feet with a humiliated touch to her face couldn't stop Nara's tirade. "You are too old to adopt these kids, Mama, and I'm sure as hell not doing it. You've got to stop this all right here. Right now. It's enough. I know what you've been through, but it's time to let it go."

Nara left the room and stomped down every stair to make sure her point was taken.

"Well, aren't you all rattles and horns today, missy!" Mama called after her.

No way in hell she was adopting three children. This whole thing just had to stop. She burst out the door of the house and walked to the stalls. She put on her horse's bridle and bit, then threw the saddle on with a grunt and pulled the girdle straps to the perfect tension.

"Blackie!" She whistled for her dog. White-socked paws pounded the dusty earth. "Come on, boy. Let's go check the cattle."

* * *

She rode until she reached the edge of the ranch and looked out over a cliff to the buttes beyond, no more than mountains with the tops flattened. The sun drifted directly overhead, illuminating the valley. Not a lick of shade to be found, except under the ponderosa pines that dotted the range here and there. The warmth of the sun penetrated the hat on her head and warmed up her scalp. She turned toward the fence and saw another break. An obvious one. "Shitfires," she swore under her breath.

Ivar's crew again. Her childhood friend Ivar Magnusson hadn't inherited the best land in these parts. Ivar's family were first-generation homesteaders from Missouri and immigrants from Norway before that. Ivar could never find anyone to marry him and join operations or land. She figured Ivar Senior had something to do with that. His father was just about the meanest bastard on two legs. Ivar had often shown up to school with black and blue on him.

She turned her horse around to head back for tools and make certain those boys were being worked hard under Jim's direction. She'd shared her suspicions about Charles with Jim, then told him, "Work those boys till they're so tired they can't cause any trouble. Maybe they'll do us all a favor and run off."

She stopped by the family graveyard to tend the wildflowers she'd planted over the years. It was a secret thing she did, could never reckon why. She had collected seed from the plants out on the range and then sprinkled the black specks at the edges of the shade where they'd get just enough sun but were still close enough to the lonely little graves sheltered by this stand of pines. Most of the headstones had been carved out of rock by her forebears, except Mabel's. Mama had ordered it special from Billings. Nara had gone with her. Each time Mama tried to tell the mortician what to engrave on the headstone, she'd choke with tears, unable to talk. Nara gently took the paper Mama had written the inscription upon and gave it to the tall man in the black suit. She didn't dare speak the words aloud, for it would make her sister's death real, something they couldn't change.

Nara ran her fingers into the grooves of those words etched into granite years ago. They'd last longer than the little bones in the ground. She knelt on one knee to pull at buffalo grass choking out the blooms, tearing and throwing thick blades to the greedy wind. The bitter scent of freshly torn grass filled the air, reminding her of that awful day, the blinding sun, spring-green grass, her sister's head at a sickly angle, the terror racing in her heart, tears that wet the ground, and now nothing. Just silence.

Her older sister, Mabel, had been swallowed up by a herd of cattle during roundup. The image of Mabel's funeral had been burned into Nara like the sunshine of that day falling all around them, the final bit of light shining on Mabel's box before it was lowered into the shadowy hole in the ground. So many nights, under her warm quilt, she wondered if Mabel was cold out here in the ground. There had been several weeks when Nara had to step in and help in the kitchen. To her shame, she'd been almost angry about it. Mama could barely get out of bed. Mabel had always been Mama's helper in the kitchen and her favorite. When they were younger, Nara had mostly just watched as Mama and Mabel did all the work. On occasion she'd be given something to do, but Mama didn't need two of them, and that left just one thing to do if Nara wanted to fit in somewhere. So she pulled on a little pair of boots, found an old pair of John's dungarees, rolled the cuffs up a good three times, and followed Papa and John instead. Papa had patted her on the head, chuckled at her willingness, always saying how cute that she was "out here in britches and little boots." He didn't make her feel like a third wheel, but vital. She had chores that were hers alone. Mama would ask her to stay back and help on occasion, but Papa needed her out on the range. It wasn't until her teenage years that either of her parents made any real objections, and she thought maybe it was because they didn't want to keep encouraging her. Her older brother, John, would inherit and run the cattle operation. All that changed when John decided he wanted a life as an artist in the big city. But now Papa kept thinking he'd come back, and she knew for a fact John wasn't going to.

She'd never really reflected on her history and choices much before. It just wasn't her way, but now she could understand why she'd chosen this life. How circumstances, her being that useless extra girl, had molded her this way and that, but life is one big river and you either swim with the current or drown fighting it. Even though what she wanted wasn't typical, Nara never thought of herself as bucking tradition. Her place was out on the range. Working every day from dark to dark doesn't give you much time to feel sorry for yourself. For that, she would always be thankful.

When her fingers were all cut up and streaky, she picked at the dirt wedged under her fingernails, then stood to straighten her aching back. She turned in a wide circle to take in the vastness, the emptiness. The pain of Mabel's death had dulled in the twenty-odd years since it had happened, but there should be another voice out here. The ear of a sister who'd listen and understand, but fate has its way.

WHEN SHE FOUND the boys with Jim, they were about one foot deep in mud and shivering. Wet dungarees plastered to their legs. Jim had them moving pipes that brought water in from the creek. She had every intention of making sure that horse thief learned a hard lesson. He'd gotten off too easy, and easy didn't belong out here. It was incongruent with just about everything in her world. You need to go to the mercantile? That's about ten miles by horse cart or wagon. You want to buy a new pair of boots? That's a trip to the railroad office to mail off your order to Sears & Roebuck or a trip into Billings by rail. Nothing out here ever came easy. Or fast.

Charles's large arms lifted the pipes up on a high, broad shoulder with seemingly no trouble. A thing she hankered for at times, that kind of strength, but she came into this world a woman.

Since those three had arrived, she had packed her rifle every day, made sure the door to the house was latched every night, and slept with her gun. Mama had furrowed her brows at all this, but nobody could deny those kids, unknown as they were, presented a potential danger to the family.

Something in Charles crackled, always ready to snap. It was in those green eyes. One minute he looked at her with those sandy brows in a V, looking like he was gonna buck and kick at anything, then in the next he'd give her a wet-eyed, stricken look like some small boy you just took a whip to for no reason at all. Added up, all it really meant was he'd learned to manipulate and lie. Mama and Papa were sure fooled.

She approached on horse, remembering she forgot to check

the cistern. Mama complained that it had backed up the other day and her sink drained slow. Normally that wouldn't make Nara smile. She sat her horse and waited for them to finish up with the pipes. Her fingers clutched and rubbed the hard twist fastened to her saddle horn. "I've got another chore for you boys over here. You're gonna cut a new ditch for the cistern. The shovels are in that shed out beside the bunkhouse—and gloves. Wear 'em. I won't have you crying you can't work tomorrow because you've got blisters on your hands."

Jim looked away, probably thought she was going too far. But she'd judged right, for Charles looked madder than hell, his eyes slitted and staring her down.

"You got something to say?"

He worked his jaw furiously and finally said, "How deep you want that ditch?"

"Jim'll let you know."

She turned from their sweaty faces and rode back to the house. Nara opened the screen door to grab some lunch. Normally Mama would call out hello and offer to make a sandwich, but she moved about the kitchen as if Nara were invisible. They had been baking bread. The loaves cooled on the sill as those two hustled around the kitchen working on supper. That yeasty smell made Nara's mouth water, but she didn't dare try her luck. Though Nara scuffed around the kitchen, Mama scarce grunted. Even Opal, if it were possible, seemed more silent. The girl followed Mama's instructions and didn't turn to look in Nara's direction once.

Mama would give her the silent treatment for a few days, three at least. Papa would cock an eye at them between turning the pages of his newspaper. He was smart enough not to get in the middle of their "woman squabbles," as he called them.

Nara put together a chicken sandwich and went to take a big bite when she heard a horse cart pull up outside. She peered out the window, grabbed the edge of the counter, and sighed. Mama came over, peered out the window, and did a rare thing. She swore. "Damn that girl. She better not put one careless foot on *my* porch."

Mama never spoke of that spring day. They were all so young. The sun was out, and the day was beautiful, until it wasn't. It was spring roundup. Ella and Nara had been lollygagging around like young girls do. All through their youngest years they had been the best of friends, until Ella had ridden fast at the herd. Thoughtless and impulsive. It made the cows panic. Nara's older sister, Mabel, had been in the middle of a swarm of furry backs, cutting calves. Mabel never came out of that stampede alive. That day burned inside her mama's gut like she'd swallowed the sun in the sky.

Throughout the years, Mama made sure Ella felt like the black sheep of Yellowstone County. When Nara was a girl, her mother taught the 4-H cooking classes in the county. All the girls had shown up except Ella. She'd come last. Maybe her ten-year-old heart knew what she was in for. Nara could still see little Ella standing there with her head down, shaded by the screen door and shame.

Mama had stalked to the door and muttered something the rest of the girls couldn't hear. When Ella didn't leave, Mama opened the door and pointed for her to leave like you shoo off a dog. The girls started laughing, and Ella finally had the sense to scoot.

As they grew older, Ella learned to keep her distance. After school, she married Art, the sheriff's son, as if that would raise her status in the county. Like many government positions out in the middle of nowhere, Art had inherited the sheriff's position once his father had gotten a little too long in the tooth.

Nara came out to the porch and stepped down, not to greet Ella, but to keep her away from Mama. Ella drove her cart, her round belly bouncing, baking up her seventh baby. A weakened condition like that made riding a horse near impossible. In the back were two of her youngest, who couldn't be of use on the small farm and ranch they kept for food more than anything else, but one had to be actively using the land to keep up the homestead agreement with the government.

Papa had often made the comment that Ella had been blessed with six boys in a row, like he'd forgotten all about Ella's part in his daughter's death, but crying wasn't Papa's way. Nara had never seen him shed a tear her whole life. Thankfully, he was out of town today buying some equipment in another county for a "good price," and more than likely casting an eye over the rolls at the homestead office. One more rancher going out of business. There was a greediness to her papa, for he grasped every bit of earth to him like there wasn't any other way to survive.

"Afternoon," Ella called out.

Nara walked up. "What's going on?"

Ella got down slowly, with her pregnant stomach. She had a freshly baked pie in her hand. Ella proceeded to the porch with a smile on her face, holding out that pie toward Mama. "I baked you a huckleberry pie, Mrs. Stewart."

The screen door slammed as Mama went back inside. Ella winced at the slight. "When is your mama gonna forgive me? I was only eight years old."

"Losing a child was hard on her."

Ella snorted. "Believe me, it's been tough on me, too. Your mama has seen to that. Anyways, I'm not here on a social call."

Nara put her hands on her hips. "What can I do for you?"

"I'm looking for some runaways."

It stunned her, but it shouldn't have. Nara merely raised a brow. "Really?"

"An orphan train came through a week ago. They jumped off somewhere between Big Horn and Custer."

"Huh. How many?"

"Two boys and a girl."

"Haven't seen 'em."

Ella's eyes scanned the ranch in a circle. "If you see 'em, the Children's Aid Society wants to know. Me and my cousin Judy are coordinators for them out here."

"I saw the posting at the train station."

If the person standing before her had been anyone *other* than Ella Connelly, she would have turned those runaways in right here and now. For the moment, she'd keep it to herself and think on things.

"What'll happen to them when you find them?"

"Take them back to New York. They've got a place there for runaways and kids nobody wants."

CHAPTER 6

"NARA, SET THAT GUN OVER BY THE COAL STOVE. YOU'RE GONNA shoot holes in my table." Mama frowned, then set down a plate of eggs and ham in front of Charles. He loved the salty smell and the brown sugar crust she baked it with.

Papa looked at the shotgun, then to Charles, who put his head down toward his plate. After all his backbreaking work, Nara went from being harsh to outright hostile, toting that gun wherever she went, watching him like you would a thief. Maybe he wasn't enough help around the ranch.

Opal sat at the table. "Good morning, Opal," Nara said.

Opal glanced her way but said nothing. Nara pursed her lips at the slight.

"Uh, Nara, is there anything you want me to do out with the cattle today?" Charles asked.

"Not until you can keep your butt in the saddle," she said, cutting up a piece of ham. "Jim will give you a horse to ride and care for. If you don't water it, the horse will go thirsty. You don't feed it, the horse won't eat."

He nodded, sure he could please her with this responsibility. "Yes, ma'am—I mean Nara."

She squinted one eye at him like one does looking down the sight of a gun.

After he finished up, he went to find Jim. He found him washing his hands under the water pump. "Nara said you have a horse for me."

Jim raised his brows. "In here. Come on."

They went into the stalls. Charles followed him with a dogged determination, but when Jim swung open the stall door and that burly mount came snorting right up to Charles and nudged him none too gently, he backed up and shuddered. To say this horse appeared intimidating might be a charity. It stood high and bulky, big boned where other horses were lithe. Its dusty coat grew splotchy gray like it had rolled in brimstone and ash. Its mane erupted from its withers short and frizzy, burned off, maybe. Though he didn't know why anyone would do that to a horse. Jim walked past the big horse and made to leave.

"Uh, Jim. How does this particular horse like to be saddled?"

Jim's brows came together, and he scrutinized Charles with those dark eyes.

"I just want to make sure I'm doing it how he likes it, is all."

Jim walked over to the tack and began to show Charles how to prepare the horse for riding. He did this with great patience and a gentle voice, such that it made Charles feel guilty for lying about having saddled a horse before. But it was just possible that Jim knew that.

He handed Charles the reins. "Take good care of this big boy."

Charles stepped forward. The horse swung its muzzle around and blinked a large eye at him, nostrils flaring. It had a black spot in the middle of its forehead where other horses would have a pretty white diamond. Its pink lips had a jagged scar.

"How'd he get that thing on his mouth?"

"Boss bought him up in Miles City a few weeks ago. Didn't pay much for him. He's an Appaloosa," Jim said, holding the creature in obvious reverence, stroking its withers.

"What's so special about that?"

"These horses were bred by the Nez Perce people. They used them for war and racing. These are ancient horses and have roamed these lands before any whites came. They are courageous and fast. If my life were in danger, I would want to be on the back of this horse."

"How do you know all that?"

"There was a time when only the Dzitsistas roamed these lands, they shared stories and traded skins."

"What do Cheyenne call white people?"

Jim smiled. "Dog face. For the hair on your face."

Charles rubbed his whiskery chin and looked around at all the other stalls. "I'm not sure I'm ready for a racing warhorse. Don't you have another one? Like that little golden horse you gave to Patrick?"

Jim shook his head. "A horse has to match the rider. His name is Charge."

And with that, Jim left Charles alone with the horse. He walked it from the stables. Nara watched from the porch. He hadn't wanted to look a fool, so he put one foot in the stirrup, but as soon as he got upright, the horse took off like a shot. Charles bumped around in the saddle, one foot out of the stirrup, trying to hang on. The devil horse aimed right for the clothesline where Mama and Opal were hanging the wash. Mama's arms flapped wildly. "No! Stop! No!"

He tried to duck. All those white things hanging in the breeze were the last thing he saw before the line grabbed him by the ear and the horse ran out from under him. He landed with a thud on his back and couldn't draw breath. At the time, he figured it might be the wet thin sheet plastered to his face, but even after Mama pulled it off, he had trouble filling his lungs. Mama crouched down. Opal's blue eyes had gone huge as she stood over him laid out in the grass.

"That's one ornery horse," Mama said, whomping him on the back. "Try to breathe."

Nara walked up, her white hat glowing in the sun, she said, "Grew up on a farm, huh? Now Opal and Mama have to rewash all this laundry."

"Don't you worry, Charles. Just an accident. Something Miss Nara had plenty of in her growing years."

Nara rolled her eyes at her mama and left. Charles picked up a wet sheet and shook it out. "I'm sorry. I can help you guys rewash this stuff."

"Never you mind." She turned to him with a serious eye. "Just promise me you'll be careful with that Appaloosa. They're not known for their gentle nature."

"Yes, ma'am."

After Charles helped pick up all the laundry, Patrick rode up on his golden palomino. "What happened?"

"My horse needs to know who's boss, that's all."

"Best ta think of yourselves as friends."

Charge had trotted behind the barn, where it nibbled on green tufts of grass like the demon hadn't nearly killed him. "You think Nara looks at her horse like a friend?"

"I seen her give it a carrot the other day."

Charles twisted his lips and narrowed his eyes at Charge, munching away. "I'll ask Mama, see what she can spare. Anyway, where have you been?"

"I rode out early ta see the wild horses."

After they had jumped off the train, they found a band of horses roaming free. Patrick had been able to get close enough to pet a few of them in the field while Charles and Opal watched in awe.

"You can't do that. You'll get caught."

"I didn't think anyone would mind." Patrick shrugged as if he didn't know what Charles meant.

"Of course they'll mind." Charles looked around and drew close. "I can't go back to New York, and neither can Opal. You're gonna blow this for all of us. Maybe I shouldn't have asked you to jump off the train with me."

Patrick's sky-blue eyes went wide, then fell. "Sorry."

The boy wouldn't look at him, just kept his head down, quiet. Charles had never felt bad for being hard on someone before. Patrick didn't strike him as someone who'd do something wrong on purpose. "Come on. Since you're so darn good with horses, why don't you show me how to ride that devil horse?"

* * *

An hour or two with Patrick helped calm both horse and rider, so that by the time Charles led Charge into the stable, he felt more confident handling the big horse, though it cost him a few scrapes and sore body parts. When he went to open Charge's stall door, he found a string of pearls hung on the handle. He ran his fingers over the silky smooth orbs. The dainty gold clasp was undone, and they had been nearly falling into the hay, where they would have been ruined. They must be worth a fortune. He looked around and then tucked them into the front pocket of his dungarees.

Charles searched for Opal and found her out by the chickens. She held a sloshing bucket of water with two hands, preparing to water the chickens.

"Opal, wait."

She set the bucket down and looked up to him.

"What've you got against Nara?"

"She's mean."

He knelt. "I know, but if we want to stay here, you gotta convince Nara."

Opal wrinkled her nose and crossed her arms.

"Do it for me, then. If she says good morning, you say it back, all right?"

She turned her head away, starting with that pointy chin.

"Boy, you're stubborn. Unless you want to see the inside of

one of those orphanages back in New York or a workhouse somewhere, you had better find it in yourself to be at least nice."

"I'm nice to Mama."

"She won't always be around, Opal. She's old enough to be your granny, and what if she dies?"

Opal looked up into his eyes with a shine in her own. It made him feel guilty for scaring her, but it had worked. She breathed out hard, which he'd come to find was her way of giving in. It was the only way one could know Opal was going to relent, because she sure as hell wasn't going to tell you.

He still hadn't a prayer of moving Nara's feelings about himself. He picked her some wildflowers he found near some pines. He'd torn off a string from the hem of his shirt and wound it around the stems and tucked them into his rope until he got back. She was on the porch. He felt stupid as he approached and handed them to her. "Found these for you."

"Where'd you pick those?"

He'd pointed in the direction of the pines, and her face went red. She grabbed the blooms from his timid hand, threw them over the porch rail into the dirt, and muttered, "Don't ever pick those flowers again, you hear?"

At dinner he sat at the table still feeling her words like the sting from a slap. He tried not to look her way, but he could see well enough from the corner of his eye. She ate quietly, a pensive air about her. Papa Stewart didn't act any different. Mama Stewart was her usual cheerful self, talking more than anyone else at the table. He couldn't imagine how the flowers could have upset Nara so much.

He wondered if he could ever do anything right, and that's when he remembered. Fishing around in his pocket, he stood and pushed out his chair. "Mama, I think these might be yours." He held up the pearls.

Her mouth opened wide. "Where did you find them?"

"Out in the stable hanging on Charge's stall door. I figured they might be yours and put them in my pocket."

Nara and Papa scrutinized him. Papa then raised his brows at Nara, who pursed her lips and stabbed at the food on her plate.

Mama took them from his hand and said for everyone to hear, "Charles, thank you so much for finding them and returning them to me safely. I can't *imagine* how they got out of my dresser." Then she glared at Nara.

The whole thing felt weird, so he was relieved when Opal padded down the steps, as it took everyone's attention from him.

As soon as she sat down, she peeked over at Nara and said, "Hello, Nara."

Every mouth stopped chewing, forks stilled. There might have been a few people around the table who wondered if she could even talk. Charles gave her a nod of approval. She puckered up her mouth, all red in the face. Nara passed her some rolls.

"How are those little chickens doing?"

"I roll the eggs twice a day like you said."

Mama praised her for all the good work Opal'd been doing in the henhouse and milking cows.

"Why aren't you eating, Charles? I thought you liked chicken," Nara said.

"Just feeling full, is all."

"Hmm. Maybe they didn't have chicken in Canada?" she said.

"Nara, leave that boy alone," Mama called from the sink, then she said, "There was a group of men, sheriff, too, out here snooping around. They knocked on the door while you were all gone, but you know I don't talk to *him*."

Nara's head shot up, and then she stared at Charles. His guts felt like a cold faucet had turned on somewhere inside. The Children's Aid Society was bound to have put out word by now. He should never have come looking for horses, should have ditched the younger two and run like hell. Divided, they would have been harder to identify. His heart thumped in his chest.

Papa looked over for half a second but went back to stuffing his pipe, then he left to go smoke out on the porch. Charles followed the old guy outside, feeling claustrophobic in the house. Papa rocked in his chair, smoking and petting Blackie. "Have a seat, young man."

Charles had been about to go out to the bunkhouse, pack a rucksack, and leave out the back way, but instead sat in a rocking chair across from Papa. The dog walked over and leaned on him. Though his hand shook terribly, he bent to pet the dog's head up on the bony crest of his skull. The fur behind its ear was soft, soothing.

"How's the horse?" Papa asked. "Paid a dollar for that gelding."

"It's . . . a strong horse."

They'd sat for a time when Papa said, "You got something on your mind, young man?"

"No, sir. Just a fine night to sit out."

"Hmm," he said. "You know, folks out in Canada, they have a certain way of talkin'. City folks, too."

Charles thought he'd been doing a good job talking without the New York accent. One thing he'd learned was keep answers short and never answer with the truth, because a lot of times they only suspect, they're fishing. "I wouldn't know, never been to any filthy city."

Papa took his pipe out of his mouth for a second, his face one part admiration, one part gall. Then he sat back, chuffed a little, and picked up his guitar. Charles made himself sit there for a while longer, sweating in his shirt even though the nights were cool enough to give you a chill, even in the summer.

He said good night and began to walk to the bunkhouse, hands in his pockets to keep them warm. Opal went after him, her legs beating the ground furiously to catch up with him. He stopped by the water pump, wondering what she had to say, for she stood there in the dark with only enough moonlight to see the concern in her face as she asked him, "Charles, you're not going to die, are you?"

He wondered if she had lost her parents, too. Her golden hair and those downturned eyes reminded him of his ma. If he'd ever had a sister, she might have looked like Opal, but taller. His eyes stung a little as he got down on his knees to be even with her. "I promise it won't happen. I'm always careful with the horses."

She twisted up her little mouth, probably remembering the clothesline. "Be *extra* careful around the cows. Don't lay down underneath them."

On the streets, he was always the protector in his pack. Having one so tiny as Opal care about him felt new, tender. Charles shook his head. Opal was sure growing on him.

"I promise I won't lay underneath a cow. You better get to bed."

He went inside the bunkhouse, wondering if he should leave in the middle of the night. Patrick stood by his bunk, fluffing his pillow. "I know yer worrying. She's gonna warm to ya."

"Nara's no longer our biggest problem. You heard Mama. People are looking around."

"Even so, I have a feelin' everything is going ta turn out fine."

"Where I come from, fine doesn't happen."

Patrick climbed into his bunk and lay down, hands on his chest. "These folks are fair, and we'll at least have that on our side. If we run off, we won't even have that. We'd much better stay put."

Charles thought about that for a moment and then readied himself for bed. He lay down and pulled up his warm covers, trying to talk himself into everything turning out all right. Waking up in a comfortable bed inside where it was warm, to a table full of food, was enough incentive to wait and see what would happen over the next day or so.

* * *

Nara wasn't much of a talker on any given day, but her silence today was louder than usual. They crossed through the valley, skirting big tufts of sage. Nara had doled out chores this morning and looked to Charles last. "You're coming with me to check on the herd at the far end of the ranch."

They rode through dusty trails he'd never seen before and familiar mountains began to disappear. She followed him from behind and gruffed out general directions on occasion. As he searched all around, it occurred to him he wouldn't know how to get back. His mind wandered to dark places. Big as he was, she made him nervous. He knew she wielded weapons with great accuracy. He had seen Nara and Jim out practicing with their rifles and targets. She shot tin cans clean off the tree stump one after the other. It was like she was trying to prove something everyone refused to see. Charles didn't think he could outrun her or her shotgun, so he kept on going, thinking.

They continued in a northerly direction. Nara remained silent. On occasion, he'd look back to make sure she followed. "Up through that narrow pass," she said from behind.

He leaned forward on Charge as the horse began to climb up a steep ravine dotted with pines that closed in all around them. When they got to the top, Nara brought her horse before a sheer cliff with a view of a valley below. He came up beside her, hoping she had a lesson for him.

The wind moaned, bringing up grit. He wiped his eyes, teared and blurry from the relentless wind, so he hadn't seen her grab the shotgun. The barrels of which pointed straight at his head, two steely holes like eyes.

"Charles, I want you to tell me one more time where you come from. And this time, you damn well better not lie to me."

Nara had him cornered, and considering the sheer cliff below, there was no good way out. In New York, he'd made an art form of getting out of tight spots. He had one option left.

CHAPTER 7

NARA STARED DOWN THE BARREL OF HER SHOTGUN, HANDS
steady. He might have returned those pearls to Mama, but he
had a past. No two ways about it. Orphan or not, insides and
intuition meant a lot out here, where people said little and hid
much. "Well?"

He continued to gaze at her without any apparent concern.
He'd been here before. She held tight to her gun, so he couldn't
knock it from her hands. "You better start talking, kid."

His horse skittered, sensing its rider's tension, and she nearly
pulled the trigger.

"Wait! We rode an orphan train out here."

"That much I know. Where'd you come from?"

"Hell's Kitchen."

"Bullshit."

"Honest—it's a neighborhood in New York City."

"Okay, what happened to your parents, then? The devil get
'em?"

His head dipped down, and something tired in him said,

"My pop died in the war, and my ma took to drinking. She was mean after that and there was never any food. After a while I just didn't come home. A few years later I went back, our rooms were empty. I figured she drank herself to death."

Nara winced. "Yeah, but how'd you eat and survive?"

"I had a little gang of friends. We huddled up at night. We ate from trash cans, swiped food whenever we could. I'm not proud of it."

Nara lowered her gun a hair.

"I heard about the Children's Aid Society. I knew they sent kids out West. When my pop was alive, he used to read me cowboy stories at night. *Riders of the Purple Sage* was our favorite. He dreamed of moving us out here . . ." His Adam's apple bobbed, choking all his words.

He told her about the stops on the train platforms. "People would poke me, squeeze my arms, put their fingers in my mouth, but they'd never look me in the eye."

Hearing that last part, she shifted in her saddle. She'd been on the platform that morning when the orphan train came through, but she was only curious. And then they showed up on her ranch anyway. Someone upstairs had a hell of a sense of humor. She laid her shotgun across her lap.

She listened to his story, everything rushing out of him in a torrent. He talked about the other kids on the train, the lucky ones who were taken away to homes. The man who'd spat on Patrick's feet, and the farmer who rejected them both at the last stop.

"I just couldn't go back to Hell's Kitchen. It's the worst place you can imagine, Nara. When we jumped off, Patrick hurt his leg, so I went looking for horses. I figured we could travel faster, and he wouldn't have to walk."

"You showed up here with bruises all over your face."

He looked startled, and something had hold of his tongue. "I . . . I slipped on rocks and fell on my face."

"Where?"

"In the river."

"Why were you in the river?"

"We . . . were fishing."

"With what?"

"Ah . . . our hands."

"Did you catch anything?"

"No."

She put her shotgun back in its scabbard. "How did you three manage at night before you came looking for horses?"

"We all huddled up in between the rocks. I'm used to sleeping outside without blankets."

That was at least an honest answer. Nara put her hands over her eyes and shook her head, trying to block out all the terrible things she'd said and done to the three of them after they'd been out starving in the cold for days and nights. She squinted at him, considering things. That boy was a wily son of a gun, his eyes vulnerable and pleading,

She let out a big belly breath. How in the hell and on what basis she'd offer this boy room and board never added up in her mind, for she was almost certain he'd gotten those bruises in New York, but he worked hard, and on that ground alone, she said, "I can't make any promises. But as long as you keep your nose clean, I'll see if you can stay on to work—for now. Papa will have the final say."

"I'll work really hard. I promise. Just, please, don't send me back." His jaw trembled and tears plopped down, dotting the leather of his saddle and dungarees like fat raindrops.

His bawling surprised her as much as his words. She looked away from his crumpled face and reined her horse around, trotting off. Maybe she should have reached over to pat his shoulder, but she wouldn't like to have someone staring at her as she broke into pieces. She rode ahead so he could pull himself together.

She glanced back, and he had bent over that ugly horse, his hands fingering that stubbly mane looking for comfort. An unbearable sight, and soothing wasn't her thing. He was almost too old to be her son, but he could be a much younger brother. And if he were, she'd have popped him on the back of the head for such an unmanly display.

They rode back in silence. She wondered why a grandmother or an aunt didn't help him after his parents were gone. Maybe he was a troublemaker, and his family didn't want to help him. Or maybe there wasn't anyone else. When Nara remembered her tirade over the bedroom frills the other day, she could have crawled up into a ball and just died. What a terrible thing to say to that bitty girl, who had stood up on that train platform day after day, being picked over like some runty calf.

Now she had to tell her parents. Papa would give her that "I told you so," and Mama would cluck over this no end. Those kids would be stuffed and coddled beyond measure. Mama would cook up every good thing, stuff them till they puked. Getting rid of them now was gonna be a real uphill battle.

* * *

Later that evening over the coal stove, the three of them huddled together, whispering over what had to be done. Nara drooped a little. Whether she was truly tired or humbled was somewhat muddled in her mind, but she relayed the whole of Charles's story.

Papa shook his head. "I wouldn't send my worst enemy to New York, much less turn these kids out. They'll end up working for some mean son of a gun like Ivar Magnusson."

"We can't hide them forever, and we're breaking the law. I've been working Charles like a dog as punishment for trying to steal a horse, and how are we any better?"

"We'll have to make it all legal somehow," Papa said.

"What? That means adoption, and who of us is in the right place to do something like that? I'm not married, and you know I'd not know what to do with them. Opal just barely uttered a word to me this morning."

She didn't want to say her parents were getting up there in age, but they were getting up there in age. Facts were facts. No two ways about it.

"I think Charles might make a damn good foreman someday, Nara."

"Whoa. You give him too much credit. He can't even ride a

horse, for crying out loud, and I don't think Charles got those bruises in a fall. They were too old, yellowed. He's lying about something."

"He probably had to fight his way out of that damn city."

"Doesn't matter—he's too big for any of us to handle. At sixteen, he'll continue to grow. Have you forgotten about the train rider from Wyoming who killed that whole family?"

"Charles wouldn't hurt a fly," Mama said.

"He's big, sure enough, but I've seen how hard he can work," Papa said.

"There are a lot of people who work hard around here," she said, hot in the face.

Papa rubbed his whiskery jaw. "I imagine he's old enough to live on his own whether or not we adopt him. The other two are young enough to pursue making it legal."

Mama must have already adopted them in her mind, for she put herself between them and went to the next step. "Who all knows they're here?"

"Ella must suspect. She was out here the other day."

"You shouldn't have waited to tell us."

"I needed time to figure things out."

"Of all the people to hold a hammer over our head. She would be the damn adoption coordinator," Papa said. "Well, let's sleep on it."

Nara ripped off her hat and ran her hands through her springy hair. "What will make our situation different tomorrow? Tell me that."

"I don't know, but some shut-eye will sure help," Papa said.

Nara nodded impatiently. "They'll still be here in the morning, and we'll still be just us three, but hell yes, let's sleep on it."

"Clean up that mouth." Mama ripped that towel off her shoulder and gave Nara a whip on the hindquarters as she escaped up the stairs to her bedroom.

NARA STRIPPED OFF her workman's attire. Men's boots, dungarees, underwear, and wool socks. The only thing feminine was the brassiere she'd bought from the Sears catalog. It was shiny and soft, but there wasn't enough of that in her to be a mama to three broken children.

There were plenty of unfeminine things about her. Too many to count. She sat down at her mirror and grabbed the pot of cold cream Mama had bought "for your rough skin." Nara leaned closer to the mirror to get a better look at the brown spots and wrinkles around her eyes and on her cheeks. She dipped her finger into the jar and slathered on the cream. It had a light flowery smell of some kind that reminded her of the flowers she'd found on the table the other day. Nobody would fess up to putting them there, but as she took up the little vase and put them to her nose for a sniff, Jim had watched her out of the corner of his eye, and she knew. The attraction with Jim could go nowhere, but sometimes when they stood too close everything went haywire in her brain.

They were out pulling a large bull calf from a heifer. The young cow had been lying down in distress when they came upon her in prone misery. Nara had felt inside for the little slimy hooves and then wrapped chains around them. Jim put his shoulder into the hindquarters to hold the cow while Nara pulled. Their shoulders and heads touched as they both did their respective duties. Something inside her must've wanted to feel every inch of him, for whenever their bodies touched, her nerve endings went on high alert, sopping up every tiny sensation. The warmth of his skin, tickly hair, the soft cotton shirt covering his hard arms.

"She isn't pushing yet. Wait a second. There she goes," Jim had said.

Nara's face had bloomed a hot red. She'd forgotten a pretty basic part of pulling a calf.

But she didn't think on it long as his thighs brushed her own and her whole body shivered like some untried young girl.

The gas lamp hissed using too much kerosene, so she reached over, shut it off, and curled up on her side. She burrowed under her worn quilts that smelled of hair and sleep, shuddering to warm them up. The feel of her familiar pillow and soft quilt made her remember what Charles had told her about sleeping outside. No bed, no blankets. She just couldn't imagine it. But feeling sorry for someone and being the right person to help them out wasn't the same thing.

* * *

The Stewarts and their neighbors drove a herd of thundering hooves against a deep escarpment of a mountain where the cattle would be trapped. The flat-topped mountain towering above did its best to keep out that mischievous wind, but on occasion a dust devil would come out of nowhere to kick up some dirt for a little grit in the eye and some between the teeth.

During spring roundup neighbors showed up to help, knowing you'd be there for them when the time came. Folks she'd known her whole life were scattered about the grassy valley. She always recognized who was who, even from a great distance. Something about the way they sat their horse, the horse itself, or maybe it was the tilt of their hat. Ivar and his crew had been earliest to arrive and the most helpful. A few hands galloped about, rounding up the remnants of the herd. Soon the air would be heavy with the odor of burnt hair.

Ivar's boys were up on the ridge taking a break. It looked like they might be tipping a flask. The one doing the most drinking was Ella's brother. Like his sister, he was a troublemaker.

Just a year before John left for the city, he'd gotten into a tussle with the boy. John came home with a scratch on his face, his shirt a little torn. Mama had looked him over and asked him what had happened. He never did say, but Nara eventually heard it from Mary. Apparently Ella's brother had approached John at the Dark Horse and asked him about his painting, and, "Do you draw fairies?" John replied with a fist, and there ensued a short scuffle, ending with Ella's brother laid out. John never told Mama where he'd been, because if she or Papa knew he'd been out drinking, there would have been hell to pay.

The branding wagon had been brought out. On one end it had all the branding irons and tools, and on the other end was a fold-down table with room for all of Mama's pots and pans filled with food. Mama and Opal stood there working the lunch end of the wagon. They'd be the busiest of anyone. Mama kept the girl within arm's reach. Mama couldn't go back in time and pull her favorite daughter, Mabel, out of that stampede, but she had Opal tethered up good and tight, right nearly under her apron. Mama was falling hard for that bitty girl.

Mama wanted to keep the three of 'em at the ranch where no one would see them, but Nara insisted they work. Papa had said they needed the extra hands, plus it was a good opportunity to show Charles a thing or three, and besides, people kept their noses out of other families' business out here. But seeing Ella's brother up on that ridge today made the hair on her head bristle. They didn't know that young man had joined Ivar's crew.

Every once in a while, Nara'd catch Opal's eye. The girl would hold it for a slim second. Opal wore one of Mabel's old dresses, but it hung too short. Mama should have had the girl wear some overalls, but it was the neighbors being around and all. A dress was a damn pain in the ass. She rarely wore them as a girl, and only on the Lord's day. Besides, she wouldn't be caught dead riding a horse in a dress. The horse would wear it before she would.

Nara got off her mount and went over to the branding irons and fire. Jim would do the branding today with a gentle touch. She came over to him as he tended the fire and irons. One of them glowed red-hot. She put her hand on the blackened iron to feel its heat and stood close to Jim. Their shoulders rubbed and it sent a wonderful feeling through her like nothing else. "This feels perfect," she said.

His body leaned against the whole side of hers as he reached over to test the iron. His dark hand covered her own. "You're right."

He caught her eye as they stood close. It held deep and strong, like he had crawled inside her with just that rich, dark eye. Everything and everyone around them blurred into a periphery of nothing she could see or hear.

Somebody whooped and Papa hollered something back. It brought Nara back into the crowd around her. A world where she'd best be seen as a man if she wanted her life's dream.

"Better get to it, then," she said.

She mounted her horse. The saddle gone warm from the sun. "Patrick, come over here and watch carefully, I'm going to demonstrate how to cut a calf from the herd."

Mama called out, "Nara, make sure he knows what he's doin' before he goes into that herd!"

Nara turned around and nodded toward Mama's terrified face.

"Patrick, you need to approach real slow and relaxed. You don't want to startle them and get them running. You could be stomped to dust. You understand?"

Patrick nodded and followed her inside the herd of furry backs. They rode so close to the cattle you could see the curl of the fur along the bumply spines.

Cutting calves was her favorite chore on the ranch, so she'd laughed when Patrick asked her if he really had to cut them. He was a soft one for sure, but he had a natural way with the animals. Out checking the herd the other day, they came upon a rattler. A lesser rider would have panicked when the horse reared up, but Patrick kept his seat and got the horse's head turned around to stop it from spooking. There were men three times his age who couldn't handle a horse so well. He'd be perfect for separating calves.

She rode into the center of the herd. Cattle brushed up against her legs, connecting her to something bigger than herself. She faced up with the calf she meant to cut and walked her horse toward it until the other cows walked away and it was separated. Her horse knew their quarry, and as soon as the calf tried to bolt toward the herd, her horse jumped in front of it. The calf jumped the other way, and her horse mirrored its moves each time.

Ivar rode up and threw a rope around its neck, while another hand ran out on foot and clutched the rope, his hand sliding down the line until he reached the calf. He seized the calf by the knot on the back of its head and set it on its flank. The cowboy tied a rope around three legs quick as lightning, then pulled off his hat and whooped. "Probably my best time ever!"

Ivar's group clapped and hollered, cheering him on. Jim came over with the branding iron and set it to the calf's rump with a hiss of smoke. The calf's legs were unwrapped, and it ran back to the herd. The bunkhouse at Ivar's place and hers would be full of big talk and stiff backs tonight.

Everyone worked together for about three hours cutting calves when they had gotten down to the last. Patrick did a fine job for his first time out, but it would be a few years before he could do it safely on his own. Papa and Ivar were slapping Charles on the back and fawning over his strength and speed. Those big manly whops on the back were a sign of acceptance. A club she'd never make it into.

Everyone crowded around the lunch wagon. Mama and Opal busied themselves with handing out plates of chow. Nara helped spread out blankets to sit and eat on. She decided to join Ivar today, seeing how he was alone. His crew gathered up on the ridge, yelling, whooping, and getting rowdy. Opal headed their way with plates in her hands.

CHAPTER 8

CHARLES LAY ON A BLANKET, LETTING THE BIG BLUE SKY FILL HIS eyes with sunshine. "Opal, tell me the truth. Did you really make this pie?"

She looked down at him, fists on her hips. "Yes."

Patrick rolled over into the grass and grabbed his neck. Gagging, spitting, and finally laughing. She swatted his leg. "Not funny, Patrick."

But Charles saw her smile a little. He dug into his pie thinking it was the best thing he'd eaten since the Stewarts had taken them in, and he'd never gone hungry in the last many weeks. They'd been working all day without their usual break, and though he was ravenous in his belly, he was satisfied in his heart.

Charles had wrestled a kicking calf to the ground, using his shoulder, knee in the gritty ground, handling the matted fur, roping its three hooved legs with a bristly rope. By the time he'd done that three times, he'd gotten the hang of it pretty well. Papa had said, "Pretty dad-gone good," and then he slapped Charles on the back.

The rest of the hands had all competed to see who could rope the fastest, with Papa calling time on his pocket watch.

"Not bad for a Canadian," Jim had said.

In the week prior to the roundup, Jim had shown them how to use the catch rope. A hard twist, he called it.

Patrick asked, "Why do they call it a hard twist?"

"This rope is bound from many fibers wound tightly. It will never break."

Jim had held the rope in his bronze hands and made another loop. He then swung it around his head like a big angel's halo. "Kiss your hand each time you swing it around your head to keep the rope open, then release it. Where the hand aims, the rope will land."

Charles took another bite of his pie now, thinking about what he aimed for. He felt happy for the first time in a long, long while. Papa's big grin as Charles had thrown that calf on its side and roped it like he was a real cowboy, that warm slap on the back. It made something click inside for him. He didn't just fancy being a cowboy, what he really wanted was to be a part of this family. Pop would have liked the Stewarts and Montana. Charles clasped his lucky horseshoe underneath his shirt.

Mama Stewart stood at the back of the branding wagon and called Opal over to her. "You've got work to do still. Take these pieces of pie over to them fellas of Ivar's sitting up there."

Opal put her hand over her eyes, squinting from the sun. Her gaze landed in the direction of three men spread out and away from everyone else. A wariness washed over her face. Charles didn't know her story, but he knew that look well enough. Opal was scared.

"Go on, and hurry back. We've got more pie to hand out."

Charles knew why Ivar's hands had gone off alone. He smelled it on their breath when they were roping, and they'd been sneaking drinks when Papa Stewart wasn't looking. By now they'd be falling-down drunk. Just like his mother.

Opal reluctantly walked over and took the plates from Mama, using that stubborn chin to keep one balanced on her arm. She walked up the small slope and stood there with her pie. He couldn't hear what they were saying to her, but the look in that one fella's eyes got Charles's attention.

Charles had been talking to that same hand after the branding was done, but Mama called him over to her, told Charles to stay away from him. Said something about him being Ella's brother, and they didn't socialize with that family. Wouldn't say why.

Ella's brother lay down with his legs all spread, relaxing. He urged Opal forward to give him the plate, and she stepped closer to him. One of his friends started laughing and rubbed his nose, looking all squinty toward the wagon where everyone else gathered.

It was enough for Charles. He walked briskly. Opal's back was to him, but he could see the rigidity in her little spine well enough. She took a step back and stumbled a little. Charles heard Opal say, "Let go of my dress."

"I just want a little peek at your panties."

Charles broke into a run, teeth bared. Opal must have heard him coming, the beast inside him emerging and growling. By the time he reached Ella's brother, she was gone. Charles jumped square on him, pinned him down with his legs, and beat the guy anywhere his fists would connect. A rib cracked under his fist. Charles rammed his forehead into the ranch hand's nose, and blood splattered, coloring everything red. Charles kept swinging, lost inside of his own rage. The other two hands came up behind and pulled him off. Charles shoved them both roughly away, for they had watched and laughed as a little girl was accosted.

When his eyes came into focus again, the hand he'd beaten lay wet and slick, covered in red from his face and all down his shirt. During that fight, Charles had been back in the grimy streets and dark alleyways of Hell's Kitchen, where only the brutal survived. There, a beating like this was a mere warning, common, but as he took in all the attention and shock around him, he remembered he lived in a different place now, with people foreign to him.

The man on the ground lay still. It frightened Charles, until the man's eye's flickered. His head lolled to the side and blood poured out of his nose.

Nara came up from behind, her face red-hot with anger. "What in the hell do you think you're doin'?"

Charles labored to breathe. "He had ahold of Opal's dress and lifted it to see her panties!"

Papa Stewart stalked up, with Ivar right on his heels. Papa looked to Nara for an explanation.

"I knew something like this was gonna happen." She stepped back, leaving Charles alone.

Two of Ivar's hands walked up and pointed to Charles. "He came out of nowhere and just started beating the tar—"

"I was protecting Opal." Charles pointed to the bloody man on the ground, who was only up on his elbows thus far. "He tried to pull up her dress." Charles searched for Opal, who had run to the wagon. She helped collect dishes and scrape plates as if she hadn't nearly been messed with. "Ask Opal, she'll tell ya."

As soon as those words came out of his mouth, he realized how stupid they sounded. Opal might not say anything.

Ivar stood, hand on his jaw, considering everything around him with those flinty eyes. "I want to talk to Opal," he said.

He walked down to the wagon and approached Opal, who ignored him and kept cleaning up. She scraped the plates with more ferocity than before, then shook her head and turned from him, ending the conversation.

Charles breathed in deep and looked to the sky as if doing so would bring on some divine intervention. Papa went over to the place where Ivar's hands had been lying and drinking.

"They have a flask of hooch. I saw it," Charles said.

One of the guys put his hands up in the air as if to say, *Not me*. The other one patted his shirt pockets and tried to look innocent, shaking his head.

"You boys been drinking?" Papa asked.

"No, sir. Honest to goodness."

Charles turned from the scene, hands on his hips. They'd ditched the flask somewhere. Probably threw it out in the sage.

Nara and Papa had their heads together, talking between themselves. "That kid is going to be your foreman someday?"

Papa ran his fingers over his brushy mustache. "I hate to be indebted to a Magnusson," he growled low.

Charles wished he hadn't overheard what they said, hadn't come so close to finding a place to belong. Wished Papa hadn't patted him on the back, told him "Good job." Charles kicked the gravelly soil under his boot and walked off down the ridge toward his mount, knowing nobody would grab his shoulder and stop him. Tell him sorry, they'd been wrong about what happened. He kept walking, no bracing warmth on his back, just a mocking afternoon wind shoving him from behind like he didn't belong.

* * *

He'd gone back to the bunkhouse to pack his stuff, but nobody ever showed up to throw him out. He sat in there waiting for the verdict, but it never came. He heard Papa playing the guitar out on the porch. Charles wanted to go out and see if Papa would talk, but he'd probably just disturb the man's one bit of peace. Jim had ridden off on his motorbike. Maybe Charles should have asked for a ride, but Jim usually went to the Cheyenne reservation, and that was too far south of the ranch, and Charles needed to get to the train station, which was west. After the supper smells stopped driving Charles crazy, Patrick opened the door uneasily, searching Charles over. It was the first time Patrick had a hard look to his eye. For some time, the boy lay silent up in his bunk. His Irish lilt split the soundless air when he finally said, "Charles, what's the worst thing ya ever done?"

"You don't wanna know."

Charles stared above, where Patrick's mattress pressed through the wooden slats. The bunkhouse went completely still, not a breath, nor an uncomfortable wiggle. Many minutes later, a soft snore quivered like contentment. A peace afforded to those without a bad conscience to keep them awake.

The next morning at breakfast, Charles walked in expecting to get the send-off, but everyone was intent on their food, quiet. The moment he sat down, Nara pushed out her chair and cleared her plate, scratching the ceramic with her metal knife. Mama's mouth pursed as she watched Nara rough up her dishes. Opal looked at Charles a few times with gratitude in her eyes. He would rather she told them what had happened, but he figured she might have, seeing as how he hadn't been tossed out.

Papa had already finished, yolk smeared across his plate, his head in his newspaper. Westerners were funny people. The more important something was, the less they said about it. Nara sipped her coffee and stared out the window. Charles ate a few bites, but all he could taste was burnt calf hair from branding yesterday. Patrick kept to himself, where most mornings he'd have a smile and something to say. Mama usually spoke more than anyone else, but she fidgeted over by her plate to make up for it.

Charles stood up and cleared his plate before he finished and put it in the sink of lemony water Mama had prepared. He imagined her fretful hands would dry it with that dish towel of hers before long. The last meal she'd ever make for him.

He left their house. Where he was going, he couldn't say. He felt lost, scared. He went out behind the barn and leaned back against the worn wood. One would think he could find a place at a neighboring ranch, but he was sure word was out by now about the fight. Nobody wanted a troublemaker, and he barely had any experience besides. But Papa apparently had talked about training him for the foreman position. Papa Stewart kept one eye on the future. For anyone to even consider that Charles could do that job was a stretch, he supposed. But for some reason, Papa believed in Charles, and he'd waited a long time to find someone who could see the good in him.

But Nara didn't feel that way at all, so it could be the Stewarts were just biding their time until the authorities in New York could be reached to take him off their hands. That gave him a shock to the heart. It would take a while for the agent to get back out to Montana, and by then Charles could think up a place to go. He would miss them, all of them. His eyes burned with the cruelty of his fate.

Papa rounded the corner. "There you are. We need to talk."

Charles pushed off the wall to stand before the older guy and take whatever he had coming but turned his heart-sore eyes away from the keen gaze before him.

"Ivar isn't going to make a big stink of it, seems to think the hand had it coming, but you're going to have to make some adjustments."

"You mean I can stay on?"

Hands on hips, Papa looked to the sky. "Do you think you can keep your fists to yourself?"

"Yes, sir."

Papa's finger thumped Charles's chest. "You do that, and we'll all try to forget how badly you busted up that young man's face. He's gonna be breathing out of his ears for a while."

"But he was being nasty to Opal."

"There's gonna be a lot of people in her life who are gonna be nasty to her like that. She'll handle it herself."

"A tiny girl?"

"You took that way too far."

With that, Papa walked away. Charles sagged against the barn wall, his heart still thumping.

Funny thing is, Papa never said how they would stay on. Surely the Stewarts would do something to make it all legal. Charles hadn't wanted to press Papa for anything, and the old guy left quickly enough. All this uncertainty was beginning to build up on Charles's insides.

CHAPTER 9

A PERSON COULD EXPECT NEWS TO TRAVEL PRETTY DARN FAST around the county when it involved a bloody fight. Nara assumed Ella would have heard Charles had beat up her brother. And she was the vengeful type. Unfortunately for everyone else, she married the perfect person for carrying out her vindictive wishes. Art was a real pushover and would do just about anything to make Ella happy. Even before they married, and he'd become sheriff, she had him doing her dirty work.

In John's last year of school, Ella had Art intimate in front of everyone that maybe John wasn't "quite right." Her brother's red, humiliated face simmered in her mind all that following Saturday, so at church the next day, Nara let her have it.

The kids usually gathered around the big shade tree out in front of the church, while the parents visited before service. It had a big tire swing, and, like most times, there would be a hopeful boy pushing Ella on it. Her legs rose up into the air, and her dress flew away from her legs in what Ella must have known was a provocative manner. Nara stomped up to the swing, shoved the boy out of the way, and when Ella swung back down to receive her next gentle push, Nara grabbed the ropes and forced it to stop, catapulting Ella into the dirt.

All the parents turned their heads to see the scuffle. Ella's mother came over to Mama and asked her why she didn't say anything to Nara.

Mama's voice shook as she said, "Your daughter looks as dirty right now as mine did when we picked her broken body up out of that field. That's why."

To this day, it gave Nara satisfaction to remember Ella standing there in her frilly dress, dirtier than a calf born in a pigpen, but as Nara sat with her erect back and prideful heart in church that day, rope burns on her hands, smiling at all the stink-eye thrown her way, she knew Papa, who hadn't said one word yet, would do his duty and punish her. He didn't like that family, either, but he kept his grief and bitterness inside.

Most kids would have had a belt over their backside, but her father often said, "A whipping only lasts a moment. The smell of chicken shit lasts for days."

Though Mama protested, Nara was made to say sorry at school the next day, a thing she despised ten times more than cleaning the coop. Ella's satisfied grin as Nara said her piece had been the worst moment of their shared past. Until now.

Nara was sitting on the porch with Papa when Art drove up. He was in his new automobile the county had paid for just this year. The black wagon had a door on the back and two bench seats for prisoners. Two dirty lamps on the front looked like eyes, and a shiny silver grille resembled a mouth. Her and Mama didn't agree on whether or not Charles should stay on, but Papa broke the tie and said he would deal with Charles man-to-man. Nara was going to keep her seat and watch how he dealt with Art, but Papa barely slowed his strumming as he whispered the words of his favorite song.

> *The ole Sidehill Gouger had to stay on the hill*
> *Couldn't walk on level ground*
> *So he went 'round the hill*
> *And never could come down*
> *So we ran like the devil straight down*

Mama came out. The screen door slammed behind her as she stood and stared at the wagon, her apron spotted with whatever she'd been cooking. Mama bit at Nara, "I told you they shouldn't have been at roundup. When will you ever listen."

Nara couldn't say what made her face burn more, her mother's chastising words or the smug look on Ella's face as she opened the door as if she were the law itself. Nara ground her bottom into the rocking chair. Papa could get himself in as deep as he wanted. She was done with the boy.

Papa stopped strumming his guitar and began tuning it as if nothing else existed in the world but him and those damn strings. Ella stood grinning, her marching orders to Art already given. He knew what he was here to do.

"Mr. Stewart, I've come to collect those kids you've been hiding here. One of them has committed battery on a young man, and the rest are runaways from the orphan train that came through here last month."

Papa finished tuning that last string, and only when he was absolutely satisfied with the tone did he gently set aside his guitar. His chapped fingers wove the pick through the strings as if he was just getting up for a glass of water. He stood to his full height, stretched his back, and said, "Arthur Connelly, when you were knee-high to a grasshopper, I taught you how to ride a horse."

Art looked at Ella, and she urged him on with her eyes, glaring. "With all due respect, now, Robert, you know I gotta—"

Ella talked right over him. "That big boy you have around here is a danger! Those train riders are all criminals, scum from the streets."

"They're not criminals or scum!" Mama yelled from the porch.

Her face red, eyes bulging, Mama looked like she might jump down the steps and strangle Ella. There's only so much a person can take from another.

"They're good kids, and they work hard here on my ranch," Papa said.

Art said, "But they're not your kids to keep. They've got to go back, and something has to be done about the beating the other day."

"After what your wife's done to this family, I say she owes us a child!" Mama shouted.

Ella looked down, almost guilty, maybe ashamed. Mama

walked straight up to Art and got right in his face. "Way I see it, Ella's brother should be up on charges for molesting a little girl. He tried to pull her dress up!" Then she looked over to Ella. "Like everyone in that family, he's a bad seed."

Mama stared Ella down, but this time an older version of that reckless young girl stared back and held up her chin.

The hay wagon lumbered by with a full load, scattering straw here and there. The boys and Jim had returned after baling the last field.

Art stepped back and calmly said, "Will the girl attest to the fact?"

"What has that got to do with anything?" Ella said.

There was no telling if Opal would say a damn thing to Art. Mama slapped her towel over her shoulder and went inside.

"She's going to fetch Opal," Papa said.

Jim and the boys approached with a worry in their steps. Papa caught Jim's eye and gave him a quick nod. He turned right around, and Nara knew he'd fetch a rifle or two. Charles glanced all around and stepped back like a wild mustang that bolts at the first sign of trouble.

The screen door opened behind her. Mama escorted Opal with both hands on the little girl's shoulders, as if Mama could manage the burden only Opal could carry.

Charles's eyes went wild. "What are they doing with Opal?"

Mama said, "They're only here to ask her questions about what happened."

Jim returned with three rifles. He kept one and set two behind Papa. Nara moved toward them and picked up one of the guns.

Art knelt and put his hands on his knees to make direct eye contact with Opal.

Papa said, "Now, you tell him the truth."

Opal went all red in the face and squirmed away, wanting nothing to do with the man crowding her face. Mama reached down to comfort Opal. "He pulled up my dress!"

Art said, "Who pulled up your dress?"

She shook her head, face all flustered. "Don't know his name."

"I need a name, Opal."

"Leave me alone!"

Charles hurried over, picked Opal up, and took her away. The little girl buried her head in his chest. "You're upsetting her. Can't you see she doesn't know who he is? And why should she?" Charles said, rubbing her bony back. "He was Ivar's hand. She never saw him before, and believe me, she won't again if I got sumthin' to say about it."

Art walked up to Charles as he comforted Opal in his arms.

"You sure talk tough for a boy of sixteen years," Art said.

The boy's jaw worked furiously, but Nara could see the control, if only for Opal's sake, but more than that, she could see he cared and would protect her.

"Still, a man was badly beaten. I should probably take you in for questioning."

Nara stood up. "Why? Because your wife says so?"

Opal leaned out from Charles's arms and batted Art away with mighty fists for their size. "No!"

Papa grabbed a rifle and nodded to Jim, who came around to flank him. The sound of rifle clicks filled the dusty air.

"Is that how it's going to be?" Art challenged.

"Arthur Connelly, get your butt back in that fancy paddy wagon and get on outta here before I shoot the tires out it."

Nara smiled. She never loved her papa more than when he stood his ground. Out in Montana, the sheriff didn't always get his way when right wasn't on his side.

Ella slammed shut the metal door she'd been standing behind and strutted on over. Her very pregnant stomach bobbing up and down with indignation. She wasn't going to get what she wanted. Ella hated losing. "What about that other boy you have here? Folks have been talking. They don't want any Irish around here." Ella sent Patrick a hateful look that made the poor boy's face crumple.

Nara stepped in front of Patrick. "How dare you say such an ugly thing to this boy!" Nara pointed at the sheriff. "Your grandpa is from Ireland, isn't he? Why would you let your wife talk like that, then?"

"His grandfather worked hard when he came here, didn't put out his hand," Ella pressed on. "It doesn't matter anyway. My cousin Judy says they've all got to go back to New York. You're breaking the law."

Papa walked up to Art. "Take your wife and get off my property."

Mama stood up on the porch quivering, gripping the rail so tight, imprints of her fingers might remain there, like the strangling pain that losing a daughter leaves on the heart. Nara took in a deep breath for courage, for her next words might make her a prison, but Ella wasn't gonna take one more child from this family, not if she could prevent it. "I've written to Children's Aid in New York about the kids." Nara put her arm around Patrick. "You should know by now, we Stewarts don't break the law."

Everyone gawped at her like she'd grown another head, except Papa, who nodded to her in respect. Somewhere in the threat of losing the kids, she realized they were hers to protect, and that made her sort of like a mother. Not the experienced kind who would read you stories or teach you how to bake, but something. Or maybe a much older sister. She just hadn't worked it all out in her mind as yet.

Ella's heckling broke through this moment like a thunderbolt does when it hits the roof of your house and goes right to the heart.

"You can write to New York all you want. You need committee approval right here in Montana."

CHAPTER 10

NARA'S CHANGE OF HEART HAD SURPRISED THEM ALL LIKE A SUD-
den gust of wind. The kind that rushes at you hard and if you
open your mouth, it steals your breath, frightens and exhilarates.

"Can ya believe it!" Patrick had said.

Charles couldn't wrap his mind around it. He had only just
calmed down as he readied himself for bed. "We don't know
what Children's Aid will say. They might just take us back, and
what if Nara changes her mind?"

Papa opened the door to the bunkhouse. He scratched at
his brushy mustache, and then leaned into the wall of the log
cabin as if he needed the moral support. Jim got up from his
bunk, put on his tired-looking boots, and left. The door shut,
rubbing in its jamb like it always did. Papa looked behind him
for a moment, but he didn't speak right away. Charles sat up.
Maybe they were too much trouble for the Stewarts to take on.
An unworthiness settled over Charles. He should have known
better than to fall in love with this life, this family.

Papa walked over to Jim's bunk and sat down, having to take

off that ivory hat to fit underneath the bunk. He set it on Jim's pillow for safekeeping. The nightbirds began to sing up in the pines, disturbing the dusky quiet.

The old guy gazed at the rough-hewn ceiling like there might be an answer in all the knots and grain. After a minute, Papa breathed in real deep, both of his hands digging into the sides of the bunk bed, then he looked them both straight in the eye for a long minute. Charles squirmed under Papa's serious gaze, waiting for the blow.

"What do you boys think about us making this all legal?"

Charles's chest collapsed with relief, but he wondered what "all legal" meant. "You mean adoption?"

"Yup."

Staying on their ranch as a bona fide family member meant more to him than he could say, but any talk of New York terrified him.

Patrick was the first to speak, though he did so red in the face. "I would like that very much. Very much, indeed."

Papa looked to Charles, but words like Patrick's never came easy to Charles. "I really like it out here, and . . . everyone."

"All right, then." Papa slapped his legs with his hands to signify it was a done deal. "You're good boys." He came over and ruffled Patrick's red-gold hair and nudged Charles on the shoulder.

"What about Opal?" Charles asked.

"Opal told me, 'If Charles says yes, then I say yes.'"

The obvious affection she held for him pleased Charles beyond measure. He never had a brother or sister. Cousins, or anyone. He didn't know why she favored him, but it might have begun the moment he stopped the jerk on the train from picking on her. Maybe no one had ever stood up for her before.

* * *

The big sky blistered with an intensity little felt when Charles had lived under the shadows of tall buildings, only the heavy air had reached him there, none of this clean sunshine. Day by aching day, Charles's back had begun to grow stronger, his walk a little taller. He didn't hunch over as much to hide his size anymore. Everyone out here worked from dark to dark, and he hoped one day his strength and willingness to work hard would be appreciated by Nara. His days were full of burning muscles, and by evening he felt rubbery and satisfied. And then sitting around the table with a real family. Three meals a day was a thing he'd begun to look forward to, and not just for the home cooking, but to hear the stories. The small talk. He and Patrick would take off their shirts in the bunkhouse at night and put their arms together to compare the tan lines made by their short-sleeve shirts. Patrick had more freckles than anything. Then they'd look at their necks, laugh, and say how they'd become real rednecks. Jim hopped up from his bunk with his bronze skin to compare to theirs and called them both "pale face." Patrick asked him how come his skin was so much darker.

Jim lay down in his bunk, his hands over his chest. His deep voice made Charles feel content and drowsy as he told them how the Cheyenne were created. "The first person floated in the water, sky all around. Tired seabirds flew in the air, looking for a place to nest, but the entire world was covered in water."

Jim told them how the creator made land using soil and then put a spirit into everything. The earth, plants, animals, man, and woman. The man and woman soon developed a spiritual relationship with the natural things around them.

Charles could relate to Jim's story, that feeling of being as much a part of the earth as a tree growing in the ground, everything connected. Being closer to nature had brought him a peace he never thought to have. The grass beneath Charge's hooves crackled as he and Patrick trotted through the rangeland. The rocky flat-topped buttes looked chalky and delicate, like they'd crumble in a rainstorm.

It felt nice to be out here, just him and Patrick. Nobody watching over their shoulders, just the sun warming them. The wind rippling through Charles's shirt like freedom. The horse beneath had begun to feel as natural as sitting in a rocking chair. It had taken him a while to catch the rhythm of riding, but now it felt as easy as walking, but faster.

It hadn't always been so easy. Charge had tested and tried him no end. Charles had wised up to the horse trying to knock him off, so then Charge had taken to playing dead. Charles had only just recovered from the clothesline incident when they had been out on the range. He felt the horse go out from underneath him like they'd fallen in a hole.

Charles had yelled "Whoa!" as Charge fell over on its side. His leg had gotten pinned that *first* time. The second time the horse pulled that stunt, Charles managed to jump off before they hit the ground together. Charles had been trying to get Charge to stand. He pulled on the reins, the bit pulling on its slack mouth. And then its head just fell limply back to the ground. "Oh, geez. You gotta quit this!"

Charles poked the horse on the shoulder and got no response. One big eye flapped.

"Why couldn't I get a normal horse?" Charles groused to the sky.

Patrick had come clopping up, his brows together in genuine concern for the devil horse. He jumped down. "Did he stumble, break his leg?"

Patrick's skinny hands felt all over the horse's fetlocks.

"Don't worry about him. He'll come around in a minute."

"He's done this before?" Patrick put his ear to the horse's ribs like he could hear what was ailing that horse in his chest.

"Nothing wrong with his heart. It's in his head!" Charles poked himself in the forehead.

Patrick was up on his haunches just staring at that crazy horse. Truly perplexed.

Charge's eyes were open and still. Its mouth had fallen agape, that scar looking ever more jagged. But when you looked close, the shiny whiskers underneath his chin were twitching like Charge held back from laughing.

"Wait," Patrick said. "Is he . . . I think he's smiling?"

"He sure is!" Charles shook his head and groaned. "Do you think Papa will give me another horse?"

The boy didn't answer, just started to run his fingers lightly over the horse's belly.

"Patrick, are you doing what I think you're doing?"

Charge's flanks began to shiver as if he were shaking off a fly. The big eyes flustering, then came a high-pitched sound and the horse rolled over and got up all at once, stirring up a mess of dust and shook off.

Charles went over and grabbed the reins, dragging Charge along. "I can't believe this is the horse I get. Some cowboy."

Patrick started laughing. "I've seen a lot of horses, and one thing's for certain, this horse is smart."

"Why am I sure that's not a good thing?"

"When you need him most, he'll use that head for good, and keep you safe."

As they rode out in search of the herd, Charles remembered how they'd been woken early and sent off. "Patrick, this feels like a test, and we've got to pass."

Patrick nodded his affable head and kicked his golden pony to a trot. Papa had come into the bunkhouse earlier than the rooster crowed. "Eat your vittles and get out there before the sun does," he had said.

They were sent alone for the first time to check the herd.

"How will we know where to find them?"

"That's easy. You'll smell 'em."

A herd gives off a musky, dirty-hair odor, but strangely enough, it has a purity to it like soil. It's earthy. Charles stopped Charge on a small hill to look over the condition of the grass and herd. Patrick rode up, and they sat on their horses in quiet companionship. The cattle huddled together in the valley below. Calves stood against their mamas' furry sides. Others played, kicking up their heels, galumphing about. The sun shone on their black coats like pools of oil.

Charge shifted around underneath Charles, and he nudged the horse forward. "Come on. Let's get a better look at the forage and see if they need to be moved on."

Charles remembered everything Nara had taught him to look for. He roamed the whole area. "Plenty of grass still around here," he shouted over to Patrick.

The boy got off his horse and played with a calf. He would pat it on the spotty back, and it would run after him, then he'd change direction, tap it again, and run the other way. The mama cow looked on, chewing vigorously. "Patrick, that cow doesn't like you foolin' with her calf."

But he didn't hear a word, just kept running circles around the furry fella.

The cow charged, and Charles kicked his horse to life. "Patrick!"

The boy looked up in time, his eyes gone big. Those skinny legs and arms pumped for dear life to reach his golden pony, a mad mama hot on his tracks. He jumped onto his pony and galloped off, laughing as he rode past Charles.

Charles shook his head, smiling. Since the Stewarts had asked them about adoption, Patrick had been more joyful. Charles would breathe easier once they heard back, when things had gone through without any questions or hitches. He trotted through a rockier part of the pasture to make his rounds and search for leppies, orphaned calves. Nara had taught him to look for bloated bellies and calves eating grass where they should only be drinking milk. Him and Patrick wove through the herd checking them all over for signs of disease and distress. That mama cow kept an eye on them both, not dipping her head once to the grass.

Charles couldn't imagine a more peaceful employment than watching over cattle. But Nara had assured him there were always trials. Wolves, breach calves, and miles of busted-down fence. Every last calf looked fine within the heard itself, but he spied one a ways off from the rest with a big stomach. He trotted over and found it nibbling at grass.

Jim had taught him to throw the catch rope. He'd practiced enough in the yard, but his fingers still shook and fumbled as he untied the rope. He whirled the hard twist well above his head, cutting the wind in two, gaining speed with each twirl. Remembering Jim's words, he aimed with his hand. It fell and looped around the calf's strong neck. At first he couldn't believe he'd done it, then he pumped his fist in the air. "Whoo!"

Patrick shouted over, "Fine throw!"

They tussled with the calf until it settled down. Patrick's eyes darted about, probably searching for charging heifers. Charles chuckled as he held the rope around the calf's neck and ran his hand along its swollen belly. The fur was curly matted and had a woolly feel. "I'll bet you've got one hell of a gut ache."

"You'll have something to talk about at the table tonight. Papa will be proud," Patrick said.

Charles nodded. "Maybe Nara, too."

Patrick's brows rose as he helped him subdue the calf with a tighter neck knot. "I wouldn't be getting me hopes up."

The calf struggled and kicked up its hind legs trying to escape the rope. Its nose rubbed against Charles's dungarees, leaving a slimy trail. It finally settled down and let out a long, pitiful moo.

Charles led the calf toward Charge. When he tried to mount, the calf tugged one way, and Charge wouldn't hold still. The ornery horse walked forward when he grabbed the horn to mount, as if the horse knew what Charles contended with. Charge swung his furry head around and nickered a little, lifting that scarred lip. "You think you're funny, but I'm the cowboy, and you're the horse."

Patrick had told him, "Grab the reins and hold on to the mane." It rhymed, that's how he taught him to remember it. Charles grabbed what little stubbly mane the horse possessed, and it stayed in place, allowing him to get a leg up and over with only the pulling calf to contend with. As he trotted off, the calf bawled and clopped on behind him. He knew this was serious and couldn't wait, so he rode back to the ranch with some pride. Jim watched Charles ride up and helped him get the calf into a pen they used for the orphans.

"Will he make it?"

Jim's mouth hooked up to one side. "Hmm. He's pretty bloated, but I'll give him a dose of clabbered milk and oil. You did good."

"Thanks." Charles petted the top of its bristly head.

Jim said, "Rub him under the chin here like this. This is how cows groom each other. It will make him gentle."

Charles scratched under its drooly chin and hoped Jim would

tell Nara or Papa about what he'd done. He went inside to get a sandwich. Opal was cleaning pots from breakfast.

"Where is everyone?"

"A funeral."

"What?"

"Nara was cussing and wore a dress this morning."

"So?"

"When Mama told Nara to wear a dress to church last Sunday, she swore and said it would take a funeral."

"Oh." He sat down, knowing where they had gone. Weeks of waiting, and finally he'd know. Opal set a sandwich down in front of him with a smile, then walked off. He took a bite, and it sort of lumped around in his mouth like he'd eaten sand.

"Is it good?"

Charles went to the faucet and gulped down some water. "Uh-huh."

CHAPTER 11

WHEN MR. MORGAN FINALLY ARRIVED IN TOWN TO CHECK ON the matter and see to the paperwork, neither Nara nor her parents had really thought about who would officially be on the papers. The adoption agent didn't want to go out to the ranch, so they met out at the church. Mama insisted Nara wear a damn dress. The shoes were an abomination. She'd already twisted her ankle twice. It was gonna smart getting up into the saddle tomorrow. Rubbing at her ankle, she cursed under her breath, "Shitfires."

Mama pursed her lips with warning. Nara could see the soap coming now. True, she was an adult, and Mama wouldn't really do it now, but a person only needs to have their mouth washed out with soap once in a lifetime.

They had waited for many minutes when a man walked in, presumably the agent. He wore pants to his knees and his hair parted down the middle. His socks had a funny crisscross pattern of diamonds that looked garish, to her eye. Judging by the way the man dressed, New York might be a whole other country.

Right behind him stood Judy and Ella. Her parents looked to each other as if to say, *Here we go again.*

Nara gave him a tight smile, then introduced herself and her parents in a quick fashion to get that nicety over and done. Then she sat down and glared at Ella. Mama's knuckles went white as she fisted her hand on the table, but she was attached to those kids and would likely suffer through anything for them.

Ella had only just had her baby. How in the hell she found time to make trouble was a real wonder. "Mr. Morgan, you should know that Ella won't be a good advocate for these orphans."

Papa nudged Nara, encouraging her to simmer down. When Mr. Morgan inquired why, Mama elbowed her in the ribs. Nara couldn't mention Ella's brother for obvious reasons, they all wanted to avoid that subject. Ella smiled at her, knowing full well what Nara struggled with.

"Well, sir. Ella here has known our family for some time. She might not be the partial advocate you might desire, and Judy here is her cousin. She's always gone right along with anything Ella set her mind to."

There came that elbow in the rib again. Mama stood up. "Mr. Morgan, would you excuse us for a moment?"

Mama grabbed her by the arm and all but dragged her out into the entry hall. She yelled in a whisper, "What in tarnation are you doin' in there?"

"I can't let her get away with it."

"You sound like you're seven years old. Are you *trying* to make it so we can't keep the kids?"

"No."

"Well, then, missy. Get your butt in there and fight like you mean it. With your big-girl manners."

Mama shoved her back the way they'd come. Mr. Morgan looked perplexed, but he would hardly want to travel all the way to Bull Mountain, Montana, only to leave without resolving things. She would bet her bottom dollar the society would rather not see the kids come back. With that in mind, she ignored Ella entirely and began asking the questions she had prepared in her mind. He nodded and listened, and then took some papers out of a satchel. "I believe our contract will make all those issues quite clear. Let's start by going through it line by line."

The first item noted that applicants had to be endorsed by the committee. Mama winced when he read that out. The contract didn't read out much like adoption. Older children were to be given board and clothes, school only part of the year, and then wages when they were eighteen as if they weren't family at all.

Papa had that furrow to his brow. He spoke first. "Sir, with all due respect, it seems to me that the older the child, the more this looks like indentured servitude."

Ella snorted and sat back in her chair. Mr. Morgan looked at his neatly folded hands, nodding. "You see, we feel that the older a child is, the less likely they are being adopted as a real family member."

"How can the society condone such a thing?" Mama said.

"I understand your concern, but the lives of these children out on the street is far worse than a good, honest life of work and the opportunity to go to school."

Nara interjected, "But by your standards here in the papers, the boys would receive a substandard education, to my way of thinking."

"Kids of their age and circumstance can hardly expect better."

"Sir, these are the minimums, are they not? So, if we feel schooling for all of them is what they need, then it's within our power to do better than this piece of paper, right?"

"That is correct. But you may not be ultimately doing the best thing for these *older* children. Most have lived terrible lives, and only a good day's hard work will correct the imbalances of temperament they have acquired in their short lifetimes."

"Well, I will tell you right now, those boys will get the same education Opal does. You have my word. We have a saying around these parts. Paper burns. Words don't," Nara said.

Judy smirked and said, "We would all like to hope for the very best in any child, Nara. But these aren't typical children. Have you been a witness to any troubling behavior since you've had them out on your ranch this past month?"

Mama spoke right up. "No, we haven't. They've all been polite, hardworking, and grateful children. Why, I haven't heard a single complaint or cross word out of any of them."

Nara and Papa agreed with her, nodding their heads. Mama cast her stern eye toward Judy and Ella, daring either of them to say otherwise. She particularly kept her eyes on Ella.

Ella smiled at Mama and said, "I feel I really must be honest with you, Mr. Morgan. Despite what the Stewarts say, Charles has shown a tendency to violence that has a lot of us here worried, including my husband, the sheriff."

"Indeed? What has he done?"

Mama stood up and pointed her finger at Ella. "Charles protected Opal, that's what he's done. I've not seen him raise his voice or hand to anyone before or since the roundup."

So much for big-girl manners, Nara thought.

Papa pulled Mama back into her chair and said, "That's correct. I myself have worked with the young man, training him up, and believe me, if he had any of those violent kinds of tendencies, I would have seen them."

Mr. Morgan looked to Judy for her opinion and she said, "I have to concur with Ella. His suitability for placement in my experience is not good. I think he should be sent back to New York and placed in a home until he comes of age. There just isn't much that can be done for a young man with that kind of tendency."

. Ella said, "We risk the safety of everyone in the county. That is my husband's opinion as well, especially after seeing how badly he had beaten Ivar's ranch hand at the Stewarts' roundup."

Nara boiled inside. "You mean your brother, don't you? Your kin! Who lifted up a little girl's dress to see her panties? That's the 'ranch hand' you mean, right, Ella?"

Now she was breathing so hard and angry enough to pull Ella over the table and break her nose to match her brother's, but Papa whispered in her ear, "Unless you want this man to think you're not a fit parent, you best cool your heels, Nara Jean."

Mr. Morgan placed his hands on the table in the form of a steeple. "In matters such as these, I'm inclined to remove the child and take him back—"

Papa raised his hand. "That won't be necessary, Mr. Morgan. I've got a firm hand on this situation and can assure you that boy will work hard and any tendencies he *might* have had to violence will be worked out of him daily till he's fit to be a preacher."

Mr. Morgan sat back in his chair considering and deliberating, but Judy was hard at work whispering in his ear.

Mama said, "I think we should all hear what our adoption coordinator has to say in this matter."

Mr. Morgan nodded. "I agree. Her advice is quite simple. We'll put him on probation until September. And if he is seen by this community as a vital member *and* has no more violent episodes, then we can consider this matter closed, and will then complete the adoption for all of them. We can sign contracts today, if you folks are amenable?"

Ella said, "If you could see my brother's face, Mr. Morgan, I believe you would judge differently. That troublemaker should be sent back to New York—on the next train. He's a monster!"

"Mrs. Connelly, I have made my decision. I appreciate your fervency in this matter, but considering the nature of the incitement, and my belief that the Stewarts have this boy under a firm hand, my word is final."

Judy whispered in Ella's ear. Something that made her calm down and smile. It made Nara wary as all get-out.

"The other matter of concern is, who is adopting these children?"

"We are," the Stewarts all answered together.

Mr. Morgan chuckled at that. "You see, we need one set of *parents* to sign."

Nara knew she wasn't an ideal candidate, and honestly, she hadn't thought much about who was going to be on the contract. She'd just figured they would work it all out.

Papa spoke up, and said he and Mama would sign, but Mr. Morgan didn't seem to like that situation any better. Mr. Morgan searched carefully for his next words. She was sure he didn't want to insult her parents. They were looking at sixty-some years, both of them.

"If it were just the boys, I'm not sure it would be an issue, but since Opal is only eight years old, we'll need a younger set of parents for her." Mr. Morgan twisted up his mouth to one side and tapped his thumbs together.

She could tell he often had to spend his time weighing less-than-ideal options.

* * *

Nara often did some of the house chores when she could. Mama was too old to milk cows in the late afternoon and then go in and make supper for everyone. Opal was too young to do both cows alone, so she and Nara sat together, each with a stool and a cow. It was nice to have an extra pair of hands around the house for chores and good listening company for Mama. The boys were covering the range this afternoon.

Nara worked the teats of her cow. The hiss of milk hitting the steel pails parted the quiet. A shaft of sunlight illuminated the specks of dust floating in the barn air. Opal's little scarred arms milked the cow. Mama had only just managed to help the girl bathe and dress.

"How is your little chicken Brownie doing?"

"She's big like her mama now," Opal said.

"They grow fast."

"How come?"

"Animals have to grow fast to survive."

"I wish I could grow fast."

"You'll grow soon enough."

Opal lifted one shoulder like she didn't really believe Nara. Nara wanted to ask Opal what had happened to her parents, but Mama seemed the best one to get it out of her. Nara wouldn't know what to do if Opal started crying like Charles had that day out on the range.

"Opal, let's take this to Mama out on the butter porch so we can separate it."

Nara carried both pails, as the girl was too small to carry hers. Opal had tried before, leaning to one side with all her might, but the milk had splashed all over the place with her desperate attempts to carry it across the yard to the back porch. She was very popular with the barn cats.

Opal hopped up from petting a cat and gave a little skip and a hop to catch up. Nara hadn't seen her do that before. That happy way of walking little kids do without thinking. At her age, Nara was certain she'd hurt herself if she tried it, but it must come naturally to the young. Nara shook her head to clear her silly thoughts. Having these kids around was making her soft.

Mama was out back waiting for them, fanning herself during her one break. Nara pitied her mama. By the end of the day, Mama's feet were swollen and bursting out of her Mary Jane shoes. She'd been rubbing them and muttering now. But when she saw Opal step up onto the porch, Mama's eyes lit up. "Well, there you are. How much did we get this time? Let me see."

Nara took Opal's pail and put it under Mama's nose for inspection. Her eyes went big. "A whole pail! Good girl. We can make pie crust with the extra butter we'll have."

Nara poured the milk into the separator, and they watched it spin and separate the cream from the milk. When that was done, she poured the cream into a white ceramic churning jar, and set it in front of Mama. Opal leaned on the arm of Mama's rocking chair, watching. The waning sun lit up the fine strands of Opal's golden hair. "Do you want to try?" Mama asked.

"Uh-huh." They sat there for a while, rocking in their chairs, as Opal churned with all her might. Mama took a turn and then Nara. They passed around the burden of the chore until the butter made a sucking noise. Mama looked happier than Nara had ever seen her. Opal wandered off the porch and went to pet Blackie. "Opal, honey, don't let that dog herd the chickens again." Mama turned to Nara. "Keeps rounding up those chickens and bringing them in the house. I wish he'd pester that ornery old rooster instead."

Nara could tell Mama had something to say, for she stared out into the wild blue yonder and fidgeted with her hands, silent for once.

After many minutes Mama said, "I've been thinking. I want

you to go out and make nice with Ella. Smooth things over if you can."

"What? How in the heck is that gonna work?"

"I don't know. With her watching over us, and these kids being on a three-month probation, then we should at least try."

"You mean me, right?"

"I've never asked much from you . . ."

Nara's chest felt the prick from the perfectly aimed arrow. "Don't be so sure about that."

Mama's eyes opened up wide to Nara's sass.

Fact was, both her parents had asked a hell of a lot from her. Mama needed her to put on an apron, be a companionable daughter, have babies, and Papa needed her to run the ranch— though he'd no sooner admit it than eat a rattlesnake.

Nara squashed her hat on her head. "I'll go, but don't get your hopes up."

* * *

Art and Ella lived in the original log cabin that Art's father had built. Nara didn't know how they managed, with all those kids in there. She stopped the horse and got down from the cart. A curtain in the window fluttered angrily. Things hadn't gone too good for Ella and Art. He couldn't work his land and be the sheriff of the whole county, so his land suffered.

Ella opened the door, her eyes narrowed with bitterness but her chest puffed out with pride. Under no circumstances could anyone be allowed to think themselves better than Ella, and if she wanted revenge for all the years of hostility she'd endured, then Nara was gonna stop that right here, right now.

Pink-skinned children stared from around their mother's skirt. "Well?" Ella stood up there expecting her due.

The thing Nara wanted to do was walk up the steps, take the baby from her arms, hand it off to the oldest child, and then slap Ella till she was red in the face. To wring her neck, and good. Nara had too many fantasies of that kind to be out here right now.

Nara cleared her throat and said the words she'd practiced on the way over. "Ella, I've come here to tell you that I'm sorry about how things have been all these years. I know you were just a girl when you ran at the herd. Mama and I want to put all this resentment behind us."

There, she'd said the words. Oh, but they choked her and made her sick, so much that she wondered if Ella sensed they weren't genuine.

"What a pretty little speech, Nara Stewart. But there is no way in heck your mama has forgiven me."

Ella walked into her house and left the door ajar so that Nara could decide to come in or not. Nara turned to her horse cart, but Mama's smile and Opal just under her apron felt more important than foolish pride. Nara gritted her teeth and went inside. What she saw took all the venom out of her. A large copper still steamed its fiery liquid into a coil that dripped into a glass jar, taking up most of the kitchen. The whole house stank of vaporous hooch. Nara wondered how the hell Ella cooked with that thing in there. Ella didn't drink, but everyone talked. She sold it for money to buy clothes for her kids, though by the look of the dirty toes in the room, Ella's side business wasn't getting the job done.

Ella raised her chin up high. "Well, sit down and take a load off."

Nara sat in one of the rickety chairs as gently as she could. The kids gathered around the table, wondering at their visitor. Remembering Ella's pride, she took her eyes off the squalor and asked about some of the folks from other ranches and towns nearby.

Ella held her resentful lips shut for a moment, but her penchant for gossip gave way.

"You haven't heard?" Ella looked at Nara like she was a simpleton. "Patsy's husband ran off with a Crow woman not two weeks ago. He'd been drinking too much at the Dark Horse and went on a real bender. When he finally sobered up, he went back out to their place to make up with his wife, and do you know what she did?"

"Nope."

"Art said when he got there, her husband was in the front yard and a frying pan laid next to his head. And a broom. He was knocked out!"

"Did Art arrest Patsy?"

"No. She told Art that her husband had been back home and was feeling bad, so he was sweeping and cooking when it all happened pretty suddenly."

"Did he believe her?"

"No, but he could hardly get a statement from an unconscious man."

"How does he keep people from killing each other around here?"

Nara winced at her ill-spoken words. Ella had a long memory for revenge, but at the moment, she enjoyed her gossip. She went on to the next bit, and it wasn't long before Nara had the tattle from three counties.

Nara took advantage of a lull in conversation to stand up. "Well, I'm sorry Mama couldn't make it out here, but you should know, she asked me to come here and speak on behalf of the family."

Nara said all her goodbyes to the little ones with wooden, awkward pats, thinking this hadn't been too bad after all. The stooping was worth it to have a little peace between everyone. Ella stood on the top of her steps, baby in her arms, jostling the child quiet. "Just so you know, I'm done crawling on my hands and knees for forgiveness from your family, and now you need mine. You coming out here one day out of the last twenty-odd years won't change the way your ma's treated me."

Ella kicked the door shut.

CHAPTER 12

THE WIND HAD GATHERED ITS STRENGTH FROM THE MONTHS OF summer. It blew out the sun like a candle each night earlier than the day before. Charles had learned the rhythm of Montana's dark-to-dark days but had yet to experience all its seasons.

School would start soon, and so they all went into town for pencils, paper, and the like. They took a train into Billings and walked around the small city, where they shopped for clothes. It was nothing like New York City. The streets were cleaner, with less people. Folks were friendly and waved to each other, made eye contact. The buildings were not nearly as tall as the skyscrapers he used to see in the skyline of his youth. If this is what country folks thought of as a big city, then that was fine by him.

At lunch, only Minnie talked to him. He just vaguely remembered her from his first week at the ranch. She looked different now. She wore a pretty dress and chatted about her secretarial job while they all ate patty melts and sodas at a fancy shop. "I can type forty words per minute now."

He nodded and smiled but didn't know what to say to her in return. At least she paid attention to him.

A week ago at the ice-cream social, a boy Charles's age had roughed up one of the Crow girls. She had been beautiful, and Charles had wanted to dance with her, but after he taught the bully a lesson in manners, they all had to leave. Charles hadn't punched or shoved the boy, just threatened him. Papa had stood at the entrance of the church and waved them out with his hat. "Billy Colfax is a neighbor and friend of ours," Papa had said angrily.

When they arrived home, Mama grabbed Charles by the arm before he went up the porch steps. Her round face and dimples disappeared into lines and a severe eye. "Charles, you've *got* to control your temper." She shook him to make her point. "If the Children's Aid Society doesn't think we can take care of one of you, then they'll take you all back. Do you understand?"

Nara had made him clean out the chicken coop the next day, and he'd taken his punishment like a man, but the worst of the fallout had been Papa. He had been most disappointed with him, for he hadn't said a word to Charles since that time. On the New York streets his size and temper had served him well. Out here, he needed to rein it in if he was going to be accepted by the family.

When they returned from the train station, he offered to carry all the supplies they'd bought in Billings by himself. He hefted them inside, then piled them high on the table. Charles stood about feeling unwanted, and unworthy. He kept his hands in his pockets to hide what they were capable of. "You didn't have to buy me all this stuff," he said.

"Your toes would have poked out of those boots by November," Nara said.

She insisted he buy some clothes and boots that fit him, but all he really wanted was one of those ivory Stetsons. He didn't dare ask for one. Patrick took his pile of new stuff and said, "I'm going out to look after the horses."

Nara was bound to notice sooner or later the "horses" Patrick referred to were mustangs. While they were in town, they saw a talkie called *Wild Horse Mesa*. The light from the screen flickered and shone on Patrick's face. Every emotion crossed over those freckles as the Navajos tried to persuade the rancher not to harm the horses. During the worst part of it, horses running and screaming, Patrick wiggled so much, Charles worried the boy would jump right out of his seat. Afterward, Patrick asked Nara if the ranchers ever rounded up the mustangs around here. She said, "They compete with the cattle for forage. I don't much care for the practice myself, but Ivar might round them up soon."

Patrick had gone pale. Charles figured after Patrick put his stuff away in the bunkhouse he'd be on his way to warn them, drive them off someplace where Ivar would never find them.

Mama stood over the table heaped with school supplies. She tried to give Opal a pencil and paper, but the girl ignored Mama. Nara came over. "Opal, Mama is trying to give you something."

Opal's little shoulders shrugged, a wary shade over her face. "What's wrong, Opal? Tell me."

Opal folded her disfigured arms on the table and put her head down on them. Her foot swung and scuffed the wooden floor below. Nara grabbed her knee to still it. "Now, be honest with me. Do you know how to read and write?"

Opal didn't look up, just shook her head. "Did you ever go to school?"

There came that little shrug of the shoulders. Charles interpreted that as a few times, or not very often. Nara said, "When you get to school, you'll start out right where you need to. All the children have different lessons and are different ages. It won't matter a lick. Okay?"

Opal put on her apron, ready to be done with the conversation, and walked into the kitchen. She peeked in the oven.

"The other kids will pick on her. She has to know how to write her name," Charles said.

He pulled out a chair, took the pencil and paper from Mama, and began to write Opal's name in big letters. He held out the pencil to her and said, "Here, copy what I wrote. That's your name, and the teacher will want you to put it at the top of every assignment. That's the first thing you have to know."

She dragged herself over to the table and took the pencil from him. It swayed awkwardly in her little fingers as she copied the letters he wrote out. It took her many tries, lots of erasing, and her almost bolting from the chair a couple times, but he sat with her, determined to be patient and teach Opal.

"Where'd you learn to write so well?" Nara asked.

"I did really well in school when I had a home and parents."

Mama and Nara regarded him with pity. It made his face burn

with humiliation, but he wanted to show them he was smarter than they realized and could do a lot more with his hands than just knock heads.

When Opal had copied her name successfully, he said, "Do it again."

And when she'd done that, he said, "Good. Do it three more times."

When she finished, he took the paper away and put a clean blank sheet in front of her and asked her to write her name. She looked stumped for a second. "Picture what you just wrote in your head."

She scrunched her eyes together, then in quick little strokes scrawled out the first letters as if she had to hurry before she forgot. "Good. Now your last name. Remember?"

She looked up, tapped the pencil on her forehead, and wrote down the wrong letter. Charles turned over the first sheet and let her peek. She put her pencil to paper and drew out the letters *S T E W A R T*.

Nara grabbed a box off the table. "I've got something to do out in the stables. Be back at supper."

Charles taught Opal a while longer and then went out to the bunkhouse to find one of those Zane Grey novels and kick up his feet. When he opened the creaky door, he noticed it straightaway. It shone bright in the shady afternoon light. Had it fallen from the skies or been sent by an angel? He ran his fingers over the smooth straw weaving of the Stetson. He tilted his head forward and pushed his hair back from his forehead. It settled snugly on his head like it'd always been there.

"You're a real cowboy now."

Charles twisted around. He hadn't noticed Jim lying there on his bunk. "Oh, hey."

There was a faded cigar box by his side that lay open. He put a photograph back in, clapped it shut, and put it under his bunk.

"Someone special?"

Jim breathed in real deep. "My brother."

"I didn't think you had a family."

"I don't."

"What happened to your brother?"

Jim's jaw clenched, and his cheek ticked. "He was shot by a white woman who thought he was a coyote. He was just a boy."

Charles's mouth hung open. "I'm real sorry." Charles shifted things around on his bunk, wanting to ask, but not wanting to upset Jim all the same. "What did they do to the lady?"

"Nothing." Jim got up from his bunk and pulled on his boots. "I'm going out north to check on the herd."

"I'll come with you."

Jim held up his hand, his back still to Charles. "Better for you to stay."

* * *

Mama had bought some fancy food at a store in Billings the other day. The smell of it cooking reminded Charles of the Italians in New York. Papa stood in the kitchen, waving his hand in front of his face, acting like Mama cooked up horse dung. "Woman, what is that smell?"

"It's spaghetti."

"Oooh, not that Eyetalian stuff. I've just barely gotten to like that chicken à la king. What's wrong with regular food anyway?"

Patrick laughed like a sneeze you catch just before it unleashes, then snorted it back down again.

"You quit your hemming and hawing. You're gonna love it," Mama said.

Charles ate heartily that evening, pleasing Mama no end. Even Jim liked it, but Papa grimaced through most of supper. Charles thought Papa might be putting on a show, lest she run amuck in the kitchen and ruin his digestion with all her fancy food.

Charles had been putting on his boots for the walk back to the bunkhouse when he overheard Mama and Nara argue as they dried dishes together.

"I gave my word, Charles would get the same education as the other two, and I'm not going back on it."

"Billy Colfax will be there tomorrow, and what do you think is gonna happen if we're not around to control him?"

"Charles has learned a lesson. I'm sure of it. Haven't you seen him moping around here?"

* * *

About twenty kids of all different ages stood around, waiting their turn to go up and into that little schoolhouse. Patrick sidled up to Charles like one of those crabs he used to pick up from the sand on the seashore when he was a young boy. Crabs walk sideways, and Charles figured that was a lot like Patrick's life. Opal followed behind. The Colfax boy from the ice-cream social waited with his friends up on the landing of the steps. They all laughed and pointed when Charles walked up the steps. A bunch of dogs itching for a fight. The only things that stopped Charles from grabbing that little jerk and tossing him down the steps were those words of Mama's about him ruining it for the other two, and then telling Nara he wouldn't be able to control himself at school. He'd felt pretty low last night, but he woke this morning determined to make them all proud.

He took off his new hat and reluctantly hung it up on the hook. Farther down, hooks for cups lined the wall and a water jug with a spigot sat on a small table in case they got thirsty. He hung the tin cup Mama had given him on a hook next to Patrick's. Opal got up on her tippy-toes to put hers on the hook. The air smelled like dusty old books. The walls were lined with shelves nearly everywhere except where small windows let in a bit of the late-summer sunshine. Out one of them he could see a tree starting to turn color. It was September. He would lament the passing of summer warmth. Shivering cold weather wasn't a favorite.

He wedged himself into the tiny desk and glanced at Patrick, who sat to his right. Opal was in the front row to see the board better. All the little ones were. Their teacher stood at the blackboard and wrote his name down. The chalk in his hand nicked and scratched at the blackboard. His hair had a shiny bald spot in the back of his head that kept catching the light from one of the little windows in the back. "Children, I am Mr. Meyer."

His spectacles were round and not very effective-looking, small as they were. He wore a pair of threadbare cotton slacks with a tartan plaid shirt. In New York, his teacher had been neatly dressed in a wool suit, bow tie, and slick combed hair.

A small flag hung over his desk. "Please rise to say the Pledge of Allegiance."

When Charles stood, the desk came with him. Colfax snickered a few desks down. Charles breathed in deep, determined to ignore him. This boy wasn't going to get his hackles up, no matter what he tried.

"I pledge allegiance to the flag of the United States of America, and to the republic for which it stands, one nation, indivisible, with liberty and justice for all."

Somebody's father showed up still in his muddy work boots. Mr. Meyer eyed the dirty boots with obvious distaste but introduced him and explained that the man would make his way around and adjust the desks. Charles would be grateful to have his raised, so he could move his legs underneath it. The desk was made of oak. The varnish worn at the edges. Etchings of students and days gone by covered the top and inside the lid. Nara had said, "Whoever finds my name or John's carved on a desk gets my helping of dessert."

After all the desks were adjusted, the teacher announced inspection. Nara had prepared them for this moment. Charles smoothed out his crisp white handkerchief on the desk. His new initials, c. s., had been embroidered in dark blue thread. Mama and Opal had been busy with them for nearly all of August, so he'd watched his as it was being made, but sitting here with the initials out there for everyone to see made him feel proud to be a part of a family. Charles smiled, remembering Nara's warning this morning. "For goodness' sake, keep it clean at all times and don't dare wipe your nose with it. That's what sleeves are for."

Everyone had their hands splayed out over their handkerchiefs, waiting. Charles smoothed the rooster tail on the back of his head to get the hair to lie flat.

"You're mighty big for a . . ." Mr. Meyer consulted his roster in his hand. "A sixteen-year-old?"

"Yes, sir."

The teacher continued to look at him with scrutiny, and it was unfortunate, too, because so did everyone else. Billy snorted and elbowed one of his friends. The old Charles would have scowled or challenged each one until they turned their heads, but he had to be nice and get along.

"Very clean hands. Smile for me."

"Brushed 'em this morning, sir."

"I need you to smile, please."

Charles breathed in real deep and then bared all his teeth in what probably looked nothing like a smile.

"I'll not have any unpleasant sort of business in my classroom, Charles Stewart. I hope we are in agreement?"

"Yes, sir."

Being commanded to show his teeth reminded him of the train inspections. Patrick had a big bright smile for the teacher, no questions asked, but despite Patrick's kindness, once Mr. Meyer heard the Irish lilt, he narrowed his eyes. His manner toward Patrick a touch cooler. Patrick stopped smiling and put his face onto his fist.

The Colfax boy's name was Billy, which sounded a lot like bully. Charles twirled his pencil with his fingers, observing that boy out of the corner of his eye.

The teacher had already prepared assignments for each of them, and they approached Mr. Meyer's desk in turn to receive them. Charles got through his too quickly, so when he was done, he helped Patrick with his.

Mr. Meyer stood up. "Time to eat lunch. You have half an hour to eat, rest, or play in the field. File out neatly, grab your pails, and no dillydallying."

When Charles got up to leave, Billy stepped in front of him.

Patrick gave him one of those don't-do-it looks. Charles gritted his teeth and fell in line behind the arrogant boy. But nothing could stop him from popping his knuckles right behind Billy's head as they walked outside. That really should have been warning enough to the boy, but apparently he was ten kinds of stupid.

Opal, Charles, and Patrick sat by themselves under a cottonwood tree, eating their lunch, when Billy came over, a smug smile plastered to his dumb face. Charles ignored every word coming out of his mouth and purposefully looked toward the church across the road, praying to God the boy would just leave them be.

Billy asked Patrick, "Is this your little sister?"

"Ya, this little lass is Opal."

Charles could have groaned aloud. Patrick would just never learn. But Charles kept staring at the church. He plucked a piece of grass to make it seem like he didn't care one bit about Billy or his stupid questions, and chewed on the end of it.

Billy laughed and didn't seem to have the mind to stop. A few other boys approached. "Hey, fellas. You want to meet a lass?"

Patrick said, "A lass just means girl where I come from."

Everything got real quiet. Charles turned around. Billy looped his thumbs through his dungarees and said, "Oh, yeah? Where is it you come from?"

"Ireland."

"So that means you grow spuds there, right?"

Patrick went red in the face, got up, and brushed off his clothes.

"In case you weren't aware, potatoes are grown right here in America," Charles said.

"But they come from Ireland. Why else would they refer to your 'brother' as a—"

Charles shot up. "What I know is ya aren't gonna finish that sentence."

Billy smiled at Charles as Mr. Meyer's voice came across the field. "Charles, what is going on here?" Mr. Meyer took off his spectacles and rubbed them on his plaid flannel shirt.

"Billy here was about to call my brother a bad name."

"How do you know he was about to?"

"Because he was talking about how potatoes are only grown in Ireland."

"Charles Stewart, that makes absolutely no sense whatsoever. All of you come inside and get sat down. I have a mind to hand out some difficult exercises to some of you."

Charles hooked up one of his eyebrows, thinking he'd finally get something that would keep him occupied. They all followed Mr. Meyer inside and took their seats. Billy passed right in front of Charles, cutting him off to get to his desk. Charles put his hands in the air, so it didn't look like he'd bumped into the boy on purpose. Clearly, that's what the little shit was trying at.

There was a time when being the top kid was important to Charles, but now it didn't make any sense at all. He had one goal in mind these days, and that was being a part of the Stewart family and, one day, foreman of the ranch. And no jerk with a small, bigoted mind would get in the way of that.

CHAPTER 13

SUMMERS PASS QUICKLY IN MONTANA. "BLINK AND YOU'LL MISS it," they say. September had settled over the land and sunk into the valleys, cooling the air. Things around the Stewart house had settled down to a dull roar. Papa began to give Nara a little more rein, inch by inch. It was the little things, like he stopped countermanding her on decisions she'd make. He asked her a question instead of giving her the answer. She even caught him reading one of her books on fall calving the other day. But when she sat down to talk to him about it, he clapped it shut pretty quick and acted like he'd picked up the wrong book.

Charles had calmed, had become a little more pliant. She felt sure he wouldn't have any more violent episodes. A life like he'd lived would give a person bad habits that required time and patience. One thing about him, he worked damn hard, and that she could relate to. The adoption probation was nearly done and through, so Mama breathed easier.

The kids had gone off to start school, leaving her, Papa, and Jim to cut up the herd into heifer replacements, steers to be sold, and so forth. Fall was the time to take your stock to market and reap the reward. They had spent the earliest hours of the morning driving cattle to the train depot and onto stock cars. Papa stood outside the stock car counting out bills and paying the temporary laborers he managed to scrape up for the drive.

Glad to be out of the saddle, Nara near fell into her seat on the train. Dust from so many hooves beating the dry ground coated her hair, skin, and clothes. Papa climbed onto the train, looking older than ever. He draped himself over the bench. The train whistled as it chugged forward to find its momentum. The countryside rolled by in the reflection of his weary eyes. They would get off at Miles City, which had one of the biggest stockyards in Montana.

Jim sat on a bench in the row across, his hands behind his head. Nara moved over to Jim's bench to give Papa room to spread out and lie down. The train went around a turn and she sat down a little too hard. A little too close. She smiled over at him to cover the awkward moment and moved a smidge away. "Jim, I know you don't care too much for trains."

He nodded.

"The ride to Miles City is a fairly quick one. Coupla hours, with all the stops." She took off her hat and tucked her hair behind her ear, then looked over at Papa and put her hat back on.

The train scraped along the tracks, taking them through the land where Custer died in the Battle of the Little Bighorn. Nara scanned the golden hills and sagebrush that should still be red for all the violence. Jim looked out onto the passing land with a stony eye.

"It's an ugly history out here," she said.

"Chief Two Moons would tell the story to us children only if we begged him. He didn't like to talk about the fighting days."

"How did it start?"

Papa grunted from his bench as if to say, *Enough chitchat*, and put his hat over his face. He didn't like the old stories. Papa had been sixteen during the Battle of the Little Bighorn. She could sometimes pry a few snippets from him now and again, the settlers' side of what had happened. Nara figured everyone had been caught in the middle.

Jim began his story anyway, because either he didn't care or didn't catch Papa's drift. Jim breathed in deep to begin, his chest swelled, and his bronze hand slid closer to hers. There were little white crescents on his fingernails made all the brighter for his dark skin.

"Chief Two Moons and his people were camped peacefully on the Powder River. One morning, soldiers stormed the camp. The men and women scattered everywhere, leaving the ponies. The soldiers stole them. But that evening, while the soldiers slept, a war party crept into their camp and took them back. They rode far to a place with good grass and clean water. Sitting Bull and Crazy Horse were gathered there, prepared to fight. Two Moons told them, 'I am here to fight the white man.' Not long after, the three chiefs fought General Crook. Many soldiers were killed, only a few Indians. It was a great fight, 'much smoke and dust,' Chief Two Moons liked to say."

Jim folded his muscular arms across his broad chest. His sleeves were rolled up to his elbows. He had veins on his forearms you could trace with your finger. She turned her head the other way. "The Cheyenne are brave," she said.

Jim nodded with pride, his chin tilted up just that little bit. "Two Moons is very old now. He only wants peace, and for Cheyenne to raise cattle and make butter."

In school, she had learned that after the railroad came here, the homesteaders followed right behind and wiped out the buffalo within two years. "Is every last buffalo gone?"

"No herds, a few stragglers. There is talk of raising them like cattle."

Papa pulled his hat off his face, then sat up a ways. "Those beasts are as dangerous as a grizzly bear, make no mistake. Can't raise 'em as stock." Then he put his hat back over his face and lay back down.

* * *

The Olive Hotel in Miles City stood tall. A three-story brick building, easily the nicest place Nara had stayed in. They'd only be here one or two nights, depending on how fast they sold the cattle, but the bed was sure something. All fancy with ruffles. Mama would have loved it for all the special stitching and frills sewn into the sides. After an early-morning cattle drive to the depot and a long train ride, she did something rare and took an afternoon nap.

Later that evening, she, Papa, and Jim went downstairs to the restaurant to eat, but when the waiter saw Jim, he said, "We don't serve Indians."

"Why not? He's as hungry as any other man in here." Nara looked around at all the white cloth–covered tables.

Papa held up his hand to quiet her. It made her temper spike to be hushed. The world would be a better place if women could speak their minds. Men danced around the edges of all their various conflicts. Nothing ever got done that way. Jim's face went dark. Not embarrassed, but angry.

Papa took Jim's shoulder and said low, "Jim, why don't you go on down to that little diner on the corner." Papa handed him some bills. "I'll see you later before bed."

Jim stuck out his chest and bumped the waiter with his broad shoulder as he walked out.

The waiter pursed his lips and then showed them to a table. After Papa went to sleep, she'd go find Jim. Nara popped out her napkin with a flourish, but not to be fancy. "I don't know why I thought we could get away with bringing Jim into a fancy place like this."

It made her sick to think this whole wide open prairie had been theirs alone. And *they* would have shared it. The waiter came around to take their order as if he hadn't just wounded a man to his core, and Papa ordered them a steak dinner like it was any other night. Nara shot the waiter a hateful look.

After the waiter left, Papa said, "I'm going to use a different commission company this time. The price we got last year wasn't good. I think they are still basing price on the droughts, but those cattle last year were good and fat from a year of rain."

"Maybe the packer buyer had some kind of side agreement with the commission company?" Nara said.

"Could be. Seems like every year someone invents a new way to be crooked."

"I can only imagine what it's like in some big city."

She cringed at her ill-spoken words, for anytime anyone mentioned a city it seemed Papa would remember his only son. And she'd only just gotten him to open up.

Papa's eyes dimmed. "The 'big' city. Hope your brother likes the place he's got himself to, but I'd wager not. I just keep thinking he's gonna get his head on straight and come home someday."

The rest of the evening was a bitter recanting of John's leaving and how everything would be better if he would just come home. There were at least two times she almost told him John wasn't coming home. She would have liked to dig up all those letters from under her bed and shove them under Papa's nose, so he'd get over it. Christ, couldn't he see his son wasn't coming back? It'd been years. Papa stirred some sugar into his coffee, and she ordered some pie to stuff her face and keep her mouth good and shut until she could escape to her room.

MAMA HAD OFTEN commented that Papa always knocked out the moment his head hit the pillow, so Nara didn't have to wait in her room any more than ten minutes to be sure he was counting sheep.

The air outside was a cool forty-five degrees, if her senses were correct. After being in that smoky restaurant with a bunch of loud cattlemen, it felt bracing. The distinct aroma of a large herd made its way through Main Street from the not-so-distant stockyards. This town had only one purpose. The cow-smelling air coats the skin in a way that's hard to wash off.

Her boots clunked down the wooden walk like they knew where to go. Her head hadn't a clue. What happened with Jim at the restaurant made her feel unsettled. Eating that fine meal after he left made her feel like a real ass. She wasn't one of "them," and more than anything, she wanted him to know that. Why it felt so urgent to tell him was a more complicated matter she didn't care to dissect.

In Miles City, there was only one watering hole, but it sat empty and silent. The sign up above read: Montana Bar. A bighorn sheep, mounted and stuffed, greeted walkers in the window where it must have sat for near on forty years, so thick was the coat of dust on that frizzled wool. Up ahead was a light coming from a diner.

Nara pushed open the door. The air was hazy, but she could distinguish men sitting at tables. They all turned at once to see who walked in, and being she was the only female in the room, maybe in the whole damn town, they kept looking. Feeling the pestilence of so many eyes, Nara scanned the room for Jim.

He stood up from a table in the back, and she recognized the bulbous shoulders she'd seen throw a hard twist and hay. Ropy forearms exposed by a rolled-up shirt, his short black hair that had a gloss even in the dim light.

"What are you doing here?"

She should have heard the warning in his voice, but her head was abuzz. "Feeling cooped up."

They locked eyes, and she got closer to him by degrees as they simply gazed on one another. Before she knew what she was doing, she stood toe to toe with him, inhaling his musky scent. The diner around her and everyone else had disappeared, no sound, nothing. His pupils went big and dark, drawing her in to him. Her eyes settled on his thick red lips. She leaned in closer and his big pupils shrank to pinpoints.

He took her by the arm. "Robert will skin me alive if he sees you in here with all these men so late."

She blinked several times to cast off the trance of her own hormones and was brought back into the loud diner by his anxious words.

"I just . . . I wanted to tell you I was sorry about the asshole in the restaurant."

Jim led her out into the brisk air. He turned her around and pulled her close, his voice low, smelling of cigarettes. "Is that why you're really here?"

She didn't have words for why and how she felt, and in moments like these, a body does what it wants, craves. They leaned in close until their thighs touched, chest to breast, hearts beating like a stampede. Her finger reached up and stroked that angular cheekbone she had longed to touch. He grasped her hand in his, so warm and gentle.

His mouth grazed over her face and hair, inhaling her, then he stood back. "Nara, your family would never accept . . ."

She began to say something, but like every other time in her life, her father said it for her. "Young lady, it's late. Get your butt back to your room."

The dreamlike state ruptured and Jim jumped back from her

like she was a poisonous snake. The cooling air between them, so much reality it hurt. She turned around, hot in the face.

"I was just coming to see if Jim found supper."

Papa's head remained down, hands on his hips.

She stumbled awkwardly past her father. "Good night," she said.

Leaving Jim to pay the price, her cowardly boots clomped back to the hotel.

HALF THE NIGHT she waited up, hoping Jim would knock on the door of her room. Now, in the light of day, she was grateful he'd kept his distance. After she finished dressing, there came a knock. She touched the knob, wishing Jim stood there, but she knew different. She crushed her hat on her head, donned a stern face, and left the room. Papa stood in the hall, pretending to look at a painting of a river. She shut her door, he turned away from her, and they went down to breakfast. The waiter had interrupted their stiff silence to ask them where they'd like to sit. Unlike last night, the waiter's presence this morning was like a godsend.

Papa pointed and grunted in a direction, and they took their seats. Her father still hadn't cast an eye over her. He took his napkin and tucked it in with way too much deliberation, then put the menu up in front of his face. The waiter came over, took their orders, and left.

"A woman ain't got no business near . . . a place like that so late."

She sipped her coffee, and Papa didn't say another word. Not that he expected a rebuttal or a response of any kind from her. They ate their crunchy toast, forked through tender eggs, and ate their greasy bacon with only the sound of their chewing for company. What she wouldn't do to hear Mama talking and fussing about something or other right about now.

When they arrived at the stockyards, the place was swarming with furry backs bulging in small pens. Cattle bawling and men shouting filled up both of her ears. Jim hadn't joined them. She imagined that Papa and he had words about last night.

A man with a scraggly long beard yelled, "You get the count on that pen?"

"Thirty-five!"

"Nah. I count thirty-two."

The stockyards had acres and acres of cattle pens. She stood in the center aisle that packer buyers rode up and down to consider the various pens full of cattle. Men counted with their hands and scratched numbers down on paper. Seeing all the ranchers roaming around, it occurred to her she might be the only female there. She searched the grizzled crowd for a woman. She'd been here before and understood the rarity of women at a cattle auction, but she never attributed her presence here to her father's leniency with her. But looking around and seeing nothing but bearded or stubbled faces, she had to confront the fact. Papa let her come here. An acceptance she'd somehow missed.

Papa stood with the commission agent going over the final tally of their cattle. Papa waved her over. "You need to watch this, young lady."

Papa had never made a point of having her listen before. She leaned in to read the tally sheet as the agent did the whole run-down. All the cattle they had raised were now tick marks. The thing she loved most about her family's way of life was the cycle of it. Every time of year had its own chores and challenges, but you always knew what you'd be doing and when. It felt good to see her contribution included in the sum of their labor.

"I've got a hundred and forty-five total in these four pens." The agent pointed to each pen.

Papa scratched his chin. "I think you missed a few. I know I put a hundred and fifty-seven yearlings on that stock cart."

When the agent went about re-counting, Papa gave her a little elbow. This was how it was done. Once they were done selling their cattle, they headed out of auction. Papa told her, "You have to watch them. They'll cheat you if they can."

After they made their deposit in the Stockman's Bank, they went to the train depot. Nara had been dreading the moment, but Jim wasn't there, and Papa made no indication they would wait. She sure as hell wasn't gonna raise the subject, being only too glad Papa had dropped it. Jim might have taken the morning train. Papa had probably given him a good earful. Her father wouldn't have done it in front of her. Men had a code about these things.

They settled into their seats, and Nara turned every which way searching for Jim. Papa barely made notice of this. It was that little bit of displeasure in his eye, gone in an instant.

"Profits were good this year," Papa said real low as he gazed out the window.

She nodded. The numbers were still a little new to her, but

from her experience out on the range not many head were lost to bloat, illness, or wolves this year. It might have been the extra help from the kids this past spring and summer. Papa would never associate it with anything she'd done. When they were cutting the yearling heifers from the herd to be sold, he kept seventeen percent of them. Normally he only kept seven percent. She figured he had a mind to expand.

"I've been thinking about this idea of yours," Papa said.

Nara sat forward. "Fall calving?"

"Yup."

She tried not to smile big, knowing how much it killed him to take her advice. "We could try it with twenty-five percent next winter. We'd have to herd them separate from the bulls next summer to keep them from breeding till winter," she said.

Papa squinted one eye, rubbing at his whiskery jaw, then tilted his head this way and that, making a show of his mulling it over, but he had likely already decided. "I thought we could try fifteen percent this winter, and if it goes well, then we'll do twenty-five percent next."

"That's a good plan."

It was a big risk for him on a few counts. One, following the advice of a woman, and two, risking fifteen percent of his stock and profits if it didn't go well. Taking it all in, she thought maybe Papa had finally accepted John wasn't coming home. Then it occurred to her that she hadn't received a letter from her brother in a while. He'd never gone so long out of touch, but she wouldn't tell her parents and worry them, too. They didn't even know she and John kept in touch.

WHEN SHE TROTTED into the yard, got out of the saddle, and stretched her back, the screen door up at the house slammed. Mama hurried out to the stables to greet them with what appeared to be news. And anything that can't wait until you've had a chance to wash off your grit is never good.

CHAPTER 14

CHARLES CLAPPED ERASERS UNDER THE SHADE TREE, WISHING IN-stead that he could knock Billy's and Mr. Meyer's heads together till they cracked like nuts. The teacher stood smoking a pipe on the steps of the schoolhouse, keeping a watchful eye through those tiny round glasses hazed over with a sheen of grease that would make an owl sightless. He probably thought Charles would run, but he didn't have a mind to do that. He'd been right. And when everyone got here, they'd see his side of things.

The wagon came up the road. The horses churned up a good cloud of dust trying to keep up with Papa's discernible temper. His strong, corded arms pulled the lines. "Whoa!"

The wagon stopped abruptly. Nara jumped down before the dust had settled from the wheels. She stalked up to Charles, fists balled at her sides. "What did you do?"

Charles brushed the chalk dust from his arms and rolled his sleeves back down. "Mr. Meyer says I can't come to school any-more."

"I really thought you had your temper licked, kid."

"But Billy was going to hurt Patrick."

Mr. Meyer knocked the ash out of his pipe on the side of the schoolhouse and then waved them all inside. Mama grabbed Nara's elbow and said, "I told you. He shouldn't have gone back."

Papa took off his hat, grabbing at his back. It never occurred to Charles that Papa could break in any kind of way. The old guy passed Charles without so much as peeking in his direction and then labored up the stairs. They all followed Papa into the shady room. A crimson early fall light settled over the room, bathing it in a silent fury. *September 12th 1925* had been written in neat cursive on the blackboard. Charles remembered the scratchy sound the chalk made as the teacher wrote the date this morning, when this place felt safe.

Mr. Meyer sat behind his desk, his eyes flashing behind those little spectacles. "I'm going to come straight to it. Charles is being expelled."

"What has he done?" Papa breathed aloud.

"During lunch Charles made Billy Colfax eat dirt."

"I'm sure he's sorry about it now." Papa nudged Charles from behind none too gently and he pitched forward.

"Yes, Mr. Meyer. I'm sorry Billy had to eat all that dirt to grind out the terrible things he said to Patrick."

Nara let out a strangled noise and paced about the room, clunking her boots on the hollow boards.

"This is just boys being boys, Mr. Meyer. I'll take care of this," Papa said.

The schoolteacher had his hands in a steeple over his desk.

"Charles nearly looked unhinged today. The kids are terrified of him."

"Billy was going to hurt Patrick and you weren't going to do anything about it. You don't even stop him—"

Nara held up her hand to quiet him, and he ground his teeth together.

Mama added, "I'm sure we can work it all out. After all, Charles must be one of your best students. All his papers come back with A's on them. Isn't that what's really important?"

Mr. Meyer smiled tightly and sat back in his chair. "If I only had one student to teach. But, Mrs. Stewart, your other two 'children' are struggling and require enormous amounts of my attention. It hardly seems fair to the other students."

Papa, who usually didn't ruffle at much, jumped out of his chair and pointed his hat in Mr. Meyer's face. "Those *children* are Stewarts, Mr. Meyer. Our ranch is a source of income for others in this town, and my taxes pay your salary. You would do well to remember that. This is just two young boys knockin' heads. I'll work this out privately with Will Colfax. I don't want people talking about this, you get my meaning?"

Papa stared the teacher down until Mr. Meyer turned red and pursed his lips. Charles hadn't realized how much clout Papa had in the county.

"We're done here." Papa slapped his hat on his head and turned to leave.

Charles left the schoolroom wishing he never had to set foot in there again.

Mr. Meyer called out, "One more incident, and I won't be able to have him back, Mr. Stewart."

CHARLES KNEW PAPA wouldn't say anything until after supper, for nothing ever interrupted the evening meal. Mama's mouth had been pressed to a thin line rather than trilling away about everything that had happened during the day. Most telling, she didn't hop up to offer him a second helping after he wolfed down the first before everyone else. As they all sat around the table scratching at their plates, Charles hoped Papa would acknowledge him for sticking up for his brother after everyone was out of earshot, but given his brusque demeanor, it didn't seem likely.

Mama's lemony dish soap filled the air as it did after every mealtime. Plates were scraped, scrubbed, and white towels rubbed everything squeaky dry, and still Charles sat at the table, waiting. Mama clinked silverware behind them while Charles studied his fists on his lap. Papa read through the entire paper, flapping the pages. Charles read the back pages as Papa went along.

Papa folded his paper once, twice, and a third time. Then, slow as he pleased, Papa stepped over to the coal stove and nodded in Charles's direction. Oddly enough, it made Charles feel like he was a part of something mature. Many times, he'd seen Papa, Mama, and Nara with their heads together over the stove.

Papa ran his hands through his salt-and-pepper hair a good three times. "We talked about you staying out of everyone's business. Billy comes from a good family—friends of ours, people we depend on if something happens," Papa growled.

"Yes, sir, but—"

Papa pointed his finger. "Ain't no buts, but the one you sit on. Patrick is a big boy. He needs to learn how to handle things himself. Part of life."

"It's hard for Patrick. Nobody out here likes him just because he's Irish."

"Men have to find their own backbone out here."

"Everywhere we go, we feel like outsiders."

Nara joined them. "People will soften up sooner or later. You can't settle every problem with your fists."

Papa said, "If I knocked the snot out of everyone who made me mad, there wouldn't be a soul left in this county."

"Billy was going to hit Patrick, but I didn't hit Billy. Not once. Mr. Meyer doesn't say anything when the kids call Patrick names. He's a bigot, too."

"That may be true. But there are a lot of bigots out here. Can't fight 'em all," Papa said.

Mama came over and got in the middle of everyone. "I think Charles ought to quit school."

"What?" Nara said.

"Charles isn't able to control himself, and besides, his grades are excellent. He can study at home."

"Charles has to learn more than math and reading. He's got to rein in that temper. How's he gonna do that out here?"

Papa chopped the air between them. "You two, just quiet down."

Mama crossed her arms and breathed out. "He ought to at least stay home until the trial period is over." She slapped her towel across her shoulder and went into the kitchen again.

Charles felt awful that Mama had so little confidence in him. Didn't she care what happened to Patrick?

Nara said, "It's simple. You ignore Billy and keep your temper in check. I don't see how you can ever be foreman if you can't do that. Now, for your punishment, you're gonna get up extra early, feed the milking cows, muck stalls, and feed everyone's horse."

Papa gave Nara a nod of approval.

All the blood drained from Charles's face. "But I'll have to get up at three in the morning to get that all done by breakfast."

Nara said, "Yes, you will. And after that two weeks is up, you're gonna go help out Mr. Colfax until it's dark."

Mama said from the kitchen, "Tomorrow I'll take Billy's mom over a pie."

"No, I'll handle this man-to-man with Billy's father. You can take your pie over later this week." Papa turned to Charles. "This is your final warning, young man. I'll get this smoothed out with Billy's father, but if you cause any more trouble, you're going back to New York."

Charles's face turned hot. He stormed out of the house, sat down on the porch, and put on his boots without bothering to tie them up. His laces dragged in the dirt as he stalked out to the bunkhouse, where he flung open the door, tore off his boots, crawled into his bunk, and punched his pillow. He thought he heard a board crack just a touch underneath. He rubbed at his knuckle, red and smarting.

Patrick had already settled down in his bunk, his dictionary propped up in front of his face. The boy was determined to learn every word in it. Patrick called from above, "Did ya get inta a lotta trouble?"

"Not any more than I can handle."

"I don't think Mr. Meyer likes any of us. He'd just a soon we didn't show up at all."

"You got that right."

Given what Billy had said to Patrick in front of all those kids, humiliating him, Charles had let him off real easy. He hadn't expected the Stewarts to come down on him like that. To Patrick's credit, he had tried to stick up for himself. He pointed his thin finger at Billy and with his jaw trembling said he wasn't going to hear any more of those ugly words come out of Billy's mouth. But mean kids can always smell fear. Billy had gotten right in Patrick's scared face and grabbed his shirt in a meaty fist. Charles grabbed the bully from behind and had wanted to pulverize his face so badly, but instead gritted his teeth till they near shattered, and reached down to the ground and pulled up dirt clods and anything else that came with them, packing Billy's mouth so he couldn't speak. Billy's face turned red from trying not to swallow and choke on that dirt. Charles held his jaw shut, while Billy tried to break the grip. But there wasn't a man around who could do that.

Patrick had yelled, "Charles, stop! You'll kill him!"

Mr. Meyer came out of the schoolhouse and yelled from the top of the steps. Then he came bounding down them. The crowd of kids scattered, and that left Charles and Billy front and center.

Billy spit dirt out everywhere. Charles slapped his hands together to get rid of the evidence.

Mr. Meyer's eyes had gone big and buggy. "What is going on here?"

Charles folded his arms over his chest. "Billy here was trying to clean out his mouth by eating dirt."

Mr. Meyer had approached Billy and put his hand on his shoulder. "Are you all right?"

Billy had shaken his head and then gone behind the tree, where he tossed up his lunch.

Charles lay in his bunk with his hands behind his head, staring at the slats above him. If the Stewarts couldn't understand why he wouldn't let a bully hurt his brother, then they didn't understand him. By his way of thinking, he'd be a rotten brother to stand idly by and let Billy have his way with Patrick. Boy, no matter how he looked at it, the whole thing wasn't just unfair, it wasn't workable. He'd rather not live in a place where people would let their brothers get their butts whooped for no other reason than they were Irish.

He lay in his bunk, tossing and turning. He probably had three more hours of shut-eye, and then it would be time to get up and be punished for doing the right thing. He was eighteen, so if he had to, he could go find work on the railroad or in the copper mines. He sat up in his bunk. His head touched the slats of Patrick's bed above. Moonlight entered the gloom of the bunkhouse in a sliver of silver light. Charles stared at his quilt for a bit. Though it was worn at the edges, it kept him warm. The air here would freeze you right through at night. If he got out of his warm bed, he'd be on his own again. No hot meals or soft bed. No family. But if he couldn't stick up for his own brother, they weren't a real family anyway.

He lay back down for a bit longer and weighed it all out in his mind. The moon was full enough to provide light for walking. Charles took off his covers and slowly got out of his bed. He felt around in the dark and put on some clothes. Jim rolled over in his bunk. Charles froze for a minute until he was sure Jim slept. Charles quietly packed some of the clothes they had bought him into a rucksack. He felt guilty, so he didn't take them all. He checked all around, thinking he'd forgotten something.

It hung on the bedpost, glowed in the dark. He could navigate this room by the light of that hat. He went over, picked it up, and rubbed his finger over the finely woven straw. Slowly, he hung it back up and crept to the door. Patrick snored, a buzzing kind of contentment. With one hand on the doorknob, Charles watched the boy. Patrick was only fourteen. He couldn't work on the railroads or in the mines, and even so, there were bigots everywhere. Patrick was safer with the Stewarts, reading his dictionary every night with a soft pillow under his head. For Charles, this life, this family had been all pretend and dreams.

He put on his warmest coat and hat, then carefully opened the door to the bunkhouse, hoping it would be quiet for once. He crept out the door and shut it just barely, then sat down on the little overhang of a porch to lace up his boots for the long journey ahead. He figured he might as well take them. Nobody else would be able to wear them.

He wondered when the next train to Butte would come

through. The Anaconda Company always needed men for the mines. Jim had told him that. But Charles had no money, so he'd have to jump on when the engineer and the brakeman weren't looking.

He turned from the house and put one foot in front of the other. His boots scuffed the gravelly dirt in a goodbye all their own. The stars were out, covering that big sky. The moon followed above, casting the eeriest shadows over everything. In the city, he could almost never see this many stars at night or even stand gazing at the moon. To linger would have been dangerous, but not out here. Montana felt safe. In all this wide-open space you could see someone or something coming from a mile away.

The city hid its filth in corners and alleys. Gloomy tall buildings blocked out everything. He'd never go back there in a million years. People crowded together yelling, fighting, trying to survive where you just can't, except to steal and lie. You can live in the country, but a city, that's for dying. Montana was his home now. He knew that in his gut whenever he smelled the sage or felt the grit of clean soil under his fingernails. But he still needed to find a place where folks would accept him for who he was, what he believed in. The Stewarts had no sense of justice.

The road ahead appeared dim; regret set in. Maybe he should have just scared Billy somehow, apologized in the schoolroom, but it was all too late now. Maybe he was doomed to be a thug, unworthy of a nice family and only good for busting heads. He hitched his rucksack higher up on his shoulder for the long walk.

In all that quiet, he easily heard the snap of a twig somewhere behind him. A small shadow crept over by the outhouse. At first he thought it might be a coyote. And, "Where there is one, there's more," Nara had said. Or, worse, could be wolves. He stopped to watch and recognized the walk. Opal.

He hadn't said goodbye to her. She would be upset, probably cry. Patrick would understand, but she might not. She continued to walk toward the house and then she stopped. She stilled in that way an animal does when it's concentrating to hear or see something.

"Charles?" her frightened voice called out.

"Yeah, it's me." His rucksack dropped from his shoulder a bit.

She walked toward him in her nightdress and boots she hadn't bothered to lace up. Her hair had been braided up tight. Mama probably did that for her before bedtime. It was silly for him to think it at a moment like this, but he wondered if Mama or Nara ever read her a bedtime story. "Opal, what are you do ing out of bed?"

"I had to pee."

He sighed. "You shouldn't drink water after dinner."

"What are you doing out here?"

Her eyes tilted down in that worrying way of hers, just like his ma's. He looked to the shadows all around, not knowing what to say. He needed an excuse that would make sense to her. Leaving people was easy. Saying goodbye was hard. And he knew from experience you had a choice. You didn't have to do both. But now, her standing there, he felt like a real coward. "I gotta leave, Opal."

"When are you coming back?"

"I'm . . . I ain't coming back."

"I won't let you go." She flung her little body against his legs and wrapped her arms around them so tight, if he moved, he'd fall over like a great tree.

He stood there near tears for the stubbornness of that single act of hers. Why didn't he ever have the courage to do that? Just tell his ma to stop drinking. To come home even though he didn't want to. He had just up and left her. And here he was about to do it all over again to Opal, who loved him no matter his faults, could see through his brusque veneer, and he loved her back, for her willful, quiet ways. She stood there and gripped his legs tighter, and he reached down to stroke her golden hair. "I just don't fit in around here."

She kept her arms tight. Her head shot up and those big dark blue eyes searched his for the answer she wanted. And then began to water and leak over the sides. "Yes, you do! Don't leave."

His rucksack slipped off his shoulder and dropped to the ground.

The screen door at the house squeaked. Mama stepped out on the porch, and when her face came into the moonlight he could see she knew what he was about. From afar, she implored him. Her ample cheek twitched in the way it does when she's unhappy. She covered her face with both hands. She'd been so upset after dinner, he hadn't thought she'd even care if he disappeared.

"Mama, I'm sorry."

"Don't go, then," Mama said.

Opal stood back to search his face for his determination.

He looked up into that big sky, blinded by all the points of lights converging to one in his blurry eyes. More than anything, he hated disappointing people. Especially people who cared about him. He couldn't just say he was staying, walk back to the bunkhouse, and go to sleep. "I was . . . just out here to start on my chores."

Opal smiled up at him and then wrapped her arms around his legs again. Mama searched him out from over on that porch, as if she could test his fortitude and get her assurances from that distance. A few wolves moaned in the hills above. Mama's head turned to the noise, then back to him and Opal. "Charles, I know you're a strong young man, but this world is dangerous, and you'll always need a family. We need you, too."

It made him feel good to hear her say that. Western folks had a way of making things simple, basic. Life out here can't be made any more complicated than right or wrong. Safe or dangerous. Charles could do little more than nod his head. "Okay, Mama."

"All right, then. Go get some sleep." She turned to the direction of the wolves. "There's darkness out here yet. Opal, come on to bed."

Glancing back every so often, Opal walked to the porch. Before Mama shut the screen door, she locked eyes with him for a moment. He was sure she'd watch him from the window over the sink. He turned back to the bunkhouse. The rubbery relief he felt in every bone of his body nearly toppled him to the ground.

CHAPTER 15

PAPA DID HAVE A FLAIR FOR THE DRAMATIC. HE'D DRIVEN UP IN THE early evening, and likely right then because he knew everyone would be gathered for supper. They all sat around the table chattering about their day when Nara heard a horn. Mama stood straight up from the table as if a lightning bolt had hit her. She went to the window over the sink. "I'll be a monkey's uncle!"

She ran out the door, everyone hot on her heels. The screen door squeaked and slammed as everyone ran through it. They lined up on the porch gawking. Papa honked the horn again a couple of times and got out of the driver's seat. "Well, what are you all waiting for?"

Everyone sat down on the porch, handing boots back and forth, putting them on as fast as they could. Mama walked up to him with her hands over her face and put her arms around Papa, who grinned bigger than the moon. He'd been gone all day, said this morning, "I'm going to Billings." Wouldn't say why. Nara walked around the blue and black automobile.

"It's a Studebaker Special Six," Papa said.

It had four doors and the top looked like it came down. It was made of some kind of canvas material. "Is it easy to operate?" Nara asked.

"Yup, I'll teach you tomorrow. It's easier than riding a horse."

Papa limped a bit as he walked around the auto, showing them all the rubber tires and wooden spokes. She half wondered if his sore back from the cattle drive and not being able to ride so comfortably made him finally break down and buy an automobile.

"Look right here, this pedal down here is the gas and this one is the brake for when you want to stop, but it's touchy. The steering wheel points it wherever you want to go."

Patrick stood by the engine area of the auto. "Can I have a peek at the engine?"

"Don't you want to go for a ride first?" Papa laughed. "Come on. Everyone get in back. Mama can sit up front with Opal on her lap."

Nara, Patrick, and Charles got in the back. He was so big, most of him hung out of the auto during the ride. Patrick sat crushed in the middle.

Jim waved goodbye to them from the porch. His solitude and exclusion always pinched her heart some. Nara put her head out, and the wind whisked through her hair like she rode a galloping horse, but she was just sitting there in that leather seat. It was noisy, so they had to yell to talk over the engine and rushing air, but they all had some silly smiles on their faces. They went back and forth down the old Creek Road that bordered the south side of their ranch until it was dark.

"I'm scared we might run off the road," Mama said.

Papa laughed and said, "Honey, about the only thing that scares me is a swarm of grasshoppers." Then he turned on the headlights as he headed down the road that led to their home. "Me and the boys will need to build a special barn to put it in, or it will get real dirty."

Patrick called out, "They call them garages in the city."

When they got back, Mama didn't even care that the food was cold. "It will be so quick to go to the mercantile for this and that, and I can't wait to see the look on everybody's face at Sunday service. Do you think I could learn to drive it?"

The whole room went still.

Papa finally said, "I'm sure you could manage it."

Nara always imagined Papa thought of Mama as a fixture that would forever remain somewhere in the kitchen. Like the sink or the stove.

After dinner, Papa said to Nara, "Tomorrow you need to go get that bull away from the fence. He's ignoring his cows."

Nara looked to Mama with her back turned at the sink, then Papa behind his wall of printed words and news, and rolled her eyes at the similarity between men and bulls.

Out here, things changed as fast as a river of cold molasses. Others, she wondered if they ever would. Between Indians and whites there remained a high boundary. Since Papa had caught her near Jim in Miles City, interactions between her and Jim had become uneasy.

The next morning she told Jim, "Let's you and me go pull those bulls apart."

Jim had been avoiding her, so he nodded without even looking her way. They each went to their horse's stall and saddled up with nary a word between them. The ride was longer for the lack of even the small conversation they would normally have. She squinted at Jim out of the corner of her eye, but his face betrayed nothing except the sheer will to keep her out of his thoughts and mind by imitating a statue.

From just over the devil's rope, Ivar's spotty bull grunted, stomped around, and pawed the dusty ground with a sharp hoof. Their bull bellowed right back, his head down, horns in the direction of the fence, giving the other bull the what-for. Sometimes this would go on for days. Nara watched those two big ugly beasts strut around near the fence, just shaking her head.

She cracked the whip near their bull to get it away from the fence. It hollered at her, but a few more near misses with the end of her leather, and it began to tromp off to escape her whip. She and Jim worked together to herd the stubborn galoot toward the herd, where his manly business would be better appreciated.

When they had finally gotten him near to his duty, they rode up to a ridge together to watch the bull mingle with the cows. The bull found a cow in heat and began to follow it around, nudging its backside to show interest. That would go on for many hours until the cow came into a standing heat, and then it would let the bull mount, but it was a painful process for a cow. Something Nara didn't know anything about. She and Jim watched for a while to make sure the bull kept to his business. Cows bawling below and whisking horse tails filled the air.

The silence between them felt lifeless, where before their quiet had crackled with anticipation, for the moments when their skin brushed, and the heady effect of their chemistry, the gentle smells and scents. What remained now between them were the words she'd left unsaid. "I'm sorry about Miles City. I just didn't know what else to do but hightail it out of there. You bore the brunt of Papa's anger, I'm sure. I feel awful about that."

He listened to her heartfelt words, staring out to the mountains beyond, then turned to her with his dark eyes. It wasn't so much the resentment on his lips, but how he interpreted the truth between them. "Flirting with me is safe, that's why you do it."

"No, Jim. You don't understand. It's not even in my control. What I do or feel, it's . . ."

"But you were ashamed of what you did, which is why you left. If I were a white man, you wouldn't be." His proud back swayed in his saddle as he rode off without giving her the chance to make him understand.

She hadn't been playing around with him. What she felt, did, said in those moments in Miles City, no other man had ever been able to pull those things from her, pierce her workingman's façade.

For many days after, she walked around feeling like she'd lost something, empty inside, and so badly wanting it back. Jim ever on her mind.

* * *

The train telegraph office was the only place in Bull Mountain where they had evolved beyond the horse and buggy. But just beyond. The people in this town were suspicious of anything new-fangled. As she opened the door, a radio played music like they danced to in the city. She thought it was called the Charleston. From John's letters, she knew about the flappers with their short dresses, cigarettes, and heavily painted faces. She remembered thinking they sounded more like something out of a bordello. Not that she knew anything about those, and that was fine by her. The city life wasn't for her by a long shot. She went to the window to say hello to Mary, who had worked at the office more years than Nara had memory.

"How's the family?" Mary asked.

"Fine."

"All of them?"

"Yes, all of us."

Mary cocked her head. "Nara, I heard you adopted them kids."

"*We* adopted those kids. They're not mine. I mean, they are. We're all raising them."

Mary just nodded, like she had pressed too far. "Okay, sugar. Everything going all right? I heard the oldest one's got a temper."

"No, he's just protective of his siblings." Nara went on, because if anyone was a mouthpiece in this county it was Mary, "He works hard. My father thinks he'll make a good foreman one day."

Mary cackled a little and got up from her stool. "You want a cigarette, hon?"

"No, thanks. My mother's onto my smoking. Says I sound like a man who's swallowed fire."

Nara admired Mary's short haircut, wondering if it would

suit. Nobody ever saw her hair under her hat anyway. "Where did you get your hair done?"

"Over in Billings." Mary primped the subtle curl that came just below her ear. "You like it?"

"Yes, it looks very practical. My mama would die, though."

"If there's one thing I'm certain of at my age, haircuts don't kill people."

Nara chuckled at that. "You got me there."

Mary eyed her for a second and then stepped to a wall behind her filled with lots of wooden slots for sorting mail.

"Honestly, you shouldn't let your mother dictate how you do your hair. Where would we be if we did everything the same way our parents did? Where's your Montana spirit, girl! We were one of the first states to give women the right to vote. First female elected to Congress, and you know what? She's probably got short hair, too."

Nara nodded right along. She knew all the history. It had happened before her very eyes while she was in her late twenties. She would sneak Papa's paper when he was out on the porch to keep track of what was going on with Jeanette Rankin's campaign. When Mama had asked who she voted for, Papa's paper stilled from across the table. His fingers gripped his paper a bit tighter. It was a rare event for her to fib to her parents. Keeping her hair long was the one thing she did for her mother—possibly the only thing. Mama felt women ought to look like women. Mabel would never have cut her hair short, not that Nara could ever fill her older sister's shoes anyway. Still, cutting her hair would be going too far.

Mary rifled through the place where she normally stashed

John's letters. She never put those letters in the Stewart box. It was their little secret. "Huh. Well, I guess you don't have any word from New York. Maybe John just got a little busy."

"Yeah." Nara stroked her chin, wondering what had happened. "Is there a chance it's in another box?"

"Let me see."

Mary sifted through the other boxes, then put her hands in the air. "Sorry."

"Thanks for looking again."

"Tell your folks I said hello." She touched the curl of her short hairdo with a wink.

Nara walked out of there chuckling, even though the pit of her stomach told her something was wrong. John wrote to her like clockwork. Twice a month. The only way back to her brother was his last-known address, which she didn't think he was at, considering he wasn't answering her letters. She decided to write one more letter, and if she didn't hear back, then she would tell Papa. He was going to be madder than a hornet, and it didn't seem fair, as it was John who left for the city. And it was John who had apparently gone missing or was hurt, dead. Hell, she just didn't know. But he'd better have a damn good explanation.

Agitated and distracted, she nearly ran right into Ivar, who stood just outside the train office.

"Oh, hey, Ivar."

"What brings you into town?"

"Mail."

He glanced down at her empty hands but didn't say anything. "I was wondering . . . Well, you know folks talk . . ."

"Yes, they do."

"Colfax told me Charles and his boy had a scuff-up."

"Charles has been punished good for that. Believe me, he's going to keep his nose clean from here on out."

Ivar nodded. "Work it out of them, they always say. Speaking of, I'm going to be rounding up those wild horses that are eating my forage."

"Why don't you take Charles and Patrick to help you out?"

"I could use some help, a strong boy."

"Charles and Patrick are a team. They work pretty well together."

"It would be better if I worked alone with Charles."

"Two will do the work faster."

He grunted a little at that.

"You know, it wasn't too long ago, it was your folks people talked about."

"Patrick doesn't look tough enough for this kind of work. He'll just slow us down."

"I can assure you, he is as sturdy as any hand out there. He's a little skinny, I grant you, but his hands work like everyone else's. I've never found him to be lazy, if that's what you're getting at."

"We'll see about that. Tomorrow, then."

"You be nice to that boy, and please don't repeat what Colfax told you."

"Yes, ma'am. For you."

That last bit made her feel funny.

"And, Ivar, I'm getting damn tired of fixing fences."

He just smiled and tipped his hat.

* * *

Papa and Ivar had managed to walk around each other, but things had heated up between them of late. The fence breaks chapped Papa's butt. He sensed them, even if he couldn't ride out with his aching back to see them. And on Ivar's side, Nara knew he resented the way Papa held him to account for his father, Ivar Senior. It was hard to say whether Ivar put the breaks in the fence out of desperation for forage, or whether he did it to get under Papa's skin. Funny thing was, she felt like that damn fence. Worn, broken, and just barely keeping them apart.

She put off telling Papa about lending out the boys until he was out teaching her how to drive the Studebaker the next day. She got into the driver's seat and tested out the wheel, turning it this way and that. If only it were just as easy to point her life in the right direction.

He showed her how to start the engine and off they went. Dust kicked up behind the auto as they drove down the road away from the ranch house. A chicken ran out in front of them, and she slammed on the brake. Papa's hand came up to keep him from going through the windshield. "Sorry, Papa."

"Those brakes need a gentle touch, young lady."

She nodded, a little frightened of the power under her. She pressed down the gas pedal lightly. The wheel vibrated in her hands and felt a little heavy to steer, but she got the hang of it soon enough.

Papa pointed up ahead. "Try and steer around those big

chuckholes. The fella who sold it to me said those will break the wheels pretty quick."

She stopped at the road ahead with a little more grace and turned to him. "Which way?"

"Crick road toward Billings."

They got going down the road a ways. Papa had her turn this way and that till she got the hang of it. Then he told her to practice applying the brake. The first couple tries were jolting. Papa said, "If you were in the saddle, you'd have gone right over your horse's head!"

It was tricky. You had to push it down easy until that point where you pressed it all the way to the floor. After five or six times, she learned how to press it real slow, so as not to throw them out of their seats.

She supposed her inability to focus on learning to drive the automobile had more to do with talking him into lending out the boys. He stared ahead. Gritty wind pummeled the front end of the Studebaker as it rumbled down the gravelly road, the sagebrush blurring by them.

"Papa, Ivar needs Patrick and Charles to help round up that band of mustangs eating at his grass."

He slapped his hat on his knee. "I don't know why he can't get off his lazy butt and put up a fence on that part of the range."

"You know he doesn't have the money or men for that."

He let out one of those long I-give-up breaths and gazed out at the horizon. "I don't like that family. You know that. But neighbors take care of neighbors. He helped us at roundup. I don't want to be in his debt. I suppose the boys can help me build the garage next week."

They had driven back down the road in relative quiet, not the easy kind. She pulled alongside the barn to keep the wind from leaving dirt inside the auto. Papa had ordered lumber in from Billings for the garage. It sat in big stacks near the house where he and the boys were going to build it. Until then, he used a canvas tarp to cover the windows of the automobile to keep the dirt out.

Patrick offered to help Papa do anything with the Studebaker that needed doing. It was nice to see Patrick interested in something. He'd been quiet lately, a troubled slant to his eyes at the table. One night, he hadn't wanted any apple pie. "No, thanks, Mama," the boy had said.

Mama had looked at him funny and then gone over to put her hand on his forehead. "No temperature. You feel all right, Patrick? I think he ought to take a few days off school and rest."

Papa had nixed that idea. "Can't protect him. He needs to face up to them kids, or he'll never grow up to be a man."

Nara watched Papa put the tarp over the auto now, his unerring and dependable hands checking this and smoothing over that. She figured he must know the right way to raise kids. After all, he'd done it already. Papa went inside, while Nara waited on the porch for the kids to come home from school. The sun set earlier in the day, and the boys would have to make double-time if they wanted to help Ivar find the mustangs. They would come home from Ivar's well after supper, so she went into the kitchen to ask Mama to make up some sandwiches for their pails.

Farther down the road, Charles and Opal rode together on

his horse. When Charles and Opal trotted into the stables, Nara followed them in.

"Where's Patrick?"

Charles handed Opal down to her and then dismounted. He walked Charge to the stall. "He stayed behind to finish his work."

Nara squinted an eye at that. She couldn't see his face. He removed his saddle and such.

"Opal, why don't you go on inside? Mama will need your help making supper—and don't forget to water the chickens. Thirsty hens don't lay eggs."

Opal nodded and skipped off to the house. She had on a pretty dress with a dropped waist in the new style. Charles came out of the stall after taking care of Charge.

"You and Patrick are going to help Ivar round up some wild horses that are eating his grass."

Charles's eyes went wide. "I can do it alone."

"Your punishment is done. Patrick can help out."

"Patrick's been tired." Charles worked his bottom lip with his teeth.

It gave her a moment's pause. "He's tougher than he looks."

"Doesn't Papa need his help building the garage?"

"Papa can wait." She crossed her arms, tired of his back talk. "When is Patrick going to be back?"

Charles shrugged.

"Well, you better get on over there. Take that gelding and give yours a rest. Mama's packed a pail with sandwiches."

She watched him busy himself, wondering what in the devil he hid from her.

CHAPTER 16

THE NORTH WIND HAD COME TO PAY THEM ALL A VISIT. PARCHING and relentless, it would dry up every lick of moisture in the air and overstay its welcome just like the Stewarts had promised. Fall had just barely begun, but already Papa talked about how they would get a real taste of Montana come winter and something about blizzards. But not to worry, he would tie a rope from the bunkhouse to the outhouse. Patrick and Charles had just looked at each other. Then Papa started laughing, told them they would learn "the true meaning of a chapped butt." Since the probation period had expired and Charles, Patrick, and Opal were officially adopted, everyone had felt a little lighter until now.

Charles rode up a dusty trail to Ivar's place, licking his chapped lips. It was nothing more than a small log cabin. There was a barn to the west of the cabin, a bunkhouse that was smaller than the Stewarts', a corral, an outhouse, and not much more. The chicken coop leaned over a little to one side trying to spit out all the chickens. One lonely pine tree stood near the cabin, half its limbs gone brown.

The porch boards felt soft and rotten under his feet. He glanced down and kept to the more solid boards as he approached the door.

Ivar opened the door before he could knock. Those icy eyes reflected the waning afternoon light.

"Heard you ride up." Ivar stepped out. "Well, we best get to it. It'll be dark before long."

Charles remounted the gelding he'd been given, took up his reins, and followed Ivar, hoping Patrick stayed away from home, so he would be spared the first night. Patrick had been out with the mustangs more often as school became harder. Charles had to tell an outright lie to Nara today about Patrick's whereabouts and was glad Opal hadn't said anything. Somebody had taught her to keep quiet.

They rode through rocky terrain, and bit by bit the ponderosa pines disappeared. The soil out here looked infertile compared to the lushness of the Stewarts' range. Sagebrush thrived, crowding the trails, but not much else. He wondered how many head Ivar had lost to bloat this year. Seeing things out here made Charles realize how lucky they'd been to wind up on the Stewarts' ranch.

The wind breathed down heavy on them, whipping away the sounds of everything all around. If someone got lost out here, their cries for help would never be heard. Charles shivered, following Ivar as he rode on for a good thirty minutes, when the wind stopped for a moment. Ivar burst out, "Whoa!"

Yipping noises reached them from the west beyond some

rocks. Charles turned in his saddle to hear better. One sounded like a squeaky door, another yipped, and a third one moaned. All together, they sang a grieving memorial for a thing they hadn't killed yet.

"Damn coyotes," Ivar growled. "Follow me."

"What will we do if we see them?"

"Shoot 'em. They've been picking off my calves."

They rode on to their grim task. Charles supposed if the coyotes took out all of Ivar's stock then he would starve. Surviving out here changes you into an animal.

They rode behind the rocks at a gallop. Ivar dismounted from his horse quicker than anyone Charles had ever seen before. Two coyotes were standing on the crest of a rock and they prowled toward Ivar without fear. Ivar shot one before it could get close, and it dropped, but the other one came at him and tore his dungarees right at the knee. Ivar turned his gun around and bludgeoned it in the head. The coyote yelped so sharp, it hurt Charles's ears, but Ivar kept at it. His rifle cracked the skull. Charles turned away. His stomach tightened at the familiar sound. Ivar kept bludgeoning the coyote's head, uncovering ugly memories from Hell's Kitchen.

Hard, echoing surfaces. Meat hanging in the back room of the butcher's shop just beyond the shiny cash register. Charles and Jonny, sweating. An unloaded pistol they found in an alley trembled in Charles's hand. It didn't go how they had planned. The butcher turned on Jonny with wild, glittering eyes and a meat cleaver. He went after Jonny, and Charles beat the butcher in the back of the head with the butt of the pistol. Charles heard a sickening crack, and the butcher had fallen to the floor.

Charles's hands shivered on the reins of his horse, his guts gone cold. The coyote twitched around on sandy dirt, colored like Montana itself. Fur of gold, white, and gray for the soil it was born from. Ivar's grunts and heavy breaths filled the air around them. Charles turned his horse and rode off at a gallop, wanting to hear anything else. The wind from his flight rushed past his ears like a train hurtling down the tracks. Over rough ground, he banged around in his saddle until his horse slowed on its own. He dismounted and stood on wobbly legs. His eyes drifted over Ivar's rangeland, wanting something pure to erase what he just saw. The grass stood brittle from the dry summer, but here and there, sprouts of fresh green escaped the ground from the rains last week.

Ivar's horse shimmied through the tall grass, coming near. "What's the matter with you, kid?"

Charles breathed in and then out to cleanse himself. "Nothing."

Ivar grunted, and Charles turned to mount. They rode together in silence, searching for the next things to kill, making Charles wonder if he'd really escaped the life of a brutal thug. When they came around a hill, they found the mustangs in the distance, huddled together to fend off unfriendly wind. There inside the band, Patrick stood with a small horse that shone blue like a stone in the river.

Ivar stopped his horse. Charles pulled up alongside and said, "Patrick probably came straight out here after he got home."

Ivar narrowed his eyes. Before he could ask questions, Charles kicked his mount to a trot and rode over to the mustangs. Patrick was stroking the muzzle of the small mustang. Its silver-blue color glowed more intensely in the light of the setting sun. Just like a pale gray cloud turns color at sunset. The mustang had scars on it like something had bitten into it. The little horse returned Patrick's affection, snuffling at his hair. The wild horses scattered as Charles drew close, the smell of death clinging to him.

"Patrick, Nara's gonna find out. We're supposed to be out here helping Ivar. I covered for you. I told Ivar over there that Nara must have sent you out here to help round up the horses."

Patrick's brows furrowed. "What horses?"

"*These* horses."

"Why?"

"I don't know. Keep your voice down."

As Ivar rode up, the rest of the horses scattered like wisps of smoke. Their manes flying in the wind of their flight.

Charles turned to Ivar. "Yeah, Nara sent him over. Where do we start?"

Ivar lifted his hat and smoothed his hair back. "How did you get so close to that mustang, kid?"

"They like me," Patrick muttered.

"We're out here to round 'em up, not pet 'em. Mount up. Tonight we've got to set up a chute and a rope corral."

Patrick's eyes shone with horror. He looked to Charles, who bowed his head, ashamed.

Orange light cast over the white-topped mountains as if a

fire flickered somewhere nearby, throwing off the last shadows of its flames on this hellish valley. Ivar worked in grunts, harsh and hurried, trying to race the sun. Since Charles had arrived in Montana, the work was always gritty, get in your eyes and make them water, but this felt unnatural. It hurt him to do this work, but he feared it would break Patrick's spirit. Whenever Ivar asked the boy to do something, he'd dare put up his chin at Ivar for a moment, then Patrick would cast his face down. His skinny legs struck the ground slow and heavy as an elephant's. Maybe he thought if he worked slowly, he could stop the whole thing from happening.

Charles looked at the hole in his leather glove, ripped from the bristly rope, and the red wound that lay underneath it, and he couldn't help but wonder what had happened to the rest of Ivar's men and why they weren't out here helping. Mean drunks like Ella's brother were better suited for this kind of work.

Ivar checked all the ties to the rope corral, circling his net.

Patrick said to Charles, "This will never hold them in. They're too strong."

"I'm sorry. I know how much you love these horses, but we don't have a choice."

"Everyone has a choice."

Patrick could never know how those words made the guilty bile rise in Charles's throat.

"Get moving, kid!" Ivar yelled at Patrick for maybe the tenth time that evening, making Charles's stomach roil.

＊ ＊ ＊

When the rosy morning light crept through the window of the bunkhouse, Charles opened his eyes. These days he could perceive even the smallest change in the sky through the skin of his eyelids. He rolled over, wishing he could catch a few more hours of shut-eye. Jim's feet slapped flatly on the wooden floorboards as he searched for his clothing and boots. He'd come in late last night and had been making himself scarce lately. Charles hadn't slept much, either. He'd been awake and heard Jim's motorbike on the ranch road. Charles figured Jim cut the engine before reaching the house to avoid waking up the Stewarts, because he didn't hear the motorbike near the house. It was probably easy enough to push it to the horse stables.

Patrick usually threw his legs over the side of the bunk above Charles's head, always happy to greet a new day, or at least he had been. Charles sincerely hoped Patrick hadn't heard what Ivar had said: "A man can earn some extra dollars turning them in." When Charles asked what they did with the horses, Ivar had said, "They grind 'em up and can 'em for chicken feed." Charles had stared Ivar down like he was a demon, and all he had to say for himself was "You think I'm cruel? People from the city don't understand how their steak ends up on the plate no more."

Charles and Patrick got dressed quietly, neither wanting to face this day, knowing what it would bring. At breakfast, Mama came by with her pan of scrambled eggs, a happy gleam in her eye as usual. She cocked her head at Charles when he shook his head. "No, thanks, Mama."

Patrick glanced up and met Charles's eye. He passed on the eggs, too, and nibbled at a biscuit.

Nara came in and sat next to Charles and Patrick at the table. "How's it going out at Ivar's?"

"Okay," they both said.

Nara stared into her coffee mug as she said, "You look . . . real tired, Patrick."

Patrick's eyes went glassy. He didn't look like he could speak, because if he did, he'd start bawling right there.

"He's just tired from the roundup," Charles said.

Patrick scooted out his chair and walked over to the sink to scrape his plate. Mama watched after him with concern. She transferred that right over to Nara. They locked eyes, having one of those silent conversations. Charles wondered why they could understand each other without words yet failed to see how hard things were for Patrick. There wasn't one kid who liked him at school. Mr. Meyer made Patrick feel stupid, loudly pointing out all his mistakes. And now he'd be forced to round up the horses he loved, shoving them into a tiny pen where they'd stay until they were hauled off to make chicken feed. Patrick wasn't sick. He was weary as all hell, beaten by this damn town.

Nara nodded her head and slapped her thighs, getting up from the table. "All right, then. You boys work hard for Ivar. He's always been there in our time of need, and he needs our help now. That's how it works out here. We don't want people thinking the Stewarts are slouchers." She patted Patrick's slumped shoulder on the way out.

* * *

Patrick's golden little mare plodded along like it knew where they were going, what they had to do. Charles couldn't think of one thing to say that would make Patrick feel any better, and so they rode together in silence and dread. Woeful horse hooves clopped through dried grass, taking them closer to something unnatural and vicious. Charles would shield Patrick from whatever he could, Ivar and his ice-cold eyes be damned.

When they got there, Ivar threw open the door of his cabin. "What took you two so long?"

"I had some schoolwork to finish up before Mr. Meyer would let us leave," Charles said.

"It's good you're attending to your studies. A man has to be able to write and count—even out here."

Charles nodded. "I work hard at school. I have all A's."

As soon as the braggy words were out, he regretted them. Patrick gave them a noncommittal shrug and turned to look out over the golden hills.

"Even with all your hard work at school, I hear you still have time to rough up the other kids."

Whether Ivar wanted him to boast or make apologies, Charles had no clue. "I was sticking up for Patrick."

"What makes you think the only other alternative was choking that boy with dirt?"

"Our teacher doesn't care if Billy is teasing Patrick, doesn't do anything about it."

"What happens when you turn eighteen and these fights get you put in jail?"

"There isn't gonna be a next time."

Patrick stood sullen, red in the face.

Charles said, "No disrespect, but maybe we oughta get on with it before it's dark."

Ivar nodded. "All right, kid. I suppose you've got to learn things the hard way.

"One thing, Mr. Magnusson. Patrick here is too sick to work. He can do something easy around the barn for you."

Ivar swung around and came to stare Charles down. But Charles returned Ivar's fire and refused to look away. Ivar finally turned to Patrick with disgust. "Too sick or too lazy?"

"He's not lazy!" Charles took a step forward, bumping chests with Ivar.

Ivar tipped up his hat, eyes wild. "Let me tell you something, kid, you knock off the back talk, or I'll kick your butt up between your shoulder blades!"

Charles fisted his hands at his sides, trying to keep his anger in check, knowing where this would lead.

Ivar stepped back and laughed. "Don't think for a moment I can't still do it."

Ivar grabbed his horse's lead, then pointed at Charles. "You need to learn things the hard way. Many of us out here do. Just don't come crying to me when you get your knocks, hear?"

With just a curt nod to acknowledge Ivar's words, Charles

turned away, thinking at the time, no way in hell he'd ever need Ivar's help.

Ivar brought out a black leather bullwhip and whistled up a couple of his blue heelers, and they all rode out. He set a fast pace. The dogs kicked up whorls of dust trying to keep up. When they found the mustangs, Ivar's eyes were bright with the chase, snapping and cracking his whip mere inches from the gleaming coats and tails whisking away in flight.

Patrick hung back and refused to help drive them, but something in the boy made him stick around. Maybe he planned to save them in the end. Charles dreaded the night's work. Thankfully, Ivar was so busy with the whip, he didn't have time to yell at Patrick straggling behind them most of the way. Charles rode to the outside of the stampeding band to keep them together, and chased down any that bolted away through the rocky parts of Ivar's unforgiving range. He and Ivar worked together in their unholy pursuit of creatures that had once roamed free and wild on this silent prairie. Now this stark, beautiful place echoed with vicious whips, mustangs screaming in terror, and thundering hooves digging into the earth for survival. There was so much commotion, Charles could barely understand and process his part in it all.

A small pinto he'd been trying to get back into the herd was dodging and weaving all the rocks when it was felled to the earth by a rock too large to go around. It screamed and struggled to get back up in a cloud of dust, but its fetlock was hanging by a thread of skin. It would never walk again. Patrick backed up and saw this and came galloping to its aid. Ivar turned to see all this and ran his horse hard to reach the struggling pinto. Before Ivar had even slowed his horse, out came his gleaming rifle. Patrick screamed something Charles couldn't hear over the thunder of hooves, and then came a bang like thunder. The horse collapsed, shivering its last. Patrick fell to his knees and placed his head on the withers of the pinto, stroking, bawling out to the big sky above.

Charles's heart felt shot through like that horse. He'd done that as surely as if he'd pulled the trigger himself, for he had been chasing that pinto when it ran into the rock. Ivar yelled for them to help keep the herd together, and all Charles could do was follow—he didn't know how to console Patrick, how to make that horse move again. His insides shivered like he'd swallowed an ice block.

After a few hours of this ugly work, wrangling and driving the mustangs, they had managed to get them all near the chute but one. Charles had been riding hard, twisting his body this way and that to maneuver his horse and keep the band together, hoping not one more horse would get hurt. The dogs yapped all around the band, and that one little blue horse kept catching his eye. Its coat shined with beautiful colors in the dusky light.

When they had them running toward the chute, Charles rode into the band after that little horse. He had only ever tried to cut a calf once, so as he joined the swarming band, felt them brushing up against his legs, he sensed Charge's uncertainty, but that big brute managed to carefully muscle its way between the little blue horse and the rest of the band. Charles cut right at that crucial moment, forcing the mustang away from the chute. Its legs kicked at the earth, running for its life toward the hills.

Charles pulled Charge to a dusty, skidding stop. Patrick watched him from atop his golden horse. There passed between them a knowing, that together, they would find the blue horse tomorrow. Maybe Nara would let them keep it, for it wouldn't survive on its own. Charles remembered what Papa had said about his having one last chance, but Charles reckoned that mustang's fate to be more important than his own, especially when he couldn't understand the difference between busting heads in a gang or wiping out something majestic to make a living.

The little blue horse ran like a thunderstorm cloud toward the mountains, dust whirling behind its hooves. Ivar's head whipped around to see the horse running off into the distance, then he glared at Charles like he'd strip every inch of skin off him with that whip. But Ivar didn't have time to chew Charles out or even chase down the stray, too busy shutting the pen behind the other horses.

Once they were all in the pen, Ivar and Charles rolled up the jute chute. Ivar worked with an irritability, barking at Charles. Ivar pointed to the connections on the fence, and they spent some time checking all the rope knots on the pen, so the mustangs couldn't get out. Ivar hadn't even asked Patrick to help. Just kept scowling at the boy with disdain, testing the rope and checking all the knots.

When they finished securing the pen, Charles hopped back

on Charge. They had done enough dirty work for Ivar. The less time Patrick spent looking at all those frightened horses in that little pen, the fewer nightmares he would have.

But that wasn't to be. Ivar walked up and grabbed his reins. Charge skittered to the side, resisting. Charles refused to dismount or meet Ivar's icy eye, unchastened by what he'd done, even as he feared Papa's wrath.

"Why did you do it, kid? Now we'll be out here for God knows how long, rounding up that damn mustang."

"It's getting late. Nara will expect us back."

"Nara will dig up the tomahawk if she hears you cut that horse!"

Patrick went to the pen and took off his shirt, using it to daub the blood dripping down one of the mares. When he wiped his tears, he streaked his face red.

"I'll go, but Patrick should ride home."

"Fine by me. That boy doesn't do a lick of work anyway."

Charles wanted to say something but held his tongue between his teeth. They rode off and circled around a small butte. He had a hard time keeping up with Ivar. That man rode like he could outrun the sun, but it was getting too dark to keep at it. Charles lagged behind, refusing to search, when a whisk of tail caught his eye. He prayed Ivar wouldn't see it. When Ivar turned in the blue horse's direction, Charles called out and pointed elsewhere to draw Ivar's attention away.

But he saw the little horse and turned hard, galloping after it. Charles chased with everything Charge had to keep up. The mustang began a steep ascent up a rocky ridge. The terrain slowed Ivar down. Charles followed him up, hoping Ivar wouldn't make it up the steep hillside, but Ivar got close enough to rope the horse. His hand loosened the catch rope tied to his saddle, and Charles shouted, "No! Let it go!"

Ivar took up his hard twist and began to circle it above his head, and just when he went to throw, his horse stumbled on the rocky land he had inherited like a curse.

"Come on, little horse. Run," Charles urged under his breath.

Ivar recovered from his near tumble and kept on its tail, but the mustang had crested the hill. Charles stopped ascending. A glossy black tail whisked about freely in the evening light. The last he saw of the blue horse.

Ivar cussed at his mount as he maneuvered around trying to find a path to the top, and only when the light extinguished itself in the western hill did that stubborn man turn around and head back. When he passed by Charles, Ivar said, "I'll just shoot it next time I see it. Too small to bring a good price anyway."

Charles's fist clenched around his reins, and Charge skittered sideways. For a guy who preached about turning the other cheek, Ivar had a twisted way of teaching the lesson.

CHAPTER 17

NARA STOOD AT THE TRAIN DEPOT, BREWING UP ONE HELL OF A headache. When she read the telegram Mary had handed her the other day, Nara's feelings were mixed. If John had a mind to, he could easily displace her at the ranch. Then the matchmaking would start back up with a fury. Maybe *she* ought to run off to the damn city. See how they like it. She hadn't slept a wink last night, wondering if she should tell her parents. In the end she decided he might not even be on that train.

There was a puff of smoke and a whistle up ahead. The tracks on the ground trembled like her hands. Holding on to her hat, she stepped back to watch the windows and faces go by, but the car went too fast for her to see John. She jogged to catch up with the coaches at the front. People were already filing out, bags in hand. She gave them all some room and waited. A baggage man nearly wheeled his bag cart right over her boots. "Watch it," she gruffed out.

"Pardon me, sir."

"I think you mean 'ma'am,'" she muttered.

He placed the bags on the platform and then went about exchanging all the mail and parcels destined for other stations. Probably hadn't seen her face under the hat, just heard the gravelly voice. Nara rubbed her chapped hands over her sun-worn skin. Maybe he did see her face.

John stood in the door of the train. His dark head of curly hair was bushy from his sleeping on it, just like when they were kids. His hand brushed at it in vain as he stepped down onto the platform. He saw her and smiled, opening his arms wide. To judge by his eyes, he was a different man than the one who had left this station years ago. Stars and dreams was how he departed Montana. Now those deep brown eyes were swollen and puffy like he hadn't slept in a week. As she wrapped her arms around him, his flesh felt soft like a woman's. He probably hadn't done a day's work in a while, but even so, his clothes hung loosely. "John?"

"I haven't changed that much, have I?"

Nara hugged him tight as she always had. But he didn't smell like her brother. He stank like liquor and stale sweat. She looked up into his eyes again to make sure it was really him.

"You had me scared there for a while." She socked his arm.

"Ooof. Sister, you still have a knuckly fist, I see."

"And there's more where that came from. Come on. I haven't told them yet."

He stopped dead in his tracks like he might get back on that train. She had a mind to let him.

"I hoped you would deliver the news before I got here."

"Coward. I'm not about to take that bullet for you." And she punched him again.

"Some things don't change." John rubbed his arm as they walked across the grassy area where she had parked the Studebaker.

WHEN THEY PULLED up, Nara could see Mama's face in the kitchen window. It went still, like an elk that's spotted you and just wants to be sure what you are. Then her face disappeared and out she came, running as fast as a woman of her age and girth could. "John!"

He couldn't get out of the auto fast enough. She grabbed him up tight, checking him over. "I couldn't believe it was you when I looked out the window."

She stood back, taking him all in, but to judge by her expression, Nara didn't think Mama saw the change in him. "Papa will be so darn pleased to see you. Come on, he's out on the range. He'll be back in a bit."

Blackie ran up to John and greeted him with an enthusiasm Nara rarely got from the old dog anymore. Apparently Blackie didn't think John had changed much, either.

Mama dragged John back to the house. She had him by the sleeve, and he sort of jogged to keep up with her. "Easy, now, Mama. I've been on a train for days now. Maybe I can go clean up first before Papa gets back."

She pointed her finger at him. "That's a good idea." Then she stopped. "But there's someone in your room right now." She turned to Nara. "We'll bunk Opal up with you." Then she turned to take John up the stairs.

Nara went into the kitchen to make coffee. After she poured the boiling water over the grounds, she watched it drain slowly into the pot. Kind of like her dreams. She poured a cup and sat down at the table, wondering what her role would be now and how long John intended to stay. She didn't care much for sharing her room, either. The right thing was to be asked to give up her room—in private. She might have been so bold as to suggest John stay in the bunkhouse. It seemed a little discourteous, to her mind, him showing up out of thin air. Selfish, even.

He didn't seem entirely happy to be in Montana again, so she supposed he didn't plan to stay long. Maybe just long enough to stir up a whole pot of trouble and then skip out like before. Papa opened the screen door and looked at her as if he could smell that trouble boiling over. "You look as tetchy as a rattlesnake."

Nara felt terrible for her thoughts. Papa would be happy to see him, and she should be, too. "We've got a little surprise for you."

He scrunched up his face. "Not that Eyetalian food again. I refuse to eat that stuff."

She shook her head over her cup of coffee. "That's not it."

Thuds from boots upstairs echoed downstairs, Mama's excited voice trilling from above like the happiest mama bird ever. John's deep laughter. She must be showing him Opal's room. His old room. Papa looked at the ceiling like they had some kind of poltergeist, then his eyes dropped to Nara. "John?"

"Yes, sir."

His face slowly changed from surprise to real happiness. It was an amazing thing to see, really.

Papa walked up the stairs. "John!"

She didn't get to see the big reunion between them, but she heard the firm pats on the back, the manly hellos, and, down here sitting at the table, she felt like the low man on the totem pole again.

Jim's motorbike putted into the yard. Nara's heart jumped in her chest, her brother forgotten. Jim walked in a few minutes later and looked upstairs to all the commotion with a question on his strong, square face. He took the Montana rooster that had been dangling limply over his shoulder and plopped it down on the counter for Mama. Pheasant was her favorite. "Shot this by the side of the road."

Nara smiled at him and said with too much brightness, "Mama will be giving you extra helpings tonight."

He nodded and began to stretch his strong back from a long ride, and for one burning hot second she thought the next time Mama or Papa talk about how she ought to get married, then she'll let them know who she'd choose. That'll teach them to fiddle with her life.

"Who is that upstairs?" he asked.

"My brother is back."

"Oh."

"Don't worry. We'll still need you around here."

"Lots of work to be done." He took off his hat and ran his bronze hands through his shiny black hair.

She had been watching every motion of him and then licked

her lips. His eyes darted to her mouth with interest. They gazed at one another for a moment, until he broke the contact. She put her face down to her cup of coffee. Her rational side waylaid the heartsick moment as she told herself she couldn't get him in trouble again, couldn't get distracted.

John and her parents returned, drubbing down the wooden treads like a herd of chatty cows, then sat around the table like one big happy family to visit. John entertained them with stories of the "big city." They sounded a little glossed over, to her ear. His clothing was fairly tattered. The soles of his boots were as thin as a layer of skin. The heels nearly worn off. She imagined that if he took them off, his toes would poke out of holes in his socks. But he went right on talking about his grand life.

"I've sold a couple of paintings, and there is a rich fella who wants a picture of Montana. A big one to put next to all his antler racks and stuffed cheetahs, lions, and so forth."

A game hunter, apparently. She wondered if this rich fella had the what-for to shoot down a charging grizzly. Probably crap his pants and then faint. She didn't approve of trophy hunters.

"A man should never kill what he's not planning to eat," Nara said.

Everyone stopped their happy chatter and then started back up again. She guessed Papa had forgot, because that's what he had told her when she brought home a badger she shot while checking cattle with John. To this day she could remember standing there on the porch, exhausted from having dragged that stinky creature up the steps, fur in her little fist, John by her side. Papa stopped playing his guitar. "Son, did you shoot that?"

"No, Papa. Nara did. It was a good shot, too."

Papa had looked at her with disapproval and said, "You shouldn't kill what you aren't planning to eat." And then he went right on playing his guitar.

Something stubborn in her made her say, "I'm planning on it."

"Well, you get out there, then. Skin and dress it. Mama will show you how to make badger stew."

She didn't think there was such a thing. She had just wanted him to be proud of her. But there he was across the table now, acting as if she hadn't been working her fingers to the bone since John left.

Papa's voice boomed from across the table. "Nara, did you hear that? Two hundred dollars for a painting of nature? I guess I'm in the wrong business. Why do they need pictures? Nature's everywhere." He held his hands wide.

"In the city you don't get exposed to it except travel and art."

Papa grunted.

Nara said, "Are you out here to paint, then?"

John looked down at his hands, and then to Papa. "Someone needs to run the ranch."

Nara nodded, knowing full well that was just a load of guff and there was a whole big story behind that lie. She leaned forward. "You think you're up to it? What do you know about fall calving?"

"Sounds risky. Folks have been raising cattle the same way for eons."

"Plenty of ranchers are doing it. I've been studying it. You've been in New York too long."

Papa squinted an eye at John, then leaned back in his chair and worked a toothpick between his teeth. Maybe the veneer of his son's homecoming started to peel like the paints John was so fond of. All gloss, nothing underneath.

Mama slapped Nara's wrist. "Nara Jean, he's only just cooled his heels under the table. You save that squabbling for later. John, I'm gonna make your favorite, chipped beef."

"John, maybe later you want to get some grit back underneath those prissy fingers of yours," Nara said.

Papa slapped him on the back and laughed. It surprised her when John got up from the table and said, "I'd be glad to dig right in."

"All right, then. Get your work duds on and meet me out at the stalls in ten minutes."

John patted his jacket and looked around as if he'd lost something. "I don't know where my work clothes are."

Mama came shining right over. "They're up in an old dresser. I'll get 'em for you right now."

"Oh. Thanks, Mama."

Nara stifled a laugh with her fist. Papa said, "They might not fit. Looks like you're but skin and bones. Is that what the city does to a man?"

Her brother just smiled, unwilling to be baited by Papa. "I've got muscles enough to throw some hay off the back of a wagon."

"Oh, well, thank goodness. You look like you're about to break in half just getting up from that chair." Papa winked at Nara.

Nara couldn't help it, she laughed aloud at John's expense. Her brother rolled his eyes and followed Mama upstairs.

Papa leaned over the table before grabbing up his paper. "What did I tell you? The 'big city' has worn off already. Hmph."

"I don't know if he's done with that life just yet."

Papa sat there working his stubbly chin with his hand. "Well, we'll see what happens, won't we?"

* * *

Nara woke determined to test John's mettle. Her lantern swayed in the dark morning hours, and she tucked her shivering hand into a pocket. The bunkhouse stood solemnly, no one stirred. With a shove, she opened the door that always rubbed in the jamb. Her boots quietly scuffed the floor as she tried not to wake up the boys, who needed rest. But her brother, he needed to learn a lesson. Coming back here, swooping in to supplant her at a moment's notice, and only because things didn't work out for him in the city, wasn't going to work out for him. She jiggled John's shoulder, his head turned toward the wall. "Get up. Time to work."

He turned over like it took a great effort, bloodshot eyes blinking in the low lantern light. Behind her the boys ruffled around under their quilts. Patrick murmured something.

"What are you doing in here?" John asked.

Nara should be asking him the same thing, since Mama had set up a bed for him in his old room. "It's time to set up the bull pens for fall calving."

He sat up and almost hit his head on the bunk above him where Jim slept peacefully, or pretended, more like.

"Papa hasn't said anything about it."

"Does he have to? I thought you were able to run the place."
John rubbed his face. "Give me a minute, all right?"

She waited for him outside, and when he finally came out, he
looked like something that had been dragged behind a horse,
and, boy, did he reek of booze. They went out to the area where
she knew Papa would want the pens and began to work.

Throughout the day, she savored every moment when he appeared to want to quit, looked exhausted, or tossed her a dirty
look when he thought she wouldn't see. But she saw it, all right,
and there'd be plenty more of those to come.

Although she had worked John hard, Papa hadn't come by to
check on them, so he didn't get a chance to observe the lack of
fitness and poor skills of his only son. Many times, she checked
and corrected his fence work, for the pen wouldn't hold a bull.
The sun roasted them overhead. She took off her hat to wipe her
forehead with her kerchief, studying his last pathetic knots, and
walked on by.

They went inside for a break, and she discovered why Papa
hadn't come around to see the pens. Over the table, her books on
fall calving had been laid out, along with the methods she had
studied by kerosene lamp when she could have been sleeping.
Papa told John to sit down next to him and then motioned to
Jim to join them. "John, I'm glad you got those pens set up."

It stung hard, but she sat at the table without an invitation.
"Papa, the books say—"

Papa held up his hand to stop her talking and turned to John.
"You're going to separate the heifers . . ."

Papa kept on giving instructions without asking for any input from her. Her hands grappled with each other in her lap. She knew far more about the process and how to manage the cows after breeding. Nara leaned forward over the table. "After breeding we have to give them wider range to find their own calving grounds, to prevent the scours."

Papa didn't look her way or give any indication he had heard her.

Nara's face flamed over. The chair beneath her grunted over the floor as she stood. "Well, I'll just start helping Mama out, since you two know how it's done."

Papa stopped talking for a moment to acknowledge her curt comment, then continued giving John instructions. Which bulls to use for breeding and so forth.

Jim's face softened with sympathy as he sat with the men of the house.

From her place at the sink with Mama, Nara observed John nodding his head, but he seemed a little nervous to her eye. His hands shook badly, but she hadn't seen him drinking too much coffee. Through the kitchen window, she watched Charles and Opal ride up from school. She glanced over to Mama, who rinsed vegetables, and wondered how a woman could just stand here at a window, hands in soapy water, watching as everyone else lived their lives. "How do you do this day in and day out, Mama?"

"You'd be surprised what a woman can endure for her family."

Mama's words felt like a slap. Nara stormed off, letting the screen door slam behind her. The kids sat down to dust off and remove their boots.

Papa yelled from inside the house, "John, here are those new Stewarts we were telling you about."

Nara gritted her teeth and went back inside.

"Kids, come over here and meet my son John."

Charles and Opal stood woodenly. None of them really talked about family stuff. Father, mother, sister, brother. They just weren't that kind of family, so the awkwardness she read in Opal and Charles made perfect sense to her.

Nara left the sink and opened the door to search for Patrick. A guilty shade passed over Charles's face, but he didn't explain the younger boy's absence, nor did she ask, lest he lie again. Considering how rough those two had had it out at Ivar's, she figured Patrick needed some space, so when Charles made an excuse "to go check on something," she didn't challenge him. Opal made a beeline for the safety of the kitchen, putting on the little apron she and Mama had sewn up special. It had butterflies all over it.

Nara helped Mama load up plates and then sat herself, forking her green beans like enemies, sawing through her beef, gulping her water, and slamming the glass down on the table. Mama scrunched up her brows and pursed her lips at Nara, while everyone else pretended not to notice.

"Papa, I'm gonna go back out after dinner and check over those ties on the pen. Some of them didn't look strong enough to hold a bull." Nara glared at John.

Papa's mouth twisted up, and he kept on eating like she hadn't said anything. She guzzled water to put out the fire in her gut.

John tried to cover the tension with conversation. He was affable that way, even if he'd let himself go flaccid and soft.

"Jim, how'd you end up working out here?" John asked.

Jim shared his experience working for Anaconda out at the mines. "One day I got up choking on black phlegm, and I couldn't do it anymore."

Mama grimaced at that, and if Nara's senses were correct, she kicked Papa under the table, but he kept right on listening, too interested in hearing Jim open up about his past life to nix the conversation over a little mucus. Jim said, "I needed something closer to the land, not tearing big holes in it."

Papa nodded. "The robber barons of Montana, sad business. Men getting stuck underground and no way to rescue them. Families left without a provider. But those big companies don't care about people. They just want their profits."

"Commercial ranching is a threat to us even now, as we sit here," Nara said.

Everyone looked to her. "They're buying up properties that have fallen behind the times."

Papa winced at her. It was the family's worst nightmare, something they never mentioned. Everyone gazed anywhere but at her. Soon enough they started chatting, while Nara planned a few ways to test John's fortitude. She knew he couldn't keep up with her, and she meant to prove it to Papa.

Everyone got up, pushed in their chairs, and stomped out onto the porch, except John and Jim. They huddled together having a quiet conversation. She walked by on her way upstairs to listen.

"Come on. We'll take the Studebaker, be back before anyone wakes up," John said.

Jim caught Nara's eye. "I have to be up early."

She shook her head as she walked up the stairs. Looks like she wouldn't need to throw her brother a rope to hang himself. He'd brought his own.

CHAPTER 18

THAT FIRST NIGHT WITH JOHN THERE IN THE BUNKHOUSE FELT funny, but on the second night, things got downright peculiar. Charles didn't know whether he dreamed it or not, but the bunkhouse door had been squeaking all darn night.

First light crept through the canvas curtains by the window. He rolled over and saw Jim's and John's bunks sat empty. He hopped up out of bed and jostled Patrick's shoulder. "Hey, get up. I think we're late."

Patrick sat up and blinked his eyes. "Huh?"

Charles put on whatever he could find lying on the floor. "Put on your duds. John and Jim are already up. We must have slept in."

Patrick heaved his scrawny legs over the side. They dangled limply this morning. Charles jumped into his dungarees, walked over, and slapped the top of the boy's lethargic foot. It was an affectionate thing his pop used to do. Funny how he could remember those little things and not Pop's face. Charles had said he was sorry about the pinto over and again. Patrick told him it wasn't his fault, he was just taking orders. But nothing about rounding up those horses felt honorable or decent.

Patrick crawled down from the bunk, as slow as the last bit of syrup from Mama's little glass pitcher that sat on the table.

"Come on. I'll bet you're hungry."

When they got to the main house, Nara asked them where John and Jim were. Charles sat down and said, "I thought they got up early, because they weren't out in the bunkhouse this morning. I thought us two were late."

"Hmm." Nara pushed out her chair and went to the sink, where she tossed a whole cup of coffee, and walked out, slamming the screen door behind her.

Charles and Patrick looked at each other and shrugged. Mama stared out the kitchen window, shaking her head.

* * *

At school that day, Patrick wasn't looking too good. He had put his head down on the desk and then came that light buzzing snore. A kid in front of them looked back. Charles had warned him with his eyes. *Don't be a rat.*

As they headed home, Patrick looked for all the world as if he might fall off his horse. Maybe Mama was right. He might be getting sick after all. Despite this, when they hit that certain fork in the dirt road, Patrick stopped for a bit, looked awful funny at Charles, and where usually Patrick would only give them a nod, he stopped for a bit and finally said, "You're a good big brother."

It felt nice to hear Patrick say that, but before Charles could find words, the boy turned his horse and trotted away. Maybe Patrick thanked him for cutting that little blue horse. He might be off to find it right now. Charles wondered if he'd done the right thing. Maybe the mustang wouldn't survive out there on its own, or Patrick would get caught trying to find it. Then they'd both be in trouble. Charles heard a rumbling above his head. A big drop descended from above and wet his cheek. Something funny, call it a sixth sense, made him think twice. He decided to take Opal home and then ride back to help Patrick find that little mustang.

"Is that rain?" Opal asked from behind where she sat on the horse's rump.

"Yep. We're gonna get wet."

She let out a little sigh.

"Hang on, we'll be home in fifteen minutes."

They rode the rest of the way down the road to the ranch. Everyone had fretted over the forecast all last summer. Papa and Nara would be happy to get some more rain. Charles tied his horse up to the rail on the porch and patted its scraggly mane just as the rain started to come down harder. The old Charles would have ridden off, telling them nothing. But somewhere out here that ruffian had disappeared, made pure with hard work and sweat.

Nara burst out the door and onto the porch, Mama and Papa right after her. "I need to tell you guys something—"

"I bet you do. We need to talk to you, Charles," Nara said.

Nara held open the screen for him. Charles looked toward his horse.

"Don't try it, kid."

Papa waved everyone inside and told them to sit down at the table. "I'll come right to the point. Ivar has been out here. His mustangs were let out of the pen last night."

They all burned holes in him with their eyes. "You think I let them out?"

"Ivar does," Papa said.

"Well, he's wrong. That pen we made probably busted down itself. Neither me or Patrick thought it would hold."

Papa breathed in real deep, scooted out his chair, and went to the counter. He picked up a length of rope that had been roughly cut. He tossed it on the table under Charles's nose. "He brought this with him."

Papa sat back down, rubbing his face like he could lie down right there and sleep forever.

"I didn't do it. Ask Patrick or John or Jim. I've been sleeping all night." He pointed in the direction of the bunkhouse.

Nara shook her head and groaned. Papa turned to her and asked, "Have you talked to John and Jim about it? If they heard anything?"

She pursed her lips. "I'm not a gambling woman, but ten to one, they will both say they were asleep and didn't hear a thing."

"Patrick was there, he'll tell you."

Papa looked at his hands on the table, worn and chapped. "Ain't nobody in this county going to believe what Patrick says."

"So, that's it? You're just going to believe Ivar?"

Nara stood over by the sink and said, "Ivar told me when you were rounding up the last remnants of the band, you cut a horse and let it go free."

She walked over to him and leaned both hands on the table. "Now, I'm asking you to tell me the God's honest truth. No lies, Charles. Did you cut that horse from the band?"

"Yes, I did."

"Why?"

"You wouldn't understand."

"Try me."

"You just wouldn't . . . I can't."

Nara stood up with a crazed glint in her eye. "I understand a lot of things. Rules, Charles. When are you gonna get your head on straight!"

Mama waved at her to calm down and sit. Nara walked back over to the sink. Papa sat back and folded his arms on his chest. "You can deny this all you want, but Art's going to arrest you. Ivar intends to press charges. You won't be able to work this one off this time, kid."

Papa's cold eyes and closed-off heart frightened Charles. "I didn't do this."

Papa leaned forward, a dark shade to his face. "Out here we have rules. They keep people alive, from getting hurt. They may seem cruel or foreign to you, but there isn't any other way to survive out here. To raise stock out here." Papa's finger stabbed the table to punctuate his words. "And because of what you've done, I'm indebted to Ivar Magnusson. Money I've scrimped and saved to expand my ranch or buy new equipment will go up in smoke."

Papa was through with him. Charles wouldn't be able to squeeze another drop of patience from the man. "What's going to happen to me?"

Papa said, "Like I said, Art's going to arrest you."

Charles shot up from his chair. "I didn't do this."

He looked to the kindest person in the room, but Mama turned from him and started fiddling around with things in the kitchen.

Opal peeked down from the stairs, standing at the top. "Can I come down now?"

Nara called up, "Yeah. You better get out there and tend the chickens before that rain starts up again."

Opal came down slowly, peering around the room at everyone. She had her hair up in pigtails, overalls on. Charles got up to follow her outside for chores.

"If you run, you'll be a fugitive, Charles," Nara said.

"I'm not running. I didn't do this. John and Jim will tell you I was in that bunkhouse all night."

For once in his life, he was innocent, but the look on Nara's face told him she didn't think so. It was like they were all against him.

He followed Opal out, and they sat on the porch to put on their boots. Opal padded down the steps in her little rubber boots and into the damp dirt to start her after-school chores of feeding and watering the chickens. Charles untied Charge and took him to the stables. He brushed his horse down, listening to fat drops hit the roof from dripping trees. He put his head to Charge's muzzle and scratched his frizzy mane. It would all get worked out one way or another, but the way the family had turned on him bothered him more than anything.

He left the stalls and looked over to the house. He just couldn't walk through that door again. Couldn't see their faces, their distrust. Opal was out feeding the chickens, so he went over to her. The usual quiet between them felt that much emptier, but it suited him right then. He liked that about her. She'd just enjoy the peace right alongside you without gunking it up with a lot of gibber. When he lived in the city, it was never quiet. Even in the dead of night.

She hopped around in a little dance, scattering crumbs. What he wouldn't do for that kind of cheerfulness. He sat on the tire swing he had pushed Opal on throughout the summer. She'd grown on him. It reminded him of a time not long ago when he thought she was a right pain in the ass.

They'd been out walking near the tracks after they'd jumped the train. The only way to cross the river was to go across that train bridge. Their feet had stopped just at the edge of the train bridge. Charles went first, keeping his feet on the boards, Patrick right after him, but Opal stopped. "My foot will fall through."

The tracks had big gaps in them. You could see the water in the river below, so he picked her up and carried her. It didn't turn out like he wanted.

Patrick stopped and turned around. "Did you hear that?"

Before Charles could answer, a train whistled from the direction they'd come from. He had thought they'd have plenty of time to cross before a train came by. He remembered the panic of that moment as he searched around for a place to hide.

He had set Opal down, and then got on his belly to look underneath the tracks. An iron brace dipped below the wooden tracks to a foundation below. There was a little cubby that would fit all three of them until the train passed over. Opal gasped above him. He stood back up. She was way too close to the edge.

Patrick said, "We can run for it."

Charles shook his head. "We won't make it." He took Opal's hand, and she resisted with all her might. "Come on, Patrick. Climb underneath. There's plenty of room."

Patrick shook his head. "The train will crush us."

The engine emerged in the distance around a bend. Opal twisted out of his grasp, and he grabbed her up.

"Trains have been coming over these tracks, and look, it's never been crushed or broken." Charles pointed to the space beneath. "I need you to go down first, so I can hand down Opal. Quick!"

Patrick looked at the oncoming train, and then knelt to climb down feetfirst.

"Hold on to the side of the bridge. Yes, right here," Charles said, watching Patrick as he climbed beneath. "That's it."

Opal knew she was next and gave him a little kick before he handed the wriggling, red-faced girl down feetfirst.

"No!" She swung her legs.

"Opal, quit fussing! You'll fall into that river."

She looked down and then stopped all her caterwauling. "You got her?"

Charles could barely hear Patrick, as the sound of the train had begun to overwhelm them. He looked at the oncoming train and kept ahold of Opal. "Patrick!"

Opal called up, "Let go!"

Charles released her, and she disappeared over the side and under the bridge. He went down feetfirst over the side and caught a peek of that steely engine coming at them so fast, it might run over his fingers if he didn't hurry. They all crammed in the shade of a cement brace just big enough to keep them from plunging into the river below. He tried not to think about that or notice the cracks in the cement.

Opal whimpered, "I'm gonna pee."

"No, you're not," Charles said.

The wood tracks above their heads began to clatter like they might split above them. Charles didn't want them to see the train go over, so he pulled all their heads together, and they looked their fill of each other like it would be the last. Everything quaked and juddered. The concrete, the tracks, the metal rails. Even their teeth. His hair felt like it would fall right out of his head, every nerve ending afire. It went dark. The train was every unbearable noise you could think of all rolled into one, as if everything on earth screamed at once.

The softest thing in the world at that moment was Opal, who clutched to him like a koala bear he'd seen once at a circus when he was littler than she was now. His sight had become blurry from the shaking of the train. Opal's mouth hung open, screaming, but all he heard or felt was that train. He tucked her farther inside of himself and ducked over her.

When the savagery above had finally ceased, they sat there

numb and lifeless for several minutes in a pool of warm pee. To her few utterings, Opal was true.

Despite all the trouble, having a little sister was worth it. Charles knew Opal would have a hell of a time with him being hauled off to jail. He put his foot down to stop the tire swing. "Opal, come here a minute."

She skipped over, chickens following in her wake. "Look, the sheriff is going to come out here and take me away. They think I stole some mustangs, but I didn't do it. Soon enough, I'll be back. Okay?"

Her little face scrunched up. "They can't do that!"

"Don't worry, I'll be back."

She dropped the tin of crumbs to the ground and ran back inside the house. He could hear Mama trying to calm her down. He wondered if he'd done the right thing by telling her. But he supposed this family valued honesty, so they couldn't very well ask him to lie to Opal.

Wrathful wind gusted through the ranch, like someone yelling at the top of their lungs. It chased and picked up the dirt, swirling it along, raking through his hair like it had something to say. Within moments, rain began to pour down from the sad sky, but he remained on that old tire swing. His boot dragged through the gravel as he waited.

THE SHERIFF MUST not have wanted to miss mealtime, or he was trying to beat the storm. He pulled up in that fancy paddy wagon, emerged from it vindicated, for now he could drag Charles off. The auto door slammed. His wife, Ella, got out right after him.

Under her breath, she kept saying something. He heard Art say, "It's enough, Ella. Get back in the wagon and be quiet."

Charles got up from the swing and walked toward the sheriff. The screen door squeaked. The Stewarts came out to stand on the porch. But they had no resolve and no rifles to aim at the sheriff this time.

"Charles Stewart, you are being arrested for thieving approximately twenty mustangs from Ivar Magnusson's property last night. I'm going to take you in and book you." He held Charles's eyes. "You're going to jail, son. You understand?"

Charles nodded. Papa stood at the porch rail with an inscrutable look to him. Mama tried to keep Opal calm, but she struggled to get away. "Don't let them take him!"

Nara finally had to pick her up and take her inside. That little girl was all legs and arms, grabbing on to the sides of the doorjamb and hollering. At least one person was on his side. Patrick still hadn't shown up yet. Nor John or Jim. Nobody to say he'd been in his bed all night. He figured it was better this way. Fewer people to see his disgrace.

He looked up into a thunderous sky busy making mud all around him and wondered why he wound up here in the best place he could imagine if something terrible like this was going to happen. This land and this family had made him a better person, but something out there was still gunning for him.

Art took him by the arm, escorted him around the back of the paddy wagon, and opened the back door. Blackie jumped at Art, yapping. Charles stepped up inside, and Art slammed the door. There were benches on both sides. He sat to the right, feeling more alone than he ever had before.

The auto started up, and Art turned the paddy wagon around to leave down the road. Through the streaky window Charles saw Papa take Mama by the arm and lead her back inside. Papa was resolute. They wouldn't help him. If he'd been their blood, they might have. He'd gotten used to being a part of something, taken care of, but now he realized he would never belong to anyone, never have that warm hand on his back, the security of a family who'd love you no matter what.

As Art continued down the road, the house had gotten small, and the rain obscured his view, blurring it all from sight like maybe he'd never been there at all.

The wagon rolled and bumped through the dirt road. He wondered if they'd get stuck. Art would have to uncuff him to help.

CHAPTER 19

IF BAD THINGS COME IN THREES, THEN NARA COULDN'T IMAGINE what next. She rolled over in her bed, woken by panicky voices and thumping feet. She squinted at her window. Still pitch-black outside. Her father bellowed at her from below. She pulled on her dungarees, hopping around the dim room, then hurried downstairs toward the ruckus. On the last step she stopped, shocked by what she saw on the table.

There lay Jim. His face all bloodied up, and his shoulder in an unnatural position. He was moaning and mumbling. Papa held him down. Mama ran around getting towels and water. John stood by the door with his head down, rubbing his forehead. "What in God's name happened?"

Papa yelled over his shoulder, "They got in a wreck in the Studebaker."

Nara marched over to John to smell his breath. Hot damn, he'd been drinking.

"Me and Jim went into town. On the way back, the rain started coming down and everything went blurry. We ended up in the ditch. If it hadn't been for the storm, we'd have been all right." Those eyes pled with her to keep quiet.

"I can't believe this. You've been home maybe two, three days? Do you have any idea what you've done?" She went to the table to help Papa with Jim.

She leaned down over Jim to smell his breath. He hadn't been drinking. Mama came over and wiped at Jim's face. He twisted to escape her nursing. She inspected his shoulder by poking it. He nearly rolled off the table. "He's gonna have to go into Billings. This shoulder looks broke."

Papa turned away and swore. "They wrecked the one thing that would be real nice to have in a situation like this." Papa turned to John. "You will never drive my automobile again." Then he pointed to Jim on the table, moaning. "And you're fired."

"Why should Jim be fired? He wasn't driving the auto." Nara stared down John. "And he wasn't drinking. Smell his breath."

"Don't sass me at a time like this, Nara Jean."

"Sass you! I'm a grown woman, for God's sake!"

"This isn't the only time I've caught Jim up to no good!"

"Just what are you implying?"

"I know what I saw in Miles City."

Nara crossed her arms, looking at her father as fiercely as she ever had, her blood hotter than hell. "You let Jim go, then you can let me go, too."

John stood there with his head down like a coward. "What do you think, John?" Nara asked.

He fumbled around, his hat in his hands, and shook his head, not meeting anyone's eye.

Papa dismissed her with an angry wave of his hand. "I'll deal with you all later, but right now we've got to find Jim a doctor."

"Fine," she said between her teeth. "We can take Jim in the wagon come morning and get him on the first train to Billings."

"No. We'll go straight there in the wagon right now. It'll be faster."

Mama stepped between. "You can't take him all the way to Billings in the back of the wagon. He'll go into shock in all this rain and cold. They'll be burying him when you get there."

Nara nodded. "Exactly. This is a bad break, and the weather isn't cooperating. The best we can do is keep him warm."

Jim moaned something. Nara stood over him to listen and had to stop herself from smoothing the stray black hair matted over his forehead. She grabbed a blanket off the sofa and placed it over him, tucking it in gently all around his shivering body. Her lungs expanded, filling herself with his musk, a muddy scent from the wreck and iron from the bloody cuts. It made her forget where she was. Her hand stroked his strong, angular face, feeling the fire of him.

Mama cleared her throat, and Nara pulled back her hand, retreating to the kitchen counter to stand with Mama, who lifted a brow at her. Nara's cheeks flushed, and she turned to the window, his scent still inside her. She stood there trying to get her head on straight and think about what needed doing.

Papa had been busy yelling at John. "Tomorrow morning, while Nara and I fix this damn mess, you're going to get your butt out there and take care of things while we're gone."

John nodded, taking his mighty small ass-chewing. He wasn't

responsible enough to drive the auto, much less run the ranch. She
thought about asking Papa to smell John's breath, but figured he'd
just make some excuse for his precious son in any case. The pickle
of it was, they needed John now. Charles was in jail, and Patrick never showed up from school yesterday. She'd gone out and
looked for him till well after dark but couldn't find him anywhere.
Maybe they'd been riding the boy too hard. Maybe the people
in this county had finally killed his cheerful disposition with all
their intolerance. Nara went upstairs to get something warm on.

She grabbed a thick shirt and then went to look out her bedroom window, hoping Patrick was out there in the bunkhouse
right now, and if not, then she planned to ask Mary at the depot
to send Art a message to be on the lookout for the boy, but an
inkling told her he had left of his own accord. She threw on her
warmest duds to go back downstairs.

Jim lay on the table, still shivering. Nara turned from Mama.
"Mama, I'm gonna make some coffee. Will you get another blanket for Jim?"

Nara could feel Mama's probing eyes on her.

Papa tromped back in and said, "No time for coffee. Throw on
your warmest coat. We're going to have to find the Studebaker."
He took his hat and squashed it down on his head. "Patrick's not
out in the bunkhouse."

* * *

The next hours were hell on earth, but not the hot, fiery kind.
More like the slow dripping, wet-to-the-skin kind. At first light,

they had wrapped Jim up in blankets and laid him in the back of the wagon. The potholes had gotten deeper from the storm. Jim grunted and cursed over every one of them. The clouds seemed determined to plop just enough to keep them good and wet.

She gripped the lines and drove the team steadily into town, careful not to push it and end up in a ditch. Not for the first time did she wonder why Papa never bought a proper carriage. God knows Mama had complained about it for all the years she could remember. Nara looked at him out of the corner of her eye. Water dribbled from the brim of his hat. His eyes squinted in misery. She'd kept quiet, not wanting to poke him after the shouting match over Jim, but she wouldn't let up. Jim wasn't going anywhere. He was the best hand they ever had. It made not one lick of sense to punish Jim for John's mistake—or hers.

Jim and Papa waited for the train out on the platform, while Nara went to talk to Mary. They needed to get word out that Patrick had gone missing. She never found so much as a freckle in the storm last night. All she could hope was the boy stayed somewhere dry in all that rain and cold.

Mary was in her little booth as usual, filling up the wooden slots with mail that came in on the train. Those big wood crates must have made many journeys back and forth, seen more places than Nara ever would. "Mary, I need you to do something important for me."

"Yeah, sugar. Whad'ya need?"

"Patrick is missing. He didn't come back from school yesterday afternoon. Can you get word to Art? Ask him to have a look around, and anybody else coming through?"

Her eyes went wide. "You bet I will. I'll send one of the baggage men to leave Art a note on the jailhouse. Oh, here."

Mary handed her a letter. It was from New York. The Children's Aid Society. Nara felt the sharp edges of that envelope and looked to the skies. "Things come in threes," she muttered.

Mary looked at her from the side and lifted one brow.

Nara folded the envelope three times and put it in her pocket, resolved to put off whatever lurked in the letter, for it couldn't be good.

All she could manage to say to Mary was "Mighty obliged."

As they boarded the train to Billings, the thing troubling her about Patrick's disappearance was the timing, him leaving and those mustangs freed all in the space of a couple of days. During the journey, sitting on that train near made her crazy. Jim was all busted up, a young boy was out there somewhere defenseless, and Charles sat in jail. But there she sat on that train sopping wet, Jim miserable, and Papa in a silent fury.

One thing was certain. She had to talk to Charles and get him to fess up. He knew way more than he was saying. And by God, when she got back, she'd pull it out of him.

* * *

Nara stood out on the porch watching the sun come up, holding on to that rail for dear life. Patrick still hadn't returned. She didn't know what would happen next to Charles, but he owed her the truth. It might not change Papa's mind, for that was set. After Art had taken Charles away, Papa had said, "That boy will take what he's got coming to him like a man, and we will not intervene." Mama protested, and all he said was "He's not of age. They won't hang him." And from that moment on, he refused to speak of it.

She knew Papa felt betrayed and wouldn't forgive the debt he must pay Ivar. Not that Papa had run right over to Ivar's and offered or anything. He was also pretty damn set on letting Jim go. He hadn't been by to get his things from the bunkhouse, so she didn't know where Jim was or how he was. He might have returned to the reservation, and that was thirty miles away, but his staying away would give Papa more time to cool off. Maybe he'd reconsider then, but the look on Jim's face when they left him in that hospital room had been a shaming moment for her. That dark eye, accusative. As they left the hospital room, she had felt torn, but if she tried to stick up for Jim any more, Papa might not think her words were genuine, because of what he saw in Miles City.

So many fires raged all around her, and only a few shovels to put them out. Thank goodness it was a slow part of the year, for they were three hands down on the ranch, and with Papa digging in instead of shoveling, that left her to sort it all out. Mama did what she could. She had it out with Papa again after supper last night. Nara heard it from her room.

"You need to go see Ivar, get him to drop those charges."

"Stay out of it."

Mama and Papa hadn't talked to each other this morning, not even their usual morning grunts. His biscuit had been fairly dropped onto his plate. No offer of touching up his eggs with a little extra gravy. His yolks were hard, not that molten gold that would spill out when he forked through them. But to all this, he just pretended not to notice and put that paper up around his head. Like stubborn was gonna fix anything.

Mama had made sure there were lots of grounds in the coffee this morning, too. It burned and sloshed around in her stomach as she juddered over the potholes in her little wagon. She'd left the ranch as soon as Art would be at the jail to let her in.

She opened the door to the sheriff's, and light shone directly into the cell where Charles sat. He had a thin woolen blanket wrapped around his shoulders. The moment he saw her, hope washed across his face. Seeing him now, she should have been madder than hell itself, but all that reliance, that need he had of her, was strangely enough a good feeling. It settled her into a better state of mind, because she had been about to peel the skin off his ears. She had no good news for him.

Art sat at his desk, blowing on a cup of coffee. "Make it quick, Nara."

Charles jumped off the makeshift bed he'd been sitting on and wrapped his hands around the bars. "Nara."

If Mama stood here now (but Papa had forbidden her to come), she might try and make him feel better, say words that would never comfortably roll off Nara's tongue. Mama had snuck Nara a sandwich in wax paper before she left. Nara passed him the opaque parcel through the bars. His big, trembling hands grasped and crinkled it, but he looked away. The kid was hungry for sure, and proud.

"How's he been treating you?" She shot a look over at Art, who sat busy at his desk.

Charles shrugged. "Art isn't around here much."

The fire had gone from the boy's eyes. They were two pools of something she couldn't see into anymore. Used to be a bright, earnest look to them. A firmness in his face that spoke, *I won't let you down*, even when words failed him. Stooped over as he was now, he looked nothing like the powerful young boy who had come to work his butt off and prove his worth, prove he was good inside. It was a shame. For a while there, she thought she could help this boy.

"What have you told Art so far?"

"When he brought me in the other day, he asked a bunch of questions. My name, where I lived in New York. Friday he's taking me to Billings to stand in front of a judge."

She figured he wouldn't have said anything to cast suspicion over Patrick. "There is a lot more to this than you've been telling me."

Charles looked down, his hands still on the bars, but his fingers loosened a smidge.

"Patrick disappeared after you were arrested."

His head shot up, eyes filled with dread. "Where is he?"

"That's what I'd like to know."

"I didn't hurt him!"

"I know you better than that, but there's something you've been hiding from me as it regards him. You began to tell me the other day, but I didn't listen."

Charles turned away, wouldn't look her in the eye.

"Time to fess up."

He backed away from the bars and paced around his cell as if he were measuring all the shitty outcomes from telling her what she needed to know.

"Patrick could be in real trouble. It's for his own good."

"I just . . . look, the only thing I do know is where he might have gone."

Nara leaned in closer to the bars. "Tell me."

"I figure he's out there somewhere on Ivar's place looking for that little blue horse I cut from the band."

"A little blue horse?"

"Yeah, it has scars on its sides like something took a coupla big bites out of it. It's out there on its own, he'll be tracking it down."

"Huh. That must be the little filly I rescued from the fence early spring. I can find the mustang, but where does Patrick sleep at night?"

"He knows how to find warm places at night. Like those old tar-paper houses from the homesteaders."

"He learned that from you."

"If you get me out of here, I can find him. I didn't let those horses go."

"You cuttin' that mustang from the band looked pretty bad, but I think I know why you did it. Papa won't post bail or hire you an attorney. It's time to talk, Charles."

"What happens to the person when they figure out who did it? I mean, it won't be bad, will it?"

"The penalty for horse thieving is hanging—when you're an adult. But since I don't believe the responsible party is over eighteen, I don't think that'll be the punishment."

Charles's face went white and his knuckles gripped the bars, with the same blanching effect.

Art called out, "Nara, I have something I need to discuss with you. In private."

She went over to his desk and leaned over it, weary as hell.

"I called New York to see if your boy over there had any priors. They've got a rap sheet on a boy fitting his description longer than a horse's tail, *and* this kid's eighteen."

"Charles is sixteen."

They both looked over at Charles, his beard gone whiskery from not shaving.

"Nara, that boy hasn't ever looked sixteen to me. This description is dead-on. There aren't that many young men that tall."

"Shitfires."

She went to the bars of his cell. Charles was breathing hard, fussing around in his cell, looking for a way out. "Art told me you're eighteen. That true?"

His eyes dropped to the cold concrete floor. "Yeah."

"You have to tell him *right now* who let those mustangs go."

Charles walked around his cell, rubbing the top of his sandy-blond head. He stopped and turned away from her. "I think those horses busted out of that flimsy rope corral on their own."

"You realize they're gonna hang you, right?"

He went to sit on his hard cot with his mouth contorted, lips pressed together, and then he stared at her with dead, bleak eyes.

She stalked out the door, cursing in words she'd never said before. Words that would provoke Mama to chase her around creation and back with a bar of soap. Patrick had to be found.

That boy would at least tell the truth. She put her hands in her pockets to keep them warm and realized the letter she had folded up was gone.

* * *

She drove her horse cart across cow trails, searching for that shallow valley with lush grass. It was probably golden and crispy by now, eaten to the nub, but horses keep their rituals. It was near dusk when she pulled up. She got down to make her way on foot. Her boots skimmed through the dried grass, legs burning with the effort. She raced the light tonight, had to find that boy. He couldn't stay out here another night on his own, and Charles, no matter his past, couldn't hang for a crime he didn't commit.

HORSES OF EVERY color scattered across the valley. She approached easy and slow on her feet. When she got closer, she saw Patrick's skinny little legs under the girth of a large black and white stallion, and without thinking, she barked out, "Patrick! Back away from that horse!"

She frightened the mustangs. The little blue roan with the scars came running by for the safety of its mama.

"Nara?"

"Young man, get your hide over here before you get pounded into the earth."

The stallion threw its head around, neighing deep, holding its ground, but strangely, it showed no aggression to Patrick.

The boy walked to her bent-headed, loose in the neck. He was pretty dirtied up and looking skinnier than ever. Mama would have fits to see him like this, all hollowed out. No meat on his bones.

"You've got us all worried sick. Where in the devil have you been?"

He still couldn't look her in the face. All she could see was the top of his orange head.

"I've been mindin' the horses. I won't let Ivar round them up again."

"Is this where you've been going in the afternoons all this time?"

"Ya."

She shook her head, wishing she'd watched him closer, and regretted the harsh punishment she had dealt Charles. Maybe she should have talked to Billy's father about his son's bullying. All of this was so new, foreign. Like feeling your way in the dark, stumbling into furniture. And then it had been her idea to have Patrick go round up horses for slaughter, a thing his soft heart just couldn't do.

"I didn't know you loved these horses so much, or I would never have offered you boys to help with the roundup. I should have gone to that school and thumped Billy in the head myself."

His Adam's apple bobbed around as he choked back tears.

She put a hand on his shoulder. "Folks around here can be damn ignorant."

"Nobody likes me. These mustangs are all I have."

"You're a part of this family. You have us."

Patrick clutched her around the middle. It shocked her for a moment to feel those wiry arms so intimately wrapped around her, but then her arm settled around his bony back. Her chapped hand stroked that orangey gold hair. His little chest quaked against her stomach as he bawled out all the pain he'd been holding in so long. "Hey, now. Getta hold of yourself. Things aren't always gonna be so tough."

"I know people are fed up with the Irish coming, but I mean ta pull me weight. These horses can pull theirs, too." Patrick held his hands out wide, tears welling. "Just look around, so much space. There's room for everybody and everything."

"There sure is, kid."

Patrick's head cuddled against her chest, warming her heart even as it broke for him. Charles might have been right to show the kids at school they couldn't pick on his brother. After all, she'd stuck up for her own, thrown Ella from that swing into the dirt. The remembrance of that childhood revenge could still bring a smile to her face, so why she thought the worst of Charles when all he ever did was stick up for family seemed beyond reckoning. One thing remained in her power, and that was to bust that big kid out of jail.

"Patrick, you tell me right now, right here, who freed the horses. Who cut that rope?"

His head shot up, those watery eyes gawped at her. "I thought ya woulda figured by now it was me."

"Charles is sitting in jail right now. Ivar pressed charges against him."

Patrick stood back. "But it was me!"

"I know that now, but it looked bad, with Charles cutting that little blue roan free."

"He did that for me." Patrick looked to where the little filly stood. "I had ta make sure it found its ma."

She patted his back. "I suppose what you did is fitting, seeing how I wrestled that little horse from the fence and brought it back to its mama early last spring."

He looked up at her, surprised. "I call her Huckleberry, because she's blue."

"That's a fine name," Nara said.

They both looked on that filly huddled against its mama, chewing the last grass of the season.

"Come on, it's cold out here. Mama's bound to have something on the stove."

"Is Papa mad?"

"He'll get past it."

WHEN THEY GOT back to the house, she ushered Patrick up the steps of the porch and called out, "Mama, you got anything to eat for this skinny boy?"

The house was silent. Papa sat at the table with that folded-up letter in his hands.

CHAPTER 20

AFTER ANOTHER DAY OF WAITING IN HIS CHILLY CELL, JOHN AND Jim still hadn't come forward on Charles's behalf. He needed them to tell the sheriff he'd been in the bunkhouse all night—sleeping. That should be enough to get Ivar to drop the charges, then nobody would have to be jailed or hanged for the crime, but as the clock ticked on the wall, the sun came up and then down, he began to panic, sweat, mulling it around in his mind. Patrick wouldn't hang for cutting the mustangs free, but the longer Charles stayed locked up, the easier it would be for New York and the sheriff to put it together.

In this desperate state of mind, he wrestled with his conscience. That afternoon, he almost called Art over to tell him who'd really done it. He'd gotten off his wooden bed, gone to the bars, then back to his bed, and back and forth. The only thing that prevented him from turning into a rat, something he despised more than anything, was Patrick.

Nara brought Patrick to the jail. The boy looked nervous, and he should be, because as glad as Charles was to see the boy he now thought of as his brother, whole and hale, he worried more about what would happen next. The resolute set to Patrick's peach-fuzz jaw said it all. Charles didn't want Patrick to incriminate himself. The sheriff only needed to know so much. "Patrick, wait, come here," Charles called out from behind the bars.

Patrick shook his head. "It's gone too far." He approached Art. "Sheriff, I let the wild horses go free. It's me that ought ta be in that cell." He held up his skinny wrists so Art could slap on the cuffs.

Art just wiped his face over and over again. "Boy, you Stewarts. When do you find time to tend to your cattle?" He glared at Nara. "All right, kid."

Art took Patrick by the arm and led him into the cell next to Charles's.

"I didn't know it was against the law ta let wild horses go free. The real crime ought ta be grinding up horses for chicken feed."

"According to law, when Ivar rounded them up, he took possession of that band. It's legal around here. They chew up forage for cattle. Even right now, those horses running free, they belong to him."

Patrick called out, "That's a stupid law!"

The phone rang, and Art picked it up. "Hello. Yellowstone County Sheriff's Office."

He put his hand to his forehead, listening for a minute. "All right. Hang on, I'll get over there." He slammed the phone down.

Charles watched him say a few words to Nara, and then he left, leaving them all three in the jail. Nara paced around, hands in her pockets, waiting.

Charles called over to the next cell, "Patrick, you all right?"

"Ya. I'm sorry they nabbed ya for it. I didn't mean for it ta happen."

"Where were you running off to?"

"I hadn't thought that far. It took a coupla days to find the little horse and reunite her with her band, and then Nara found me."

The phone began to ring again on Art's vacant desk. Nara looked over and away out the window. That phone kept jumping around on that table, making an awful noise. After a good minute of that, she swung around with an aggravated eye, stalked over, picked it up, and slammed it back down. She turned to walk away, and it rang out like something stubborn. She turned in disbelief and squinted, same as when she aimed her rifle, which, if she had it, there'd be a smoking hole where the telephone sat now.

Nara reached out with a strong, chapped hand and growled into the phone, "Yellowstone sheriff."

With the telephone to her ear, Nara slowly turned to Charles, searching him over, crawling deep inside with just her eyes. What she meant by it, he didn't rightly understand, until she finally spoke into the telephone.

"Yeah, this is Art Connelly."

Charles gripped the bars and strained to hear.

CHAPTER 21

NARA HAD LIVED HER WHOLE LIFE IN THIS ONE COUNTY IN MONtana, insulated from the world by the barbed wire around their property. A place where rules and law kept her safe. In her wagon, she bumped on down one of the five roads that existed in Yellowstone County, trying to reconcile the image of Charles as a brutal thief with the young man who'd shown up on their ranch, that tiny girl hidden under his arm, willing to do every dirty chore to earn his keep.

When she left the jail, she had never felt so naive in all her life. Charles had lived a life she couldn't conceive of, and in a place so far away, her imagination couldn't reach it. When she had found him stealing her horse, he'd been desperate but never threatened her in any way, and he only came for horses because Patrick couldn't walk. The few times he'd been violent with anyone they had provoked him, hurt someone he cared about. If she were to judge him solely by his actions in Montana, then she'd have to say the boy had a moral compass so strong it pointed straight up to heaven. So, when the New York police asked if they still had that boy in custody, she said no. He'd been cleared of all charges and left town. Didn't know which train. Kid didn't say where he was headed. Charles had listened the whole time, knew what she did.

Those tears of relief and grateful look were all she needed to know that she'd done the right thing. But after some reflective time in her wagon, she thought impersonating an officer of the law must be a felony.

For the first time in her life, she decided to conceal the truth from her folks. One, for the way she handled it, and two, because they may not understand how anyone could be so desperate and turn dark inside. But all creatures on this earth, man and beast, do ugly things to survive.

In any case, things were bad enough. Papa had found that letter. It must have fallen from her pocket and dropped to the floor of their house like a great rock falling from a mountainside. Papa said he'd handle it, to keep it quiet until he figured out what in the devil was going on. "They put so many kids on those trains. Doesn't make any sense."

Nara passed the road leading to her family's ranch and toward Ivar's little place with the intention to get him to drop the charges. The only way to fix the problem to everyone's satisfaction was to settle things privately. She was sure Ivar had enough justice in him to see things clear about the mustangs. But her task would be no easy thing.

While she'd been out checking the winter pens early this morning, Papa had gone out to Ivar's place to make "amends." He didn't want Charles to hang for a crime he didn't commit.

Not after Patrick looked him in the eye last night and told him word for word how he'd cut that rope corral and let those horses run free while Charles was asleep in the bunkhouse. Unfortunately, Papa had decided to go out to Ivar's by himself.

When Papa stomped back into the house, he said he offered Ivar reparation for the mustangs, which the "Norwegian mule" refused, saying, "I won't take your charity."

Folks out here would rather starve than take something that could be perceived as a handout. She could only imagine those two alone in a room together. Like two angry bulls in one small pen. So Ivar refused to drop the charges, and Papa threatened to "shoot every damn cow that comes through my fence." And that's what happens when men try to work things out.

She walked up to Ivar's cabin door and steeled herself. Her knuckles rapped on his rough-sawn door.

For the first time in their lives, those icy eyes cut her through. "What are you doing here?"

"Come on, Ivar. I'm just here to talk."

He stepped back, waved her in, and said, "I may as well have every last one of you Stewarts over. Beggin' your pardon, but I'm out of tea and crumpets."

Knowing he always did have a soft spot for her, she took off her hat, put it against her heart to plead with him. "We can settle this just between us. I've got these boys under control. Honestly, I do." She batted her eyes, stood too close.

He focused in on her with a suspicious tilt of his head and drilled right through her thin veneer of femininity with just a squinty silver eye. She never had the knack for the wiles of women.

"Nara, after all he's done, at some point you're gonna have to ask yourself, is this boy *able* to change? He's busted the face of one of my hands and nearly choked the Colfax kid to death with dirt."

"Charles has a past, but I know he's on a different road now, or I wouldn't be here. You know me, Ivar."

He folded his arms across his chest and leaned back. Of all the times she'd let him off easy, mending those fences, sending him back his bull instead of a steer, his attitude really chapped her ass. "Patrick let the horses go. Charles did *not* help him. He swears it to me, and so does Patrick."

"I don't believe a word that comes out of either of their mouths, especially that little Irish boy. I'll have you know, he didn't do a lick of work while he was out here."

"Coming from a man whose parents crossed the Atlantic in a boat and were processed in Ellis Island like every other immigrant, that's some fine talk." She folded her arms across her chest.

He waved her off. "I can't help Charles now, and besides, it won't matter what I do. Do you honestly want him around your place? How are you going to defend yourself and everyone on your ranch from that big boy? He's a menace. People with that anger in 'em, they don't change. A life like he's lived out on the streets. It molds a person. Besides, he's burned me good. I took him and Patrick out and taught them a thing or two. Those mustangs were going to help me get by this winter. Unlike you Stewarts, I didn't make a whole lot at auction."

"Papa said he'd pay you back."

"I don't want your father's money."

"It's not charity."

"I'm going to round those horses back up. I'll make my own way." Ivar shook his head. "I don't envy you. You've got a lazy horse thief and a volatile thug living in your bunkhouse."

His ugly words raised her hackles, but she cooled herself to say, "At least come and hear what they have to say. Make your decision then. You owe them a hearing."

Ivar crossed his arms over his chest and stroked his chin. "I don't know. I'm gonna be damn busy rounding up mustangs."

She breathed out heavy and turned to leave. "Guess there isn't much else to say. I'm sorry about the mustangs."

"You come out here in the saddle?"

"No, I've got the wagon."

"The wolves are getting bad out here at night."

* * *

Nara slept fitfully. Her mind a tangle of things she couldn't understand and problems she couldn't solve. What Ivar said about Charles being too dangerous, broken beyond repair, had tormented her. Maybe she shouldn't have covered for him. Somewhere in the middle of a frigid evening, she gave up on the sandman and went downstairs in her nightshirt to brew coffee.

She sat at the table in the dark, watching the sky go from its darkest shades to light, wondering how the hell everything was gonna get set to rights.

Mama came down, her wild hair a muss, looking just as bad. She poured herself a mug, and they sat in silence until Papa's stubborn feet came pounding down the stairs. Opal had been staying home from school and came down, too. There was no way for her to get to school with her not riding yet and the Studebaker broke down. Mama and Opal made heaps of breakfast. Papa watched the two of them together, wistfulness in his eye. It didn't happen often, but his shoulders sagged.

John came in, poured himself a cup of coffee, and sat down. Papa's jaw tensed up and he tossed his fork on the table. Mama looked over at her table splashed with egg. Papa was still ticked about the bull breaking out of the pen. Maybe she should have fixed John's shoddy work instead of playing childish games, but at least Nara had warned Papa, who might have gone out and had a look, but instead he trusted his only son. Their priciest bull had hightailed it off their range somewhere. Once she got things squared away with these boys, she'd go out on her own and find that brawny galoot herself.

Papa began ticking off the chores on his fingers like John was simple in the head. Her brother nodded his head curtly. Not once did Papa look her way, dole out a chore or anything else. Papa finally asked him, "Did you find the bull?"

John pursed his mouth. "Not yet."

Papa looked to the ceiling and shook his head. "Check the

northern range. And when you get it back in that pen, make damn sure it'll hold this time. If part of the herd doesn't repro-duce, there goes our profits for the year."

Papa finally glanced at Nara and then toward the window. There was a moment of regret there in his eye, for he knew she would have made that pen strong enough for a bull. The other thing likely peeving him was Jim could pick up the tracks and find that bull quicker than anyone.

Nara lamented there not being enough hours in the day to manage it all, for she had wanted to go down to the reserva-tion and look for Jim, but that was a whole day's trip and back. Besides, Mama looked at her funny anytime Nara mentioned Jim's name, and if Papa found out she went to the reservation, Jim would never get his job back. His motorbike had vanished. She figured he probably walked all the way here to retrieve it, his prized possession, but all his clothes and things were still in the bunkhouse. She had pressed one of his shirts to her face, the smell of it like nothing else, forbidden.

After Mama picked up the breakfast plates, Papa snatched his ivory Stetson from the hat rack. "Me and Nara are going down to the jail."

After she told Papa last night that Ivar wouldn't drop the charges, he said he'd go down and see Art in the morning, get it worked out somehow. She wished there were a better way to get it settled.

Papa looked at the rifle she packed in the wagon. "You plan-ning to break him out?"

If only he knew. She just had an itchy feeling she'd need it.

Maybe she'd shoot the ringer out of Art's damn phone. Nara gnawed at a tough piece of cuticle. Papa noticed but said nothing. She tapped her feet on the wooden floor of the wagon, trying to settle her nerves.

Papa held the leads of the wagon team and kept giving her sidelong glances like he had something to say. They hadn't spoken much, what with the fight over firing Jim and his giving John all her responsibilities.

Papa breathed in real deep like he was gonna say something, but then closed his mouth tightly like someone had glued his lips together. She raised her brows. They passed by the Colfax ranch. Horses ran to the fence, nickering hello. A few more bumpy minutes passed, and he startled her by bursting out, "I regret letting John take over. It's pretty clear his heart's not in it. But yours always has been. Maybe you should have been born a boy, hell, I don't know. But from here on out, you're gonna run things." Papa looked her straight in the eye. "Just promise me one thing?"

She sat stunned. "Okay."

"You won't ever marry Ivar Magnusson."

"Wasn't planning on it."

"All right, then."

He kept on driving the team like he hadn't cleared a whole lot of air, made his first apology to her—ever. Hadn't just handed over the reins to the family stock operation. She could only just nod her head. For as long as she wanted to hear those words, her shocked response felt mighty small, but she needed to sip on those words. Such a revelation couldn't be gulped down at a moment's notice. Had he really thought she'd marry Ivar? Papa had a myopic way about him at times.

When they pulled up in the wagon at the jail, Nara saw Ivar's horse tied up. He must have softened up last night, was all she could hope. Maybe his conscience got the better of him. Or, worse, he was here digging in.

She went inside. Art stood up from his desk, looked out the window where Papa tied up the team, and grimaced. "Can you keep him and Ivar from tearing up my damn office?"

"I'll try. Any news from New York?"

She held her breath.

"Haven't heard a word."

She felt relieved, for the moment at least. Her secret, and Charles's past, weren't going to come flying out of Art's mouth.

Art must have taken pity on them and locked them up together last night. The boys stood together at the bars of the cell they now shared, faces hanging low, looking so darn pitiful. For certain, they had learned a lesson. About the horses anyway. Ivar leaned on those bars like he hadn't slept, listening to the boys. The door opened again, letting in a shaft of sunlight. Papa walked in, ripped off his hat, and tore Ivar clean open with just his eyes. Ivar stood up straight and pushed out his chest, glaring right back.

She was going to love the next many minutes as much as getting two teeth pulled. She walked between them and held up her hands. "Now, listen, both of you. I think we all want what's best for these boys and justice to be served. Am I right?"

Neither one of them heard or saw her. Art stood up from his desk, his hand fingered the pistol in his holster.

"I never thought you'd outdo your old man, Ivar. But apparently your cruelty knows no limits."

Ivar shook his head and pointed at Papa with his hat. "All these years you've held my father's actions against me has set things good and straight in my mind. Because of you, I know my old man wasn't the only damned tyrant out here. You're just as bad. Way I see it, makes us even, you and I."

Papa got right up in Ivar's face. But Ivar held up his hands. He wasn't gonna fight a man twenty years his senior.

"Papa," Charles called out from the cell.

Everyone turned toward the boys.

"Fighting won't fix this," Charles said.

Papa put his hands on his hips and looked away, shaking his head. It was rare for Nara to see her papa caught up by his own lecturing words. Charles's past had begun to sink into her bones in a way that made her think she might not be able to help the young man. But to see him urging Papa to turn the other cheek was the glimmer of hope she needed from the boy. It made her smile, and her eyes burned from the dusty ride—tears, if she was honest with herself.

Ivar said, "I've spoken with both your boys. It seems to me that Charles wasn't involved in letting the mustangs go. It was Patrick, and sitting up here in this jail isn't going to teach him the proper lesson."

Papa said, "And you think you're the one to do it?"

"I do. I'll drop the charges if Patrick here will agree to help me round them back up—alone."

Papa thought about it for a moment and looked to Patrick. The poor boy shook his head and stepped away from the bars. He turned his back on everyone, shoulders shaking. Charles put his hand on Patrick's shoulder and spoke low in his ear. Patrick shook his head again, and Charles kept right on whispering.

Nara walked to the bars. "Patrick, those mustangs will be captured again whether you do it or not."

"I'd rather rot in this cell! Why do I have ta do it?"

"Because you'll do it gently," Nara said.

Charles patted his back. "Nara's right. It'll be easier on them. Besides, sometimes you gotta do things because it's the rules. You don't have to like it."

She shouldn't be so proud of two boys in a jail cell, but she felt something nice swelling in her heart, seeing them like that.

Ivar said, "Just so you know, kid. I don't like doing it any more than you do. It just needs doing."

Ivar looked back at Papa, who nodded his head in some kind of peace offering. Nara shook her head at them. Here stood two of the most stubborn men Montana had knocking around in its southeastern corner.

Art jingled his keys, unlocking the cell. "Well, it looks like you boys are set to go. Ivar, I'll just need you to sign a statement saying you're dropping the charges."

As they all walked out the door, Nara turned to say thank you to Art, but he shooed her out the door with a couple flicks of his wrist, looking glad of some peace and quiet. Couldn't say she blamed him. Nara squinted at the strong, clear sunshine. Papa slapped Charles on the back and said, "I'm sorry we doubted you, young man."

Charles simply nodded his head. This may have made the two of them feel all right, but she had other ideas. "Charles, before you hop up into the wagon."

He turned around with a wary look on his face. A plea to keep his secret.

He wasn't gonna get off so easy. "Hold up your right hand and repeat after me."

He slowly held up his hand.

"Swear to me, you'll always tell the truth even if it means someone else is going to get in trouble—and if I tell you to do something, you do it. No questions asked."

"I will, I swear."

"All right, then. Let's go home. I'm beat to heck."

Nara consigned her nagging doubts to the wind as Papa drove the wagon home.

* * *

By the time everyone had sat down for the evening meal, she thought there wasn't one person there who didn't feel bone-weary and relieved, except maybe John. The way Papa and John avoided each other thickened up the air. Everyone ate, their utensils barely touching the plate, except Papa, who cut his meat with a little more vigor, the knife scratching into the ceramic.

"The Studebaker ought to be fixed someday, I expect. Must have driven it all of twice before it was put in the ditch."

John turned a shade red and stabbed at the meat on his plate, head down.

"I should have known better than to buy something new like that. Automobiles are for city folks who need the *fast* life."

Mama gave him a look, but Papa was undeterred. "That wood I had delivered for the garage is rotting out there in the mud." He pointed outside with his fork. "Don't expect I'll need it anyways."

John's chair scraped as he shoved it back. "I told you I was sorry. What more do you want from me?"

"I want you to settle down and think about doing a hard day's work for once."

"So I can be like you? Up to your elbows in mud like animals—"

"John!" Mama stood up. "You better taste those words before you spit them out."

Nothing ever got under Papa's skin more than when someone rejected their way of life. Or made him feel like some muddy hick, because he chose to stay out on the soil where other folks were moving to the cement.

Papa roared, "Everyone wants the easy life these days, but who is going to grow and raise your food if everyone lives in the city? Big companies like Anaconda? You'd trust those robber barons to grow what you put in your mouth? What we do out here is vital, but it sure enough isn't easy. Maybe it's not good enough for you—"

"You think painting is easy? Putting myself out there? Being rejected time and again? It's not about easy, it's about different. I don't belong out here."

Papa yelled right back, "What do you mean? Don't belong? You sprung from this earth right here."

Papa stood now, his fists resting on the table, and nodded to Mama. "Show him what you found."

Mama got up and went over to a cabinet. She brought a small, empty bottle and put it on the table in front of John. "I found this in your pocket," she said.

"Now you're snooping around in my things?"

"I was *doing* your laundry."

"Well, Pop. Looks like you fired the wrong man," John said.

Papa looked to Nara and nodded. "I sure as hell did."

CHAPTER 22

THE NEXT MORNING, PATRICK SADDLED UP EARLY. IT WAS SATUR-
day, so Ivar would have him for the whole weekend. Charles followed Patrick into the stables. "I hate that you have to do this
alone, but Papa has forbidden me to help you. I just can't break
their rules anymore. I've run out of chances with the Stewarts."

"I don't want ya ta get in trouble, too. It will make it worse all
around, but there is something I have ta try."

"Patrick, you aren't gonna set them free again?"

"That's exactly what I'm gonna do."

"Patrick, don't do anything crazy. I mean it."

It was hard to watch his brother ride off, because, one, he
didn't know what in the devil the boy was going to pull, and
two, knowing he'd be sitting around here with a day off, except
for checking the cattle, had made him feel restless, worthless.
If Mama and Papa knew the truth about him, they wouldn't
want him anymore. Part of him didn't believe he deserved to be
here, but he wanted to change, keep his temper in check. John
had been given most of the duties that Charles had before he

went to jail, so he couldn't help but wonder if they needed him anymore.

Through the bunkhouse window, Charles watched John come from the direction of the pines. He went into the barn. Charles hopped up and threw on his boots.

"Hey, John. I'll come out and help you check the herd."

"All right, kid." His voice was a bit slurred.

They saddled up and rode out on the north cow trail with the wind to their faces. John swayed around in his saddle. Charles wondered why a guy would blow the chance to have all this by drinking. John stopped and put his hands up to the mountains ahead like he was framing them. Charles rode alongside and stopped.

"You see this?" John said.

Charles nodded.

"No, *really* look."

"Those are . . . mountains."

He laughed at Charles and took a swig off a flask.

Charles couldn't understand this guy and shook his head.

"You think you've got this life figured out, don't you?" John grabbed the horn of his saddle and smiled to the sunshine.

"I've seen a lot more than you might believe, and I know drinking yourself to death isn't the way."

"Lots of people drink in the city. Out here it seems to be a crime."

"It is. It's called Prohibition."

"You're pretty young to have such a strong opinion. When you get older, you'll think on things differently."

"No, I won't. My mother was a drunk. It ruined her, and along with that, my whole existence."

John quieted at that. "What happened to your pa?"

"Died in the war."

"It's tough for a mother on her own. Not a lot of work for women."

"Yeah, but she didn't have to ruin everything like that."

"The war did that for her. Do you have any idea how hard it is to make your way in this life when you're a woman?"

Charles hadn't thought about it that way before, hadn't realized how tough his mother had it. He'd only been thinking about how rotten his own life was after his pop didn't come back. Charles stared up at the blue sky, wishing he'd helped his mother out instead of blaming her, wished he'd never picked up that gun so he could eat. He should have found work somewhere, somehow.

Charles glanced over at John. Out here, these Stewarts had a family pact. Nobody got left behind. They took care of each other, worked hard to make one life together, and that left just one way of thinking and doing out here. Go outside of that, and . . . he supposed that was how John ended up leaving.

Papa had talked about the cost of losing that bull, the delays in breeding. Charles needed to think about grown-up things like that from now on. "Let's go find that bull."

WHEN THEY RETURNED from the northern range empty-handed, Charles felt deflated. Opal came knocking at the bunkhouse. He figured she wanted to make sure he was still there, because she'd never come into the bunkhouse before. He told her to hop up on his bunk, and he'd read Zane Grey's *Desert Gold* to her. He skipped over some of the rowdier parts of the young men on the Mexican border, and somewhere in the first couple of chapters, she fell asleep.

He lay there reading to himself until his arm and neck became stiff. "Hey, sleepy."

Little blond lashes fluttered, and she looked all around. Her head was a little sweaty from where she had rested it on his arm.

"Let's go see if Blackie is chasing your chickens."

She rubbed her eyes, then hopped off the bunk.

Charles walked over to sit on the swing, while she played with the chickens. Blackie had curled up in the fading sunlight over in some grass. It wasn't long before Patrick rode up wobbly in the saddle.

The screen door squeaked open. Mama stood out on the porch, distress etched over her forehead in deep lines. She ducked back inside quickly. Charles and Patrick looked at one another. Charles followed Patrick into the stalls. "What did you do with those mustangs?"

"They are still in the pen as far as I know, except the little blue roan, thankfully we never found her, but I don't know how she'll survive alone."

He cocked his head at Patrick and just stared him down.

Patrick held up his hands. "My plan doesn't involve *me* setting them free. Ivar is going ta do it."

Charles squinted an eye at him like he'd seen Papa do. "Hmph."

They left the stalls and sat on the porch taking off their boots.

Patrick said, "I'm not sure I want ta go in there. Why don't we take a walk somewhere?"

Charles twisted around and grabbed Patrick's shirt. "Tell me the truth. Did you do something with the mustangs again?"

Mama opened the screen door, and Charles released Patrick's shirt real quick. She studied Charles for a bit, then Patrick, then Charles again. "You boys get on in here. We've had some news from New York."

The screen door slammed shut. Patrick whispered, "See, I told ya."

Charles grabbed the handle of the screen door wondering if he shouldn't turn right around. Every instinct he'd learned on the streets told him to run.

"What's wrong?" Patrick nudged him from behind.

"Forgot something."

He jumped back into his boots and padded down those wooden steps as quietly as he could and then busted into a full-on run for the stalls, trying not to trip on his boot laces. He whipped open the door to the stable and grabbed his tack. He flung open the stall and prepared Charge. The wily horse neighed and stomped, wanting its one bit of rest. He figured this was stealing again, but there was nothing else for it. The Studebaker was broken down, and in any case, taking that would *really* make Papa mad. When he went back out of the stall to grab his saddle, Nara held it in her hands. "Where you goin' so fast?"

Charles threw his head up in the air, looking to the heavens through the slats of the roof.

"That telegram isn't about you. It's Opal."

Wondering what Opal could have done, he followed Nara back inside, where everyone had gathered around Papa. He sat with his hands folded under his chin as if he didn't relish what would come next. The telegram was at his elbow. He fingered it for a moment and then looked up at Mama, who burst into tears. Nara's leg tapped underneath the table at a furious pace like she needed to use the outhouse.

"I won't labor the moment. We've had some bad news from the Children's Aid Society." He looked at Opal, who sat with wide eyes. "Opal, this concerns you, I'm afraid."

Her little chest began to rise and fall quickly. Mama brought her under her wing and held her close.

"The Aid Society says that your mother has inquired about you at the orphanage. Did you know she was alive, Opal?"

At first she wouldn't look at Papa, but Mama told her it was all right and to "Tell him what you know." When her head finally came away from the crook of Mama's arm, it did that quaking thing, like a shake of the head to say no, but part of her wanted to be honest and it came out more like a noncommittal quiver.

Papa asked, "Why didn't you tell the Aid Society your mother was still alive?"

She buried her head inside Mama's arms. "Look at her. She can't go back. There's no way we can let that happen."

"I agree," Nara and Charles said together.

Papa rubbed at his eyes like they all wore him out so darn much. It made Charles ashamed of all the trouble they had caused the Stewarts. He wondered how much more the family could take, all the many problems they presented. Charles remembered what the nice lady had told Mr. Morgan at the station about making sure Opal didn't come back, something about her mother. So the lady from the society knew and still put Opal on that train. Whatever happened to Opal must have been awful.

"Opal, tell us how you got those burns," Charles insisted, drilling her with his eyes.

"It's okay to say," Mama said.

Opal's face went red. "I was hungry and tried to make something on the stove."

Everyone looked at poor Opal with shock and just shook their heads as if they couldn't imagine a scenario where a child would go so hungry in a home, become so desperate. But Charles could.

"They'll just say that was an accident," Charles said, knowing there was more to her story than hunger.

* * *

The next morning, Charles went out to the chicken coop where Opal scattered crumbs, and wherever Opal was, Blackie was never far away. The dog walked up to Charles wagging its tail. He stooped over to pet the dog, remembering that first morning when the dog had leaned into him like an old friend.

"Opal." She didn't look up or stop scattering crumbs. "Opal, I know you can hear me." He bent down and put his hands on his knees. "If you don't tell Mama what happened to you in New York, they're gonna take you away. Do you understand?"

She didn't look up. "They're gonna do it anyway."

Charles stood upright in shock. "How do you know that?"

She finally looked up at him. "Cuz they've done it before."

Opal was a runaway.

He went straightaway and told the Stewarts what he knew, and Papa shook his head. "Runaways are treated like criminals in this state."

Charles went back outside to convince Opal to talk. He'd had friends on the street who never said a word about their past. They'd found a way to build a wall around the pain, so they could live with it. The Stewarts would never understand that kind of scar. If he didn't find a way in, she'd be sent back.

He found her throwing sticks for Blackie. She sat her bottom down on the swing and held on, kicking her little legs. He walked over and gave her a gentle push, and she swung in silence for a few minutes. He pushed her about ten more times, and then let the swing slow down of its own accord. He came around to the front and bent down to meet her eye.

"Opal, please. They're gonna take you away from us. No matter how much it hurts you to remember, you've got to tell the Stewarts what happened in New York."

She'd just pursed up her lips as if he wanted her to eat something awful. He begged her, but she never relented. He went back around and pushed her some more on the swing, thinking of some way he could get her to talk. He walked in front of the swing and knelt again. "You didn't let me leave that one night, and I won't let you. Not without a fight."

He stared her down, waiting. But she got off that swing, took up a stick, and scratched it in the ground, making a jumbled picture in the silty dirt.

"Think about what I said, real hard. I've got to go and check the water troughs." He turned to walk away.

"They never believe me."

He turned around. "We'll make them. I'll make them."

That wall went back up, and she turned away like he wasn't there, like nothing was.

For days, each of them in turn would try to get Opal to talk, but her little face pinched shut, like those words might hurt her more on the way out than whatever it was she had to live through.

* * *

Since Papa had read them the final deliberation from the Aid Society, nobody talked about it. Charles waited. It wasn't that he didn't care, for he decided if he ignored those people coming for Opal, then it wouldn't happen. Mama worked her worries away in the kitchen, Opal following her around in that little apron, disappearing more each day. Nothing would be the same without Opal.

It was Saturday afternoon. They all sat on the porch to enjoy the last of the sunshine, though it was nippy and put some goose bumps on Charles's arms. Papa strummed his guitar and whispered his song "Footprints in the Snow." Papa told Charles a girl had gone missing on her way back from school in a blizzard years ago. The song was for her. Charles kicked his feet up on the porch rail and listened with his eyes closed, feeling those last warm rays on his face. Opal crept up and sat on his lap, burrowing into him for warmth. Charles opened one eye and patted her back. Thinking on the coming winter only made Opal's leaving more painful for Charles, like everything going dark on him at once.

Mr. Morgan had sent a telegram. Opal's mother would pick her up within the next week, as she was on her way to California and "desperately" wanted her daughter back. Charles doubted the veracity of those words, knowing her mother's kind. All he could do was hope and pray her mother would change her mind, but it was not to be.

A fancy new automobile came speeding into their ranch, swirling dust up behind it. Mama stood up from her place on the porch and glared at the approaching auto, her face contorted in misery.

Charles recognized Mr. Morgan getting out of the backseat of the auto. Charles hadn't seen him since that day out on the platform when the lady fell and accused Charles of pushing her. The day Mr. Morgan told them they'd all find parents at the next stop. He'd been sure of it. Charles had been a green young man then. He'd thought the agent was one of those upstanding grown-ups, but now Charles saw him for the shady salesman he was.

Nara stood up. "Mama, I'll handle this, okay?"

Mama nodded, her hands covered her face, trying to block out the sight. Opal jumped off Charles's lap and went inside. He could hear her little feet beating the stair treads and then her bedroom door slamming. If he had a keener sense of hearing, he might have been able to hear a lock clicking, too. Mama followed Opal, her breath ragged, chest heaving. "I'll help get her things together."

Papa grumbled beside Charles. "I wish I could train my rifle on that fella and make him go away. But they've got the law on their side. Just doesn't make any damn sense." Papa put his guitar to the side, weaving his pick into the strings.

"This is wrong." Charles banged his fist on the rail of the porch.

"Charles, if there's one thing I've learned in my time on this earth, there is no justice. It's something people aspire to, sure enough, but our hearts and our heads are forever locked in a battle seeking out the true meaning of right and wrong, because for one fella it means one thing and to another fella it means something entirely different."

A lady stepped out of the passenger's side of the auto. She had brightly painted lips, white-dusted cheeks, a short platinum haircut, and a dress even shorter than her bleached hair.

Nara said, "Boy, she's young. Must be ten years my junior."

Charles didn't have to see much more of Opal's mother to know her past. He'd seen them before. She had the confidence, but none of the class. She tried to pretend elegance in her walk, but her heeled shoe hit a hole, and she was forced to tippytoe around like the sly kind she was. For a married woman with a man taking care of her, she was awful thin. Opal's mother approached the steps and put her bony hand over her brow to block out the sun. She stepped under the shade of the porch.

"Ms. Stewart?"

"I'm Nara Stewart."

"I'm Clara. Opal's mother."

"Who's that man in the auto? Your husband?" Papa gritted out. "I think he ought to come up out of there and introduce himself."

The agency rationalized giving Opal back because Clara had married. The agency felt it would settle her and make a stable home for Opal, but Papa hadn't believed the convenient husband story.

Clara turned around. "Oh, yeah." She waved the man over, and he came to meet them at the porch.

"This is Benjamin Friedman." She giggled and then added, "He's a film producer." Her fancy little purse swung around on its sparkly chain. "We're goin' to California to get married. I'm gonna be a star in his next talkie."

Papa crossed his arms and shook his head. "We were told you were *already* married. Boy, you folks in the city have a whole other meaning for honesty, don't you?"

Benjamin pulled his face into a tight smile and cleared his throat, sticking out his hand to Papa. "Benjamin Friedman. Pleased to make your acquaintance."

"We aren't 'acquaintances,' Mr. Friedman." Papa went inside without asking him in.

Nara stood before the door. Charles could picture her with a rifle in her hands to match the look on her face. "So, Clara, you're gonna be a star, huh?"

"Uh-huh." She smiled all pretty, like Nara meant it nice.

Nara squinted an eye at her. "You one of those flappers? I've heard about those 'ladies.'"

Clara pursed her lips. "I've done some dancing in my day."

"From what I understand, those ladies drink cocktails and dance to all hours of the night in speakeasies."

"I've gotta get up early for my auditions. Ain't that right, Benji?"

The man just brushed his lapel as if this whole conversation weren't worth his time. "Things in the city might seem foreign to you folks." His disdainful eye roamed around their property and returned to Nara as if she were an oddity. "It's hard to imagine, I'm sure."

"Not really, Mr. Friedman. We read about you New Yorkers all the time." She leaned forward and talked to him as if he were numb in the head. "We-get-the-paper-out-here."

"Sometime you ought to come out and visit for yourself."

"Mister, I'm pretty sure hell will freeze over about five times before I set foot in New York City, or any other big city for that matter."

Mr. Friedman snorted and glanced back toward the auto, where Mr. Morgan shuffled around papers in a briefcase, dropping several on the ground. He bent to fetch them and fanned them in the air to get the dirt off them.

Papa came back out and let the screen door slam behind him. Mr. Morgan approached and came to stand at the foot of the steps. "Well, Mr. Stewart. I do have a few business things to tidy up. Some papers that need signing."

Papa pulled his mouth into a grimace. "I ain't signing nothing."

Mr. Morgan froze. "But, Mr. Stewart, there are some legal obligations I have in the matter."

"I don't give one goddamn about your obligations. You gave me your word and turns out it isn't worth the paper you and I signed on. And that woman is not married."

"Well, surely you mean to hand over Opal to her mother?"

Papa just stared at him for a bit. Charles watched with fasci-nation. He hadn't expected this resistance from Papa. Charles came to Papa's side, hoping Papa would point a rifle in Mr. Mor-gan's face.

The standoff lasted longer than Mr. Friedman's patience, and he said, "I'm sure the sheriff will be happy to clear the matter up with you, Mr. Stewart."

Papa smiled at Mr. Friedman. "You see Art out here any-where?"

Mr. Friedman whispered something to Mr. Morgan, who said, "I'm certain Mr. Stewart doesn't want any trouble with the law."

"Maybe I do, maybe I don't." Papa stepped down the treads of his porch. "You listen up good. If you two don't do right by that little girl, there won't be one place on this whole damn earth I won't find you. Understand?"

Clara and Mr. Friedman cowered under Papa's pointing fin-ger as if he could shoot them with it. Clara put her hands on her hips. "Opal's my girl. Nobody tells me what to do with her. Where is she?"

Clara began to walk up the steps. "Opal. It's me. Come out of there now."

There was nothing but silence from the house. A dark, un-readable screen with more than one dead fly sticking to it from Mama's towel.

"Opal!"

The little girl came to the screen but didn't say a word or lift her eyes. Clara went to the door and tried to open it, but Opal must have set the hook in the eye lock.

"Opal. You open this door right now and come out of there."

Opal just stared.

Clara looked around, red in the face. "Come on, baby."

Opal walked away.

"You get out here right now!"

Nara went flying up those steps and got straight up in that painted face. "She'll come out when she's ready. As she's run off a number of times, and has burn scars all over her arms, we all know how you treat your daughter."

Nara's hand fisted and shook at her side. That place she'd gone to, Charles understood well. Blurry, red, and violent. It makes you capable of anything.

Clara's eyes went fierce and wide. She looked over to Benjamin, embarrassed maybe. But she ran down the steps and across the dirt yard. Her heel stuck in another hole. She took off the shoe and limped toward the auto. Before she shut the door, she pointed at her fiancé and said, "Benji, get me my girl!" Then she slammed the door.

Mr. Friedman said, "There's no need to admonish Clara. She has assured me that she has always been a good mother. Opal, as you can see, is . . . at times a little stubborn."

Mr. Morgan held up his hands to get everyone's attention. "Let's all calm down. Clara still intends to marry, so I don't see a problem in this case. I know emotions are high right now. I assure you it will all pass in due time."

"Don't you dare try and assuage me, Mr. Morgan. You and I exchanged words, which out here mean a hell of a lot more than paper. And now you stand there with more papers—which I will not sign—and tell me to calm down. My wife"—he pointed inside the house—"will never be the same after this. That young whatever in the auto over there won't *never* love that girl better than my family. And it burns me deep inside that the one person who will have to live with your decision is Opal."

Charles breathed out heavy. Papa didn't mean to fight for Opal. Tears stung until they flowed down his face. He didn't care who saw it. He looked over at Patrick, his hands over his own face. Inside the house, he could hear Mama and Opal, or, more rightly, a wrestling match.

"I'll help Mama." Nara went inside, and the three of them scuffled.

Everyone on the porch could hear it. Mama and Nara trying to soothe Opal but having to capture her all the same. Just like when Patrick had to wrestle up those mustangs. Charles went inside the house. His hands shook so bad, he didn't know what to do with them. He bent down, searching for anything that might make it easier on her. "Opal. I think your mama's changed. This time things will be different."

She stopped her fighting and regarded him with contempt. "You're not really my brother."

Charles hung his head. Under Opal's scrutiny, he'd never felt so rotten in all his life as he did right then. He promised her that day on the swing, he wouldn't let her go without a fight. People like Clara don't change. He had friends on the streets with mothers like her.

Mama had let go of Opal and doubled over in her own pain. Nara kept one hand on Opal, and with the most reluctance he'd ever heard in her voice, she said, "Charles, we need you to help us."

He knew what she meant. They needed him to use his size and strength to subdue Opal and get her in the auto. "We can't let them take her. I know something bad is gonna happen."

"Charles, as hard as this is, we don't have a choice. The law has decided."

"We can take up rifles! I don't think you understand what she's in for!"

"Listen to me right now. You promised me to follow the rules, do what you're told. You swore to me!"

"How can you ask me to do this to Opal?"

Nara ripped the hat off her head and threw it across the room, running her fingers through her curly hair. "I hate that we have to do this, Charles. But I don't see any other way."

Papa called through the screen, "It's time."

Charles couldn't fight them all, and if they wouldn't help, Opal would be put in that auto anyway, and they might toss him out on his ear. He'd be on his own again.

Mama had Opal wrapped up in her arms, eyes crying down them both.

He couldn't swallow the thick lump in his throat and could barely speak with it. "I promise you. We are *all* gonna regret this." He stood up. "Opal, you've got to go get in the auto now. I'm so sorry."

"No!" she shrieked, snot running out of her little nose.

He took his kerchief from around his neck and wiped her face. "Please. This is hard on all of us. Nobody wants you to go."

She batted his hands away for the first time ever. He'd become that low in her estimation. He took her as gently as he could around the middle. Mama's fingers slowly let go of Opal's dress. "Don't fight me, Opal. Please. Nara, I don't know if I can do this . . ."

Opal banged around like a wild animal in his arms, screaming he knew not what as he walked out the door with her. "I'm sorry, Opal," he cried out as he passed Mr. Morgan and Papa.

"Please, Charles. Don't put me in there! Please!"

Blackie jumped all around Charles, threatening to bite.

Nara called out, "Blackie, get down!"

Charles stopped walking and bent over with the little girl in his arms, sobbing into her hair. "Opal, I've never had to do something that hurt so bad in all my life."

He started walking again to the back door of the automobile, where a very smug Mr. Friedman held open the door. Mr. Morgan came up behind and got in first. "Hand her in to me."

Charles stopped and held her away from them. "You be gentle with her, you hear?" He looked at Mr. Morgan with the most menacing look he could muster, making the man go white in the face.

"Opal, stop fighting me for a second. I want to tell you something." He turned her around to look at him.

"I hate you!" She pounded on his chest.

He bent over with her in his arms. The blows might have come from a cannon, for all the power. "Well, I love you. And I'm just . . . you write to me. I want to know how you're doing. Promise me."

He peered into her red face, eyes scrunched up as if she could make it all go away, and gave her one last, long hug. So tight did he cling to her, he could scarce draw breath. His arms shook as he handed her down to Mr. Morgan, who pulled her into the auto. Of all the terrible things he'd done with his hands, by far, putting her in the car had been their worst crime.

Mr. Friedman slammed the door and tried to walk around Charles, who stepped in front of him and scowled down into Friedman's face. Charles quaked all over, that red place just at the edges of his vision. So easy to step into and unleash his wrath. "You make sure Opal is taken care of." He breathed so hard he could barely talk. "If you don't, I'll tear you into so many pieces, they'll never be able to put you back together again."

Mr. Friedman winced at him with all the arrogance a man can who knows he's just about to get his face broken. He stepped around Charles and ran to the driver's door. Charles bent down to look inside. Opal was doubled over. Her face in her lap. "I meant what I said, Opal. Write to me."

The engine fired to life, and the auto sped off. The wheels jutted over potholes in the road, dirt spewing out the back.

Charles's legs gave way, and he plunked down on the road, feeling the hard earth beneath him. He clawed at the soil on both sides of him and howled up to the sky, "Why?"

CHAPTER 23

FOR ALL THE FIGHT IN THAT LITTLE GIRL, THEY SHOULD HAVE KNOWN
she wouldn't stay put in that auto. She'd been a runaway before
and was on the run again. Nara cursed her own stupidity as she
paced back and forth, wanting to kick over chairs and throw
plates. Charles had been right.

"Where did Opal jump out?" Papa roared.

"They stopped alongside the road so the little girl could re-
lieve herself, and she disappeared," Mr. Morgan said.

"Where? When? What road? How many miles?" Nara yelled
to the back of Mr. Morgan's head. If she sat down at the table
with him, there was no telling what she would have picked up
and thrown in his face.

Art said, "Yesterday, on the road into Billings. Clara didn't
know how many miles, but she'd guessed they had been driving
for . . . half an hour?"

"Yesterday?" Papa walked toward the stove and leaned over it,
breathing and heaving as if he meant to tear it off the wall, but

Nara knew he was just trying to calm himself down so he could think.

Papa said, "I'm going to get in the Studebaker and drive a half an hour. I'll look for her tracks to see where she headed. Nara will ride the back way through Ivar's and toward the road." Papa looked to Nara. "Pick up Ivar on your way, we're gonna need his help."

Mr. Morgan nudged Art. "Wait just a minute. Sheriff, I thought you were going to gather a group of men and look yourself?"

"Looks to me like we've got one right here," Art said.

Nara went to the table and leaned into Mr. Morgan's face. "Where are these 'parents' of Opal's? And why didn't we know this sooner?"

Mr. Morgan wiggled a bit in his seat. "Clara is waiting in Billings, though Mr. Friedman is threatening to leave on the next train."

"You made the wrong call, Mr. Morgan. Now Opal's out there. God knows what's happened to her!"

"The law is on the mother's side."

"Well, God's on ours." Mama must have heard the commotion. She stood on the stairwell in a housedress, her hair hastily pinned into a bun that wasn't gonna last five minutes of stirring a pot, much less the rumpus in the room.

Mr. Morgan fingered his hat and stood. "If she turns up, please send for me. I'll be in Billings for the next few days."

"Couple days, huh?" John snorted.

Art stood up and motioned for Mr. Morgan to come with

him. "You better come on with me. I'm going to take you to Billings. This is a local matter now. Robert, let me know what I can do."

Papa nodded. The agent snatched up his hat, and Art took him by the arm toward the door. "I expect to be apprised of this situation on a daily basis."

Papa ignored Mr. Morgan and walked over to John. Papa said low, "Go find Jim. Tell him what's happened. I know he's sore with me, but you make things right. He's the best tracker I know. I'll start by the road to pick up any trace or step I can find and then make my way to Ivar's ranch. If she's backtracking, she'll go right through there."

"I know where I can find him. I'll get him here. I promise."

"All right, son." Papa patted his shoulder.

Nara filled a Stanley bottle with water. Mama came right behind her, wrapping up bread and cheese.

"Nara, put on your heavy coat. We might be out there all night, and we've got to beat the wolves," Papa said, shrugging on his own coat, his eyes shined over for the first time in her living memory.

Nara's heart jolted, and she ran upstairs to grab her warmest jacket, then stomped back down the stairs. She shouted on the way out the door, "Mama, when the boys get back from the winter feed lot, tell them to pack up, bring rifles, and head out to the west end of the ranch where we've heard those wolves. Charles will remember the place. From there they should ride north of Ivar's and into the Colfax place."

Mama nodded. Nara ran out the door to put on her boots.

Papa sat in the Studebaker. He tried to start the auto, but it wouldn't turn over. He tried again. This time the engine didn't even shudder. Papa put his head on the steering wheel.

Nara rode over to where Papa fiddled with the wires under the auto's hood. "Papa, Patrick will be back soon. After he fixes the automobile, you and the boys can scout for her tracks from the road. I'll meet you at the Colfaxes' place."

Papa nodded. "Be careful."

She patted her rifle scabbard. "Got it handled."

She rode hard through their ranch and into Ivar's range.

Sharp white teeth and bristly gray coats of fur never wandered far from her mind. Opal would be the easiest meal they'd had in a month of Sundays. She covered the ground widely in a zigzag pattern, shouting out the girl's name to the wind, but wily as ever, it carried off her cries.

As she continued through Ivar's ranch, the rocky soil slowed her down. Shod horse hooves made an awful clopping sound against the rocks. She would never ride a horse so hard if it weren't for that little girl, standing out here somewhere alone, freezing and scared. And to think she could have prevented it. If there existed better proof she would never make a good mother, she sure as hell couldn't think of it.

Ivar's little place sat in the distance. A wisp of smoke came from his chimney. He must have heard the hard, urgent pounding of hooves, because he swung open his door with a rifle aimed right at her. He lowered it immediately. "Nara Stewart! You scared the hell out of me."

"Ivar, I don't have time to cross words with you. I need your help. Opal's missing. She might be coming through your land from the west."

"How in the hell?"

"Just saddle up! I'll tell you later."

He ducked back inside his house and came back out with a rifle and heavy coat, then ran to his stables. They rode on west, and when the terrain slowed their pace, she told him the whole story. He just shook his head. "Your poor mama."

"We've got to find her tonight, Ivar. I just don't see how she can survive out here another night. Let's spread out about a half mile apart and head west at a trot. She had on a pink coat and a blue dress when she . . ."

"We'll find her. Don't worry."

They split up a ways. She figured they had about three or four hours of light left. Her eyes scanned the sagebrush while every other part of her lamented. She cursed the agent to hell and back in her mind, then alternatively begged God to help her find Opal, prayed she was okay. Nara yelled to the echoing canyons, "Opal!"

Her eyes scanned a shady hillside where a dense gathering of pine trees would provide cover. Nara whipped around to have a closer look, and her horse faltered in a hole. She keeled forward, using everything she had not to go over the top of her horse. When her mount righted, she jumped off and tugged it along at a trot behind her. Approaching the trees, she stopped to listen.

"Opal?"

The wind whispered, fooling her ears as it mimicked the voice she wished to hear. She grabbed her rifle from the scabbard and began to wade through clumps of sagebrush that scratched and clung to her dungarees. Something padded around in the gravel underneath the shady trees. On quiet feet, she stepped toward the pines. Whatever lurked in there might not be friendly. She studied the ground for prints and didn't see any to match a little girl's Mary Janes. Steps scuffed about again. She crept inside the trees, and a jackrabbit sprang up, then ran to a nearby clump of sage.

She pointed her rifle to the sky and gazed up, catching her breath. She jogged back to her horse and took off at a trot to catch up to Ivar. She looked back out over the range. "Opal!"

In the distance, she could hear Ivar faintly. She had been right about the distance. A half mile was all they could split up to cover and not much more, or they might trot right past her.

Once again, she fumed over Mr. Morgan's not coming to them right away, then forced the regrets from her mind to focus on the range ahead and find that little blond head.

Nara liked to look at that golden hair, but never wanted to soil Opal's pretty head with a chapped, dirty hand. The girl might have been abused terribly by her own mother, and then passed over by farmers and ranchers on account of her scrawny size, but here she filled a big hole in the family.

Her bare hands went numb. She had run out without her gloves. After a while, she and Ivar had ridden straight through his land and into the adjoining ranch. Not long after they crossed over, she heard Papa's voice on the breeze. That same desperate call. "Opal!"

"Papa?"

"Nara?"

She rode to the direction of his voice. He had been on foot. She didn't hear either of the boys. "Where are the boys?"

"I sent them on to the Colfaxes'. They're going to ask for help. She might not have known her general direction, might have headed farther east. I found a few footprints, but I lost them about two hundred feet from the road." He ripped off his hat and scratched his head, scanning the horizon. "Nara, if we don't find her tonight . . ."

"I know." She looked around through blurry eyes.

A motorbike putted from the direction of the road, making her heart do funny things in her chest. Jim would be a comfort to all of them right now.

They both hightailed it back to the road. They found John and Jim, heads down, searching for prints.

Papa walked up and took Jim's hand in his, giving it a firm shake, while she had to stand back and pretend seeing him didn't matter.

"I sure am glad to set eyes on you, Jim. I've been looking all over heck for you," Papa said.

"Robert."

She shouldn't have been surprised to hear her father admit that, but she was glad in any case, for she wondered what Jim'd been up to. His shoulder was still wrapped in dirty white dressing, but he appeared to be managing just fine.

Papa's humbled fingers fondled the brim of his hat. "I owe you an apology, Jim. I was madder than hell that night, but that wreck wasn't your fault."

Jim nodded uncomfortably, then looked around. "This is where she left the auto?"

"Near as we can tell," Papa said.

Nara put her mind back to finding Opal. "Papa, I'll go catch up with the boys and ask Will Colfax to scan his ranch to its easternmost point." She indicated where she and Ivar had been. "We combed straight through there." She pointed. "I'll take the boys north of that and John and Ivar can go south of that. If Jim doesn't pick up her trail here, you and Jim can take the auto home and update Mama. She'll be crawling the ceiling by now."

"I don't like you being out here." Papa peered at the darkening sky. "But I'll be damned if that little girl isn't, too. Why in the Sam Hill didn't they come to us sooner? Damn them to hell."

Nara felt Jim's reassuring presence, was drawn to it. She patted his good shoulder like he was any old hand, but her beseeching eyes tried to tell him her heart's true words. "I'm glad you're back. Broken shoulder or not, we need you back at the ranch."

Jim reached back out to her with those dark eyes, an understanding in them, longing. She realized her hand was still on his shoulder, and withdrew from him, dazed by the force that arced between them.

Papa either didn't notice or didn't want to. He said, "That's right, you've got a job and a place, if you still want it."

Papa and Jim walked off together like two rocks that if you knocked them together, they'd just make sparks. When all of this was over, she'd bum a cigarette off Jim and apologize to him for everything.

The boys trotted up on borrowed horses from the Colfax family.

Charles asked, "Have you found her?"

Nara shook her head, unable to face the boy after he'd warned them. "I can't believe she's already been out here two days and a night."

"If I ever see those people again, I swear—"

"We've got to find her first."

Patrick's eyes drooped. He made the sign of the cross against his chest and mouthed a little prayer.

"Let me go talk to Mr. Colfax. You boys wait right here, I'll be back."

She rode out and found Will Colfax. In the distance, she could hear two of his older sons shouting out for Opal. "Sir, we are going to take this route along here to the north and east back through the Magnussons' and onto our land. Can you and your boys comb through your land? We don't know if Opal headed in the right direction after she left the road."

"Yes, ma'am."

"Thanks, we're mighty obliged."

He lifted his hat and rode off, whistling to call his boys to him.

It was a stumbling journey back through the dark, but as luck would have it, the wind breathed gently, and they were able to spread out farther. Yips and yaps from coyotes filled the brisk air. But to the south she heard the moaning of wolves. It raised every hair on her head and neck. "Opal!"

WHEN THEY GOT back to the house late that evening, light glowed through the windows. She told herself Opal would be in there, eating soup or tucked into bed. They all dismounted, tied their horses to the porch rails, and went inside. She swung the door open. Papa, Jim, John, and Ivar sat around the table. They didn't exactly seem comfortable in each other's company, but camaraderie wasn't the only thing missing.

Charles stared at Opal's empty place at the table. Hands fisted at his sides, he paced around, knuckles white. Nara felt she deserved his anger. His eyes rose to hers. Everyone felt the coming storm, mouths and forks stilled. Mama walked to the table with a plate of sandwiches and stopped in her tracks.

"I followed your rules. I let them take Opal. *I* put her in that auto." Charles's face screwed up in agony. "I'm going out there to find her, and I'm not letting them take her again. I may not be a part of this family, I may not be her brother, but if anyone comes for her again, I'm not letting them take her. No matter what I have to do!"

He kicked a chair in his way and stalked out of the house, leaving them all speechless. Nara rubbed her forehead and followed him out. From the porch, she watched him walk Charge out of the stable and jump on that mighty horse like he'd been riding all his life. Together, they galloped down the road.

Papa's boots settled beside her. He put his arm on her shoulder. "Let him go. He'll fight you till hell freezes over and then skate with you on the ice. He ain't gonna sleep anyway. Don't see how any of us can."

"We shouldn't have let her go without a fight."

"You got that right."

Papa went back inside. If Charles never forgave her for insisting he choose between wrong and wrong, she wouldn't blame him. They should have broken the law. For an unjust law is no law at all. Looking to the skies, she searched for the answer to her misery. Begged the Lord above for a better justice for Opal.

Standing outside in the crisp air, she couldn't help worrying how the girl would keep warm tonight. Maybe she had already grown too cold for this world. Nara shuddered at the thought and went inside for a coat. "Papa, I need the keys to the Studebaker."

"You can't go alone."

Jim scooted out of his chair and rose. John stood up right after. "She won't."

Ivar put down the sandwich he'd been eating.

"Take your rifles, all of you," Papa said.

Mama hurried on with a Stanley bottle and sandwiches wrapped up in wax paper and handed them to John. "Take these. You need your strength."

As Nara walked to the auto, a dreadful feeling came over her. A deadly end waited for someone, angels urging her forward. Without sense or reason, she broke into a run. Fumbling, she turned the key in the ignition, but the damn engine wouldn't turn over.

CHAPTER 24

CHARLES CALLED OUT HER NAME TO THE DARK SHAPES IN THE DIStance with only a sliver of moon and icy stars to guide him. To think putting her in that auto might have killed her ate a hole in him bigger than the cruel sky above. Charge had lathered from the run, but never stumbled or swayed once. The ornery horse must sense the grave urgency.

Charles regretted he didn't take Opal somewhere. The Stewarts could have said they ran off, but none of that would have been in keeping with their rules.

From a raw throat he called out, "Opal!"

He left the road and went to search through some boulders. As he drew closer, a shadow moved behind them. Though he urged his horse forward, Charge refused and walked backward, letting out a fearsome, deep noise Charles had never heard before. "What's the matter with you? Opal might be in there!"

Frustrated, he threw his leg over the side, jumped off, and pulled the rifle out of its scabbard. He'd lived out here long enough to know you don't dismount without something in the hands. He walked toward the outcropping of rocks, wishing he could see over the top of them. "Opal?"

He heard feet shift in the gravel, four of them, and heavy. Something breathed out, filling the air ahead with steam. His heart leapt in his chest. He backed up, ready to jump on Charge. But the horse had run, reins dragging up dust. He cocked the gun and walked backward to the road, looking in every direction. A shadow leapt out. He turned and fired on it. Acrid gunpowder and a sharp yelp filled the black night. His ears rang as he watched a blur of fur and blood writhe around in pain. The wolf's jaws snapped at the air around it. When the initial shock of the bullet wore off, it limped toward him, determined and snarling. Yellow eyes followed his every move. His feet stepped backward, and he stumbled over a rock. Another pair of glowing eyes came from the other side of the boulders. Bristly coats of silvery white fur shone in the moonlight. He tried to remember how to use the gun in his hands, needed to cock it for the second shot. The wolves came close enough for him to smell their hot breath. One snapped at him, and he jerked away. His fingers searched uselessly on the rifle, his mind a jumbled mess. He swung the end of the rifle around to ward them off. "Get back!"

Their teeth snapped and scraped at the barrel.

He scuttled in the gravel closer to the road. In all his terror he hadn't seen the car coming.

Headlights and a rumbling engine came upon him all at once.

The auto slammed to a stop just short of him, blinding him to everything except dust floating in the air and two shadows with rifles. One bang erupted after another in bright sparks. Sharp yelps and shrill whining pierced his ears. Charles ran to the other side of the auto for cover. Gunshots continued until the wolves ceased to make a sound. Hunched over the engine, he couldn't bear to look.

Nara searched him over with her hands, wild-eyed. "We saw Charge running hell for leather down the road. You all right, kid?"

He couldn't speak at that moment. He'd never be all right again. Through the dust and gun smoke, he could discern two lifeless piles of silver fur smudged with blood. Splotches of red covered the dirt road, catching a shine from the moonlight. Charles went behind a bush and tossed up the foamy yellow contents of his stomach.

"Jesus! It's a good thing we got here when we did. Those wolves were about to make a meal out of you," Ivar said.

Ivar and John grabbed the wolves by their tails and dragged them off the road. "The turkey vultures will be fat by next week," John said.

Charles wiped his mouth, shivering uncontrollably. He turned from the sight of those creatures, and all he could think was, somewhere out here Opal shivered, too, wolves circling her. No gun, helpless. "Nara, we have to find her. We have to. She's out here right now. Somewhere." His head spun in every direction. "Maybe she heard all the shots."

"You're in shock. You better get in the auto."

"No!" He searched for Charge. "I'm not giving up."

Jim appeared from the bushes. Charles hadn't even seen him

get out of the automobile. "There are more than two wolves in a pack," he said.

"What's your plan, Jim?" Nara asked.

"We stay till dawn. Find the rest of the pack, or at least keep them on the run. If she's nearby, she might come to us. But so will the wolves. They'll smell the blood."

Charles said, "I'll stay with Jim."

"I'll stay, too," Ivar said.

* * *

The full light of morning shone brightly in his bleary eyes. They crossed through the big gate to the Stewarts' ranch. An *S* had been burned into the wooden gate many years gone by. For the shaky promise of staying on this ranch, he'd let Opal down in the worst way, trading her in.

He brought Charge into the stall to feed and brush. Its patchy black and gray legs shook with exhaustion. Charles patted its flanks. "You're a good horse, Charge. I should have listened to you."

Patrick came up from behind. "I'll do it. Ya better go get some shut-eye."

Charles grabbed his shoulder. "Thanks. If anything happens, be sure to wake me up."

"I will."

TRUE BLUE WITH his promises, Patrick nudged and jostled at Charles's shoulder what seemed like only a few minutes later. In his haze, Charles thought he heard Nara's voice. "Let him sleep. He's had one hell of a night."

Charles sat up straight and smacked his head on the wood slats above his bunk. "Ah!"

"All right, you're up. We're heading out in half an hour. Suggest you spend every moment of that filling your belly." Nara left the bunkhouse, Patrick right behind.

Charles stood and hastily put on the clothes he'd dropped to the ground beside his bed. The smell of his stale, tangy shirt reminded him of sleeping on the streets. He jumped into his boots and jogged up to the house, forgetting to take his boots off.

Mama whirled around. "I couldn't sleep a wink last night. Those damn wolves."

He'd never heard Mama cuss before. She grabbed both sides of his face none too gently, and then gave him a kiss on the cheek. It made his face warm with something like embarrassment and not feeling good enough for the gesture. No one had shown him that kind of affection since his ma, and he'd let her down, too.

He sat at the table, and two seconds after that Mama had a heaping plate of food before him. He gulped it down and started hiccupping. Mama brought over a glass of water and patted his back. "Here, slow down or you'll choke."

Charles filled his toast with bacon and eggs and stuffed it in a napkin. "Thanks, Mama."

"You be careful out there, and promise me one thing."

"Okay."

"You'll find that little girl for me."

An urge to hug her came over him, and he stood there for a moment. "I swear to you, I'm going to find Opal."

EVERYONE STOOD BY the water pump. Papa scratched the ground with a stick. He turned around and put a hand on Charles's shoulder. "Listen up. Jim found some tracks at Ivar's place. His door was left open and a jar of peanut butter is missing. Tracks indicate she's headed north. Jim thinks she's nearby, just can't find her way. She doesn't know the range like you boys. I've told everyone to keep their chimneys going today and tonight. Ivar says he had a fire going last night, and she might have seen the smoke."

Every nerve ending in him prickled with hope. "She's alive."

"We sure hope so. But we gotta find her today, make no mistake. Go get saddled up. Take mine, your horse is burnt. You and Patrick will go with Ivar. He knows the northern range better than anyone. John and Jim are going to cover everything we combed through last night. She might be walking circles around us, for all we know. I'm taking Mama to get her brother in town. We might need a doctor, and we can't risk taking Opal into Billings. Nara will stay here and hold off Art or anyone else who shows up asking about Opal."

Nara's fingers turned white around the stock of her rifle.

CHARLES, IVAR, AND Patrick passed through the northern part of the ranch and climbed up hills unfamiliar to Charles's eye.

Not that they didn't all look alike, but it was the way they were arranged. The valleys and such. The way pine trees gathered and stuck together in different shapes. Charles called out in a raspy voice, "Opal!"

Something moved and caught his eye.

He whipped his head around as sagebrush rolled by in the valley below. He drew in a frustrated breath and called out for her again.

They had ridden for roughly two hours, crossing over hilly grassland, when Ivar whistled for them to come back. Charles's heart hammered with the idea one of them found her. He ran his horse toward Ivar and Patrick. His horse slid to a stop. A dust cloud passed over them. Charles took off his hat and slapped his thigh.

"Careful, you're gonna bake that horse," Ivar warned.

Charles crushed his hat back on his head, then looked around. "Whose land is this?"

"Bank owns it. Family went belly-up in the drought three years ago." Ivar scanned the range, squinting his silver eyes at the sun. "Finding that tiny girl out here is like hunting for a whisper in a big wind."

Sunlight struck Patrick's watery blue eyes as he put his hands over his brow to search beyond, with a wish in his eye even Charles could see and feel.

"There's a band of mustangs over there!"

"No time for that, kid."

Charles searched the small band, wondering at their harmonious shades of brown, black, and white, all the mixed colors and spots shared between them. He wished people could be more like mustangs.

A flash of pink caught his eye. He froze, straining his eyes to see that far. From the burst of his heart, he kicked his horse to a run. Ivar and Patrick rode up behind him, and Charles slowed, afraid to spook the mustangs. He gulped in air. "It's her! The pink jacket she wore, look!"

Ivar got ahold of Charles's reins. "She's lying on the ground. We have to go in there slow as molasses, or they'll trample her!"

"Ivar's right. Better ta go on foot."

They all dismounted and got close to her by turns. Each slow step was agony, for Charles yearned to leap across the prairie and pick her lifeless body from the ground. But he'd been in Montana long enough to know he'd be signing her death warrant. Ivar carried a rifle and walked through the grass low and steady like a predator. Charles shivered. When they got close enough, mustang heads popped up and ears turned in their direction. "I better go in alone," Patrick whispered.

"No way," Charles said. "I'm going with you. Besides, you can't carry her."

"But ya have ta be calm and gentle around them."

Ivar walked over to a nearby rock and propped up his rifle aimed at the mustangs. "If anything gets near her, I'll shoot it."

Patrick said, "The worst thing we can do is shoot at them. Trust me."

"Boy, you better have your head on good and tight."

Patrick nodded and moved ahead slowly. Charles followed, shadowing his every move. That boy knew these horses better than anyone, and Charles would do anything to keep her safe.

Opal lay lifelessly in the grass, her arm at an odd angle like a broken doll.

"Maybe we should call out to her?" Charles said.

Patrick just shook his head. They were within twenty feet of the band when Patrick held out his hand and called to a mare in that funny language of his. Sounded like Gaelic, but he whispered so quietly like it was a secret. Patrick held still, and the horse stared at him, chewing grass. He moved a little closer and the mare didn't shy away. Charles spotted the little blue horse in the middle of the band. It stood nearest to Opal, and from time to time the mustang would go over and nudge her and snuffle over her hair, bringing up golden wisps of it in the sunlight. Charles shuddered at the vulnerability of her tender body lying among the deadly hooves. But if he ran over and grabbed her up, it would get the whole band running. He yelled to Patrick in a whisper, "Patrick, that blue roan is over there. Look, in the middle by Opal."

"I saw, but I have ta get through the mama horses first."

Charles balled up his fist and pounded his thigh. A mustang's head shot up. A large black and white stallion moved away from them. Some of the mares followed. Charles cussed at himself, at his temper. He'd need patience and gentleness. Knuckles wouldn't get this done. Patrick moved closer. About an inch an hour, Charles figured.

With the stallion moving off and the mares following, he believed there was enough time to snatch Opal real quick. "Patrick, I'm gonna go get her."

"No."

Charles stood fully upright and pushed out his chest. He walked among them gentle and calm, but the stallion threw its head all around. It meant to protect the band. The beast lined up with Charles, nostrils flaring and snorting.

Charles held his ground as the big brute ran at him, his whole body quaked, hands out, ready for the fight. The stallion's hooves pounded and dug into earth. At the last moment, the horse went around him. Charles swung around. It came up from behind, bucking and rearing.

"Come on!" Charles roared at it. "I'm gonna get Opal, and no damn horse is gonna stop me!"

The horse trotted a ways and then stopped, calling out from deep inside its powerful belly.

Charles walked backward toward Opal, maintaining eye contact with the stallion. It lowered its head and watched. The remaining mares began to scatter, but the little blue mustang stood close to Opal, guarding her from her own kind, which he could honestly understand right now. Its little ears were back on its head in a show of strength, a hoof stamped the ground. Charles turned to Patrick.

"She won't let ya touch Opal. Let me try and charm her."

Patrick talked in his peculiar way and the horse cropped up its ears to listen. It still hadn't moved, but at least its ears weren't back anymore.

Patrick came up behind Charles, and the horse took two steps toward them. It looked curious now. Patrick closed the distance and petted its mane. "Ya remember me."

Charles couldn't wait one minute more. He slowly walked around the horse and bent to pick up Opal, braving the back end of the mustang. She felt like a limp rag doll in his hands. All the strength and stubborn had fled her little bones. Terrified she might not be alive, he made for their mounts, jogging over rough and uneven ground. Ivar shot off his gun three times and the rest of the small band scattered.

"Opal, can you hear me? It's Charles." He touched the side of her face, swollen and crusted with blood. Her eye on that side completely closed over, red and blue. He felt her hands for signs of warmth and life. "My hand is shaking too bad. Patrick, check her for a heartbeat."

Patrick put his hand on her neck and nodded.

"Oh, thank God!" Charles trembled all over and then shouted to Ivar, "She's alive!"

Ivar smiled for the first time Charles had ever seen. He trotted up, got off his horse, and ran up to them, leading their horses behind him. He handed the reins to Patrick. "Good work with those horses, kid."

Charles handed Opal to Ivar and mounted his own horse. "Hand her up to me. Careful of her arm, I think it's broke. She won't wake up."

Charles's eyes went blurry as he took her soft little body and settled her in his lap. Her head lolled over the crook of his arm as he tucked her in carefully. They rode achingly slow, afraid to hurt her further.

"Please wake up, Opal," Charles whispered to her.

As far out as they had ridden, it took several hours to get back, but each minute he must have said a prayer, said her name again and again, hoping she'd wake. Ivar would occasionally break up this solemn chanting by riding ahead at a gallop to make sure no one saw them bringing in Opal but the family.

Just before they reached the ranch, Nara approached, her horse at a run. She circled Charles's horse, trying to get a good look at Opal.

"Thank God! Stop for a second. Let me see her," Nara said.

She probed Opal's neck. "Did anything look broke to you?"

"Yes, her arm. She won't wake up."

Nara continued roving over the girl's limbs and then lifted Opal's one good eyelid and pressed two fingers to her neck. "God bless her. You did good, Charles. Real good."

The words of praise he'd waited to hear come out of her mouth had only the barest second to make him feel good, because holding Opal's limp body in the crook of his arm didn't feel like he'd done something good. He had put her in that auto, and he hadn't found her in time.

"I'm going back to the house and keep Art and anyone else clear of the ranch. Shoot off your gun once as you approach. If you don't hear a shot back, wait until you do. Patrick, come with me."

Nara turned her horse on a dime and galloped off. Patrick followed. Charles held Opal to him as if doing so could give her some of his strength. "Come on, Opal. Just a little farther. We're almost home."

When they trotted up to the house, everyone stood alert on the porch. Papa came down the steps, shouting, "John, go ride out to the road and keep watch. Don't shut the gate or let anyone see you. Just come back in a damn hurry and warn us if someone is coming."

John nodded and ran to the stables. Mama rushed to Charles, still mounted, Opal limp in his arms. "She won't wake up."

"Dear sweet God." Mama's hands felt over every part of Opal's little body and stopped at the arm, the face. "Let's get her in on the table, quick."

Charles had never seen Papa wear a frightened face. For the longest time, Charles didn't think anything scared Papa, but the older man's gray whiskery jaw trembled as he took Opal from Charles like she might break. Papa carried her inside the house, Mama followed, tears tumbling down her determined face. Opal's bloodied pink coat dropped to the dirt. Patrick walked by, looked at it for a moment, then set it on the porch steps.

Minnie had come in from Billings. She placed quilts on the table just before Papa gently laid Opal down. Patrick ran around the house, taking marching orders from Mama. Water, blankets, a bowl in case she got sick. A man Charles had never seen before came down the stairs, black bag in hand, stethoscope around his neck. Must be Uncle Bertram, Minnie's father. His daughter stood dutifully by his side, calm as her father placed the instrument over Opal's heart and chest. His fingers then gently roamed over her face and inspected her head, neck, and back. He moved over her legs and handled the joints until he was satisfied they were in working order. When he got to her arm, Charles burst out, "That's broken, be careful."

The doctor nodded without looking up and assessed the arm gingerly. When he was done, he put his stethoscope away in his bag. "She took a terrible fall. This side of her head is badly damaged. The swelling's not just around her face. She's probably been concussed, which accounts for her unconscious state. The arm on this same side is broken."

Nara said, "I think we oughta take her into Billings."

Papa snapped, "She'll wake up. Just give her a minute."

"Papa, this is no small injury. She could die!"

Charles chimed in, "Maybe they can admit her under another name?"

Mama looked between them all, a mess of misery, shaking her head. "It's a small town. If we take her in, they'll know she's been found."

"But at least she'll live!" Nara shouted.

The doctor held up his hands. "Everybody stop hollerin' and calm down. This ain't good for the girl. We've got to keep quiet and let her rest. If I think she ought to go, then I'll tell you. Now clear out of here, alla you. Except you two." He pointed to Mama and Minnie. "I'm gonna need your help getting these clothes off. Get some scissors."

Duly chastised, they all filed out onto the porch. Charles sat on the steps and began to chew his fingernails. Patrick sat next to him and patted his back. "She's gonna be all right. I just know it."

Charles nodded, hoping Patrick was right. Everyone stood

silently until Papa spoke up. "We'll do what Bertram suggests. We can't keep her here if she'll die, but if she'll be just as good here as any other place, then she's staying."

Nara nodded to that and then looked out to the hills beyond. John came galloping into the yard, yelling. "Got a car coming. A young lady and a few men," he managed to say between big gulps of air.

"All right, everyone act like they're going out to search." Papa yelled into the house, "Pull the curtains shut and keep quiet. Mr. Morgan and the mother are coming up the road. I'm going to tell them we're going out to search. I'll keep 'em away from the porch. Just don't make a sound."

Mama yelled in a whisper through the screen door, "Robert, you shoot 'em if you have to." Then she shut the door quietly.

Papa raised an eyebrow to that and looked Charles square in the eye. "Well, you heard Mama. Everyone make like you're going out to search. We're not running a lodge here. They'll get out of our hair pretty quick."

Everyone bolted off the porch and began to mount their horses and fool around with their rifles and such. The car came down the road, it's fancy tires thunking into potholes. The wind kicked up just as they hopped out of the vehicle as if it didn't want them around, either. Clara's dress whipped her legs, exposing the emaciated bones of an opium addict. The woman winced and her hands covered her face to block the blast of silty air.

Papa stalked up to them. "Have you found her?"

Mr. Morgan looked aghast. "We hoped you had."

"Well, I'm not the responsible one here, now am I? But as you can see, we're doin' our best."

Opal's bloody pink coat lay on the steps. Charles walked over to it, unsure what to do other than block it from sight.

Mr. Friedman narrowed his eyes and said, "Maybe we ought to hire a private crew to comb the area."

That got Charles's heart racing, his mind thinking. He picked up the bloody jacket and approached Morgan. "Look here. This is all we've found of her, and a mess of wolves' prints. They attack in packs. We probably could have found her in time, had you bothered to inform us right away." Charles threw the bloody coat in Morgan's startled face.

Clara shrieked and then began to contort her body like she might faint. Friedman held on to her. "Don't worry, dear, I'm sure they'll find her."

Mr. Morgan fingered the bloody coat and breathed out real deep. "Did you find anything else? Any sign at all?"

Papa spoke up. "We found a swirl of blood nearby in the dirt. I don't think I have to tell you how wolves kill and eat in a frenzy."

Clara collapsed in Friedman's arms, and he tried to carry her off to the car. She fought him tooth and nail. "I have to see. I have to find my girl! Show me whatever's left."

Friedman cooed and grappled with Clara in turns as he put her back in the car.

Mr. Morgan eyed Papa and said, "If you find a body or . . . anything, please contact me so I can settle the matter officially."

Papa's jaw set angrily. He put his finger in the air. "I'll do that one last thing for you, Mr. Morgan. Now get yourself and those people off my property, or you'll *all* be taking a dirt nap by sundown!"

Papa headed to the stables, stiff-backed. Mr. Morgan's cheek twitched, a smugness to his face. He placed his fancy hat on his head and walked to the auto.

* * *

Several nights of worrying at Opal's bedside had made them all a little tetchy. Not with each other, but with the situation, the helplessness. Papa ran Uncle Bertram ragged and insisted he do "more than just watch her sleep." Mama put herself between her brother and husband on more than one occasion. Nara kept hollering they better take Opal into Billings. Minnie tried to console everyone. Charles mulled over all the consequences in his mind, while Nara and Papa argued back and forth, dug into their viewpoints as if they stood in trenches. Nara had tried to bring Charles over to her side, but for once in his life, he didn't know the right move.

It seemed like everyone was angry about something, but mostly at not being able to do anything for Opal. Charles turned that anger against himself, as he remembered those moments when she had begged him not to put her in the auto. He sat alongside her bed, gazing at the paper-thin skin of her closed eyelids, the little red capillaries. He remembered tears streaming down her face as he failed her, let her go without a fight.

He grasped her small hand and wondered if Opal knew he sat there. Her little arm from shoulder to finger had been wrapped tight with torn bedsheets and anything else Mama could find to make a rigid cast. Uncle Bertram had used flour and water to set it good and tight.

EVERYONE HAD BEEN sleeping when Papa came to the bunk-house, gas lamp in hand. They shot out of their beds in the eerie shadows of that lamp, and in a flurry of frosty air they wrestled to put their clothes on. They ran to the main house under the starry sky and gathered in the hallway near Opal's bedroom with whispers and shuffling feet.

When Mama came out to tell them Opal was awake, Nara yelped out loud, covered her face, and cried at the news. Sobs strong enough they might break her sturdy back wracked through that tough woman. Her brother held her tight. Charles exchanged watery smiles with Patrick as they all huddled around Opal's bed talking softly, encouraging her to fight. Opal appeared groggy and didn't open her eyes much. No one expected her to say anything. Not long after, they were all shooed into the hallway by Uncle Bertram to worry all over again.

No matter what happened, they were family. People who'd be there for each other no matter what. People you could trust. Standing shoulder to shoulder in that hallway, everyone together, he wished to be a full-fledged part of them, to have that security, that feeling of safety he just barely remembered. Vague images of his pop reading him stories in bed. His mother standing in the kitchen, steam rising from pots when she was still happy. That warm hand on your back that won't let you fall, and even if you do, it'll pick you right back up.

Nara came up from behind and gave him a pat on the back. And there it was, that warm hand. "She's gonna make it, kid. You found her in time."

Charles nodded, swallowing the lump in his throat. The knuckly hands buried in his pockets came out and grabbed ahold of Nara and held her tight. She felt rigid at first, but then she relaxed, and her arms came around him, rubbing his tired back. Nara might never be motherly in the traditional sense, but she was dependable as a sunrise. Patrick came over, gave him a rub on the arm, and Nara pulled Patrick into the hug.

They watched through the doorway with red, watery eyes, all of them, as the doctor examined Opal with his many instruments. Charles didn't think he could breathe in those minutes watching, waiting.

"She's going to make it, but she'll need to rest in a dark room for a few weeks at least." He turned and tenderly prodded at her eye. "I'm not sure she'll ever see out of this eye. We'll know more about the arm in a few weeks, but it was a bad break. It may never work like it used to." He shook his head.

Charles didn't care if her arm or eye ever worked right again. She was back, and that's all any of them wanted.

Mama put a sheet over the frilly curtains in Opal's room, and in the next days, things settled down some, but anytime someone spoke too loud, Opal flinched at the sound. Charles read to her in his softest voice, grateful she forgave him for putting her in the auto. She didn't say the words, but after she woke up, he had apologized to her, promised her no matter what, he wouldn't let them take her again. Her eyes were closed, but her cold little hand came out from under the quilt and clutched his fingers.

Nara had behaved strange around him for the last many days. He figured it was the hug. Things had shifted between them, he could feel it. So when she finally approached him out on the porch one evening after supper, he understood the bent of her thoughts.

"You've been working yourself to the bone. Mama's worried you're losing weight."

"Might be." He looked off into the pitch-black sky like it wasn't no big deal, but his hands were fidgety on the rail, giving him away.

"With everything that's happened, I was thinking you might be worried about your place out here. We just wanted you to know that how old you are doesn't change anything. The Children's Aid Society sure as hell doesn't have to know. Things can be just like they were. I wanted you to know that you belong here now."

"Does that mean I'm a Stewart?" His chest swelled up all at once with the thought of it.

"Yeah, that's what it means."

His face broke out into a big grin. It embarrassed him, so he turned away. They gazed out at the shadowy hills in silence. The chickens clucked and scratched at the ground nearby. Charles figured with all the grit and fire they possessed between them, they were blood by their very natures. But thinking about his nature reminded him of his past, and his face fell. For all this time, he'd pushed it away, what'd he done, but now he had to wonder if he was good enough to be a part of a family.

"Something on your mind?"

He nodded, tears welled up in his eyes. "I just . . . sometimes I wonder if I deserve you guys."

Nara stood straight like she braced herself for a slug in the gut. That day in jail, they must have told her over the phone what he'd done. He sat in the rocking chair and clutched his own shoulders. His whole body began to quake with the suffering of so many years, mistakes nobody could fix. He hadn't meant to hurt the butcher. The gun didn't even have bullets. When the butcher had turned on Jonny with a meat cleaver, he knew it was no idle threat. Charles and his friends had slept in the alley beside the butcher shop, and the man and his wife lived in rooms above. Many a night they heard his wife's wailing, the slapping, then the silence. Everyone in the neighborhood watched her walk on by with a hat pulled low, wrapped in a shawl that couldn't hide the bent of her back.

Even if the butcher got the justice he deserved, you can't pull a stickup job like that without permission from the gang who owned the territory. Charles's head had grown high enough to be seen, wanted. The thugs found him easily enough, but Charles refused to bust heads for the mob, so they beat him bloody and tossed him in an alley, believing he'd change his mind. But he hadn't been born for that life, that place. He'd run to Grand Central to leave New York for good, and he'd been running ever since. Trying to push it all away, be that young man his father would be proud of, someone this family would want.

"I didn't mean to hurt the butcher. I was starving—"

Nara put her warm hand on his back. "Sometimes people do things they don't mean to, or even want to, they're just desperate, cornered. I've seen it in animals, and I've seen it in people."

He gazed up to the night sky. Stars began to emerge one by one. He got the feeling she didn't want to know, but someday, he'd tell her everything. Now just didn't seem the right time.

They sat quiet, listening to owls hoot to find one another. Dusky wings would barely disturb the night air as they swooped about to slay their evening meal. After a good many minutes, Nara said, "Come on. It's getting late."

Charles followed her inside. Papa fussed around, searching for something around the coal stove. "Has anyone seen my shotgun?"

Nara looked to Charles with a question on her face.

CHAPTER 25

THE ASPIRIN UNCLE BERTRAM HAD LEFT WITH THEM RAN OUT, SO Nara grabbed the keys to Papa's automobile and told everyone she was going to the mercantile. She rolled away from the house and on down the road to avoid kicking up dust. Her elbow laid on the window and her chin rested in her hand, every part of her stiff and tired. It struck her how she'd always lived in a world of right and wrong, black and white.

But that wasn't how the world really worked.

Just a few months ago, she would have turned that boy over to the New York police, but her mindset had shifted, adjusted to the reality of the world. Whatever Charles's sins, his remorse had been boldly worn the other night, and since they hid a young girl from her mother, Nara didn't think they could denounce him. They were the desperate ones now. Shoe was on the other foot. She couldn't predict what they'd do if Clara showed up again. One thing was certain, it wouldn't be lawful.

These kids had shown her how awful the world can be even when you're just a bitty kid, but she wouldn't lament the loss of her ignorance for one moment, because with all that pain had come some badly needed additions to her family. Two young boys she could train up to run the ranch when she was too old and frail, and a feisty little companion who was just as tough on the inside as Nara was on the outside. But some things would always be missing. Holes that couldn't be filled by any old shovel.

She'd went to talk to John the other day to smooth things over before he left. He was out building Papa's garage as a means to an apology. She watched him measure boards with a pencil tucked behind his ear. Folks don't often linger and watch others work, and by his words, he seemed to know what was on her mind. "Don't worry, I'm leaving pretty soon. New York is where I belong."

"That guy who said he'd buy a painting of Montana from you for all that money, was that just smoke?"

"It's real. It's just . . . what they want one minute in New York, they don't the next. But I sent that fella a letter. I'm going back. I've gotta make it work."

"You may not want to live in Montana, but Montana's in you. Paint it and share it with those fancy New Yorkers. Let them hang beauty up on their walls. Something they won't ever see in the city."

"It's funny, folks there think Montanans are nothing but a bunch of gun-slinging cowboys."

"Well, don't disappoint them. Paint it for them. Just don't forget the cowgirls."

She walked away from her brother feeling like they'd healed things over, only to see him swaying and walking funny toward the bunkhouse later that day. People must find their own way in this world, knock their head, and figure things out on their own.

The street before her sat bare and quiet, just the way she liked it. The only other rig was an old horse cart in front of Chief's. She parked the Studebaker and walked up the steps, the doorbell jingling behind her. Her boots clomped hollow along the old store floorboards. She approached the counter unaware of anything or anyone around her. "Chief, I need some aspirin."

He lifted one brow to the admission. Aches and pains were to be expected, and Papa never spent money on frivolous things. Chief would know that better than anybody.

He set the bottle down, and she picked it up to read the directions. "How much would you give a small child?"

Somebody had stepped up behind her, stood a little too close. She turned around, staring into the eyes of an embittered woman.

"That for you?"

"I've never been sick a day in my life. This is for Patrick."

Ella folded her arms. "You Stewarts. You think you're better than everyone."

Nara gave her a tight smile, wondering what Ella had cooking up in that vindictive little mind of hers.

"Art told me what happened to Opal. I'm sorry to hear it. A kid like that will always break hearts. Judy tells me that some of these kids are just habitual runners. Can't stop. Like that ungrateful mutt that runs off when you're not looking."

Nara slapped her hard across the face.

Ella grabbed her red cheek, smart enough to back away,

for the next blow would be a closed fist. Chief for his part just cleared his throat as if to remind Nara they were in the middle of a transaction.

"You're gonna regret that, Nara Jean Stewart."

"No. I don't believe I will." Nara turned to Chief and signed on their account for the aspirin, then turned back to Ella. "Everyone knows you cook up hooch in your kitchen, so you better not go threatening my family if you want your husband to keep his job. From here on out, you damn well better mind your own business."

Nara turned her back on Ella and grabbed the aspirin off the counter. Chief nodded at her with an air of respect.

She jumped back into Papa's Studebaker and wondered if Ella had heard her ask about dosing for small kids. Ella didn't outright say she heard, but that wouldn't be her way.

When Nara arrived back at the ranch, she meant to go straight to Papa and Mama and let them know they might have trouble coming, but Patrick and Ivar were out on the porch talking. When Patrick saw her, his face brightened, and he jogged up to the auto. "How's it runnin'?"

"Like ten horses under the hood."

Ivar walked up to the auto with a swagger that was just a touch more humble than usual. He leaned into the window and said real low, "Nara, I've got a proposition for you and this boy."

Patrick near jumped out of his boots as he said, "He told me he wants ta train the mustangs."

Ivar chuckled at Patrick's enthusiasm. "Those mustangs seem to like the hills around my place. Can't get rid of them, and they're eating my grass anyway. Might as well have Patrick here take a few and see what he can do with them. I'd pay him, of course."

Nara looked at Ivar from the corner of her eye. "Patrick, let me talk to Ivar while you go shoo Blackie away from those chickens."

"All righty!" He fairly skip-hopped over to the coop where Blackie terrorized the chickens.

"You wanna hire my *Irish* boy?"

Ivar breathed out real hard as if admitting he was wrong would steal him of all his strength, and he was saving up for it. So long as they'd known each other, Ivar knew it was time to eat crow. "I will admit, when he came back out that second time, he worked as hard as any cowpuncher I've ever hired. You know, when my folks and your grandparents came here, they took homesteads and worked their butts off. People who come here now are just looking for a handout. Things have changed."

"There isn't any more land to give away, and anyway, it was never the government's land to give in the first place."

"True enough." He nodded.

"You know Mama won't like it one bit."

"I don't think they'll hurt him. He's got a real way with them, whispers funny words to 'em, and they nuzzle him like he's another horse. Strangest thing I've ever seen. Something tells me this is Patrick's path in life."

Nara raised a brow to that, Ivar not being much of the "feeling" type to make such an observation. "I'll talk to my folks. They'll want Patrick to be happy more than anything."

Ivar thumped the auto a few times on the hood and waved his goodbyes. Patrick came running over.

"Well?" he said with all his smiling teeth.

"I have to talk to Papa and Mama, but I think you should do this. That's my take."

He jumped up in the air and pumped his fist a few times.

"Patrick, you've got to be extra careful out there. A wild horse is a dangerous creature. We need you here. You're an important part of this family, kid."

Patrick blushed. "I will, promise. Ivar says he wants me ta start gentling a few of them on the weekends and after school sometimes."

"All right, but during the busy months and spring we'll need you around here more."

"That sounds fair. Ivar wants me ta show him 'that Irish magic stuff' I use on the mustangs ta get them ta be calm."

Nara got out of the auto. "Is he gonna use it on himself, or the mustangs?"

Patrick cocked his head and then laughed. "I don't think it will work on him."

Nara climbed up on the porch to take off her boots and consider that young boy. His feet barely touched the ground as his joy spread around their place like warm waves. There was a time when it didn't even occur to her that if she didn't marry and have a family, then there wouldn't be a Stewart to take over the ranch. And she hadn't spent one working minute wondering who would keep her company after her folks died. She'd just had her head down, digging in, trying to find her own place. It's funny how a person can be so shortsighted. She squinted over at Papa, who fiddled around with his steam tractor out in the yard. Maybe it was hereditary.

Later that evening after supper, Nara took Opal up to bed while Mama cleared the supper things. She didn't normally help Opal dress, but these days everyone had to pitch in wherever and whenever. "How's that arm feelin'?"

Opal twisted her mouth. "Okay."

"Just okay?"

Opal nodded.

"All right, I'm gonna help you on with your nightdress."

Nara gently wove her broken arm through the hole Mama had cut for her cast. Opal wasn't able to help out with too many chores just yet, though Mama had Opal down on the couch to keep her company. Opal must have read Nara's thoughts.

Her eyes tilted down with shame. "I can't take care of the chickens or help Mama in the kitchen."

Nara felt stunned the girl equated her worth with work, but on a moment's reflection, she shouldn't have been. "We're all just glad to have you back. You're important to us no matter what."

Opal gave Nara one of those smiles a person does when they liked what they heard but were afraid to show it. Opal said, "Am I gonna get better?"

"Mostly. It'll take time, and you'll have to learn how to do things with the one eye, but don't worry about that."

"Is my ma coming back?"

"No. I mean, she might try, but we aren't going to let that happen again."

Nara wrestled with what she ought to say. "Go to sleep and let the adults worry about keeping you safe."

Opal looked at her with a trace of skepticism. Nara couldn't blame her, couldn't hold the girl's eye. Nara felt so damn guilty for what happened. Her hand grasped the doorknob, but there were words to be said. Nara turned around. "Opal, I'm sorry I let them take you." Nara's eyes burned with tears. "All this is new to me. I did what I felt was right at the time, but it won't happen again. I promise."

Opal gazed at Nara so long and wordlessly, it nearly unnerved her. Finally, the girl nodded.

"Okay, get some shut-eye. Good night."

* * *

They had a few days of peace and quiet before the sheriff's wagon showed up in the yard. Art came to the screen door, took off his hat, and shot Nara an expression of apology. She shook her head, wondering when that man would get a spine and stop doing his spiteful wife's bidding. She let him in, but when Ella tried to come in after him, Nara slammed the screen door shut on her. "Patrick, go and fetch Charles."

"Nara, are you really going to make me stand out on your porch?"

Nara would have liked to push her down their porch steps, but she turned her back on Ella and contemplated the whole scene. Opal sat in her room, and the plan was she would remain there and keep quiet. No matter what she heard. Nara hoped that girl was on her bed, because even a little footstep could be heard from down here. Nara stomped around making as much noise as she could.

Papa sat at the table. "Take a load off, Art." He motioned to the table, but Art just shook his head.

Whatever he was out here for, he planned to do it standing.

Patrick and Charles came through the screen door. Charles had that feral, shiny aspect to his eyes. Without so much as a word, they walked up the stairs as if they had rooms up there themselves. Before Charles's head disappeared upstairs, he shot a murderous look at Art. It gave Nara the shivers.

John and Jim were both gone to the winter pens and wouldn't be back till sundown. If push came to shove, it was just her and Papa. The boys had been told to stay with Opal. Mama would stay in the kitchen. She tossed her towel over her shoulder and turned her back as if their visit meant nothing to her. Mama and Papa hadn't been speaking since Mabel's headstone had been moved and a wooden cross with Opal's name had been placed over her sister's resting place, the ground roughed up. It was just about the most harebrained plan they'd ever come up with, but after hours of arguing the other night, they couldn't conjure up anything that would work better than faking Opal's death.

Art cleared his throat and said to Papa, "Robert, I'm awful sorry to disturb you folks. I'm here because the Children's Aid Society and the mother have requested the body be sent on to California."

Mama slammed a pot down on the stove and kept on rummaging around the kitchen. Though Nara had never seen her mother so riled, Papa didn't even jump at the noise coming from the kitchen.

"Opal is laid to rest out here on my property. I can show you her grave, but there isn't anyone digging up anything on my land," Papa said.

If Nara's senses were right, Art didn't want to be here, for he fiddled with his hat for a time and finally said, "Will you show me the grave?"

Papa narrowed his eyes, considering Art for a good minute, but that man couldn't hold Papa's stern gaze and turned toward the window.

Eventually Papa scooted out his chair and stepped to the door. Nara and Art followed right behind. Ella stood on the porch with her arms folded across her chest. "I'm here as a representative of the Children's Aid Society. I have a right to be here."

Nobody paid her any mind. Papa put on his boots, slow as he pleased, while Nara watched the door to make sure Mama didn't come storming out of the house with a pot to pop Ella on the head. Art grabbed his wife by the arm and took her away to wait in the yard. Two automobiles pulled up. Ella smiled. One of them was a truck with an open bed and shovels. Nara's heart spiked at the sight. If Papa saw the autos, he gave nothing away.

"It's a bit of a hike." Papa waved his hand and ushered them toward the burial site under the pines.

The walk over to the grave site was stiff-backed, every nerve ending on fire. People had to believe Opal was buried there, but if they dug it up, they'd know for sure Opal was alive and, either one of those two things would just about kill Mama. Ella walked in front of Nara, with her fat bottom bumping around under her dress like the queen of something. Nara wanted to reach out and snap her damn neck. Times like this, she could truly understand how Charles could beat someone so bloody.

They proceeded through some taller grass and walked under the shade of the pine trees. An aroma of pitch fell over her. It brought back memories of pine needles rustling in the wind. Mabel being lowered into the dark ground, never to see the sun another day. Nara worried her sister would be cold. She had asked if they should bury her with blankets. Mama had looked at young, naive Nara and hugged her awfully tight, but they never did get blankets for Mabel.

Doors opened and shut from the automobiles parked on the road. One of them was a state trooper. He got out of his auto and put on the tall hat with the wide brim that troopers usually wore. Papa was forced to acknowledge their presence.

Papa only pointed to the grave where Mabel rested underneath the cross with Opal's name. Nara supposed his mouth couldn't say the lie. Maybe they should have let Charles run off with Opal. But two of them on the run didn't seem workable.

Workingmen got out of the pickup and began to pull shovels out of the open bed. Her mind raced for an alternative, another way. They'd see that coffin had been buried for years. Papa's jaw began to tense. He put his hands on his hips and walked up to the state trooper. "Can I help you?"

"Mr. Stewart?"

"You're looking at him."

"It seems you have a body on your property that doesn't belong to the family. I have papers signed by a judge in Billings right here."

"I don't give a damn what those papers say."

The trooper came face-to-face with Papa. "I don't want to have to put you in handcuffs, Mr. Stewart. Please stand aside."

Papa shook his head with a shine in his eyes. "You're not gonna pull that little girl from her rest. No God-fearing man out here is gonna do that."

Papa held the trooper's gaze.

The trooper for his part appeared unsettled and turned away from Papa to look out to the mountains beyond. "I have a job to do, Mr. Stewart, much as I don't like these New York people telling us how to do it. We've got papers signed by a judge here in Montana."

"She wasn't embalmed. How will you transport the body all the way to California like that?" Nara said.

From the look on the trooper's face, Nara could tell he hadn't been made aware of that little detail. Ella put herself into the middle of things. "Embalmed? I'm guessing Opal's not even dead. Your family is so stubborn. The law is *the law*. The girl was never yours."

A gunshot banged through the air like a cannon. Pine needles dropped all around their heads like nails. Everyone dropped for cover.

"Mama! You're gonna kill someone."

"I sure aim to!"

With just a small amount of experience, she cocked the other barrel for her next shot like she'd been doing it all her life. Those who hadn't dropped to the ground ran behind the tree trunks. But Papa stood his ground, chest out.

The trooper hadn't brought a rifle or pistol with him from the auto. "Ma'am, put down that gun!"

Mama squinted down the sight and pulled the trigger. A thunder of buckshot sprayed the air. Papa dropped to the ground, and more needles rained down.

On the ground, with a hand covering the top of her head, Nara watched in disbelief as her mother cracked open the shotgun, pulled slugs out of her apron pocket, shoved them into the back of the gun, and snapped the barrel closed. She trained the gun on Ella, who darted for cover. Nara jumped up and took off running. "Mama! No!"

Charles came out of nowhere and dove for the shotgun. His big hand swatted the barrel toward the ground just as it exploded, spraying the ground with pellets. Nara ran up from behind and grabbed the shotgun from Mama. She searched Charles over. It was a wonder the boy had managed to stay out of the spray of the gun, but he clutched at his ear, no doubt ringing from being so close to the shooting end. He waved his hand around in the air, burned from the barrel.

"God help me, I hate that girl with every fiber of my being."

"I know," Nara said, her breath struggling with a heavy chest. "Mama, they are going to . . . I don't think you ought to be here right now."

Mama went to her knees and her whole body shuddered. "How many times does that *girl* have to take Mabel from me?"

Nara crouched down to comfort her mama. Art was over calming the trooper, hands expressive. God only knew how, but Art must have convinced the trooper Mama was harmless, for he directed the men with shovels to resume their work. Spades sliced through the sandy soil. The shovels jammed in deeper. Mama sprang up out of Nara's hold and onto her feet. She ran to Mabel's grave and the young men with shovels. "You're gonna burn in hell for this. Don't you do it! Don't you dare!"

When they wouldn't listen, she wrestled with one of them for his shovel. He dropped it, and she picked it up and took off after the other digger, sending him scurrying. Then she turned to Ella with a look venomous enough to make Ella back up toward Art. She stumbled over a tuft of grass.

Papa saw what was about to happen and wrestled the shovel out of Mama's hands. With his sinewy arms, he threw it to the ground at Ella's feet with a look of undiluted hatred. "You are a foul creature, Ella Connelly. Get off my property before I let my wife do what's she been wantin' for near on twenty-five years."

He spat at her feet, all while keeping Mama from rushing at her. Charles tried to help Papa, but it was clear the boy didn't want to hurt Mama. Papa pulled and pushed, dragging Mama away from the grave site. She was beating on him. "You never once shed a tear over that grave! She was too young to be out there on that horse in the middle of the herd! I told you. Get that evil woman away from my baby's grave. Murderer!"

Ella's eyes went wide with understanding, and she put her hand over her mouth. "Oh."

To see Ella now, Nara could almost believe Ella felt guilty for causing the stampede that killed Mabel. For breaking Mama's heart not once, but twice. Papa managed to get Mama back to the house in all her bitter muttering and slapping at him.

There was only one other time Nara could remember seeing a look of remorse so boldly stamped across Ella's face. Not since they were up on the train bridge. Just young girls. They'd found white baby owls bundled up safely in a nest that lay underneath the bridge in a trestle. They held them like precious objects. Fluffy snowballs with gold eyes had blinked at them in wonder. A misplaced trust. Ella had said now that they'd touched them, the mother owl wouldn't take care of them, so she dropped those owls one by one into the river. Little plashes of white into the river, floating away.

Nara had yelled and Ella felt remorse in the end, but some things can't be undone. Nara would never forget Ella's crumpled face as she stared at those helpless babies floating away to their deaths. And she couldn't take it back. And now there was that same face. Ella covered it with her hands as Art ushered her across the scrubby grass to his paddy wagon.

Nara approached the trooper and his boys, ready to give everything she had to get them to leave. No way was anyone taking her sister's body from this soil. As she drew near, the trooper gave orders to his boys.

She stood before this man, hard chiseled jaw, stiffly pressed uniform. He was the law, justice, a thing her family needed more than air right now. The trooper averted his gaze from her and looked toward the house with softened eyes where Papa had led his heart-sore wife, stumbling in her misery. The trooper shook his head and said to Nara, "I don't give one damn what that bench order says. If the judge wants that girl dug up, let him come out here and do it himself."

Her mouth shivered with relief. "Thank you."

She strolled through the pines that sheltered her kin, walking off the adrenaline, thinking on things. Maybe it was the razor-sharp pine pitch or the brisk air, but it struck her that justice doesn't come about through rules or law, but rather it rises from the courage of just one person. Someone who holds power, and a strength of mind that yields to the better judgment of their heart. It doesn't matter whether they're a nobody, a somebody, or a big shot, so long as they have the temerity to put one finger on the scales.

* * *

Over the next many days, the Stewarts got back to their chores, cattle, and the coming winter. But everyone felt the weight of what lingered. The only thing they had on Ella was the still in her kitchen, and Papa made it clear he planned to use it. Most of the families in the county were dead set against liquor and wouldn't take kindly to the sheriff breaking the law in such an appalling way. He'd talk to people and make the threat of re-moving Art as sheriff as real as need be. Papa said he'd wait and see what Art and Ella would do first, because they'd need to hold that over their heads for a good long time, and he didn't want to use it unless he had to.

So when the automobile doors slammed out in the yard, nobody was surprised. Except Opal, who looked around like a scared fawn and then scuttled up the stairs. Papa and everyone else were out on the range. Nara shook her head, wondering why in God's name it was just her and Mama. "I'll handle this, all right?"

Mama didn't stop toiling at the sink. She just pursed her lips and looked out the window.

Nara closed her eyes, said a little prayer to the ceiling, and then opened the door. They stood there, faces long, unreadable. Nara waved them in with an unwelcome hand, but this had to be done. She'd have to make the threat herself, though it would frighten them a whole hell of a lot more coming out of Papa's mouth.

Ella wore overalls for perhaps the first time in her life. The knees dirty like she'd been tending her kitchen garden. Ella's gaze very smartly darted over to the kitchen with fear, but Mama didn't even turn around when they came in. She kept rattling around in the kitchen with a bang and a thud. Nara wasn't going to invite them to sit.

Art took off his hat and began without preamble. "Me and Ella went up to Billings and spoke to the judge who signed the order to exhume the body."

All the noise from the kitchen stilled. If a piece of straw hit the floor, Nara would have heard it. She grabbed the back of a chair, so full of rage the wood might have snapped under her grip.

"As a representative of the Children's Aid, my wife convinced the judge that Opal should be left to rest and the matter should be dropped. Children's Aid won't have any reason to come poking around out here." He handed Nara a copy of the bench order.

Nara leaned over the table for support, feeling like she'd just run her horse across the ranch and back. She took the paper in her hand and shook it in the air. "So this is done? You won't tell Clara or Children's Aid that Opal is alive?"

"This stops here." Art nodded toward Ella.

Ella stepped toward Mama, who kept her back to them all. "Mrs. Stewart, I'm sorry about everything. Trying to take these kids from you. I've been spiteful, but you should know that what happened all those years ago, it haunts me every night, you can't imagine."

A piece of silverware dropped to the bottom of the sink as Mama's hands went idle.

"Yes, I can. Every night when the lamp goes out, I see my girl in her last moments, and me helpless to save her," Mama said quietly, her broad back to Ella.

"I'm so sorry. I was just a girl. I'm sorry." Tears slipped down Ella's face.

Mama dried her hands and turned around. She looked at Ella good and hard, and then breathed out what Nara rightly hoped was all the bitter poison of twenty-odd years of grief that had been coursing through her mama's veins.

"It was hard losing Mabel, and . . . for so many years—I suppose too many—I've been hating you for it, but I reckon you regret what you did."

"I do. I wish I could go back to that day. I wish it so much, but I can't ever make it right."

Nara looked at Ella's troubled eyes and remembered that same look in Charles's, for they must surely feel the same about their past. Nara mourned how long her family had hung Ella out to dry. They should have forgiven her a long time ago. Things with the kids would have gone much smoother. It's funny how things come back on the people you love when you fail to forgive. That bitterness like poison until someone lets go, bleeds it out.

Mama nodded. "I've done enough wishing myself, so for all of us and my sweet girl, Mabel, I forgive you, Ella Connelly. Now, let that be the last of it."

Mama turned back around, her shoulders heaving.

"Thank you." Ella burst into tears and put her hands over her face. Art took her around the shoulder and guided her out the door.

Nara embraced Mama from behind. "I'm so sorry about Mabel. I know she would have been a better daughter to you than me." Nara's voice quavered.

Mama turned and took Nara's shoulders in firm hands and shook her. "Don't ever say that. Never. I couldn't ask for a better daughter, all I could ever ask for is to have both my daughters with me." Mama hugged Nara till all breath squeezed clean out of her lungs. "One thing I know is you're all different but perfect in your own way. Now go on out there and make sure their words stick this time."

"Okay, Mama."

She got a swat on the butt as she left for the porch. From the looks of it, Ella had all but run to the auto, likely needing a reprieve and a private moment. Didn't they all? Some time later, she'd go to Ella and ask her forgiveness for the years between them that lacked any kind of mercy.

Art stepped down off the porch and held on to the banister as if there was something he couldn't let go of. He fidgeted around for a time and then said, "I hope you can see your way clear to keep silent about the still in the kitchen. The money she makes feeds my young ones, or, I swear to you, I wouldn't let her do it. But I just don't have any other choice."

"I understand." She stared him down for a bit, remembering her own moment of desperation. The law she broke to protect Charles. "You know, Art, sometimes people do things in tough situations. Things they never thought they would, if you get my meaning."

He nodded. "I think we understand each other."

AFTER SUPPER THAT evening, Mama stood up and put her fists on the table. "I want Mabel's grave set to rights this very moment. I won't sleep a wink unless it's done."

Papa stood up and told everyone to get their butts out the door and put their boots on. "Jim, could use your help, too."

Nara jumped upstairs and put on a dress. A fitting tribute to Mabel, and a gesture to Mama of respect and love, and if she were being totally honest with herself, she wanted Jim to see her in it.

As they walked out to the family graves, the sun lay low, burning the sky with fiery rays. Like even that sun held on to a grievance and wouldn't rest. Papa signaled for everyone to stop, then whispered something in John's ear. Her brother nodded his head as if he'd been given the holiest command. He called Jim, Charles, and Patrick to him and the lot of them went off to the barn as if they all knew what happened next. They came out with some tools, Mabel's old headstone, and several roses wrapped in canvas. Mama put her hand over her chest and went over to the wheelbarrow and gazed at the white roses budding. She ran her fingers over white petals, glowing all the more in the low light.

"You remembered," Mama near whispered.

Papa nodded. "Mabel loved roses. I've always remembered. It's just never easy to talk about, think about."

Mama hugged him tight around his middle, and he rubbed her back as she sobbed into his shirt. "Shhh, now. That little girl has always been in a better place. It's just hard letting go."

Papa's eyes dripped with some of the first tears Nara had ever seen from him. Everyone stood around just then, somewhat in awe, until Nara began to walk. The others followed on, leaving Mama and Papa to their healing. All this time, Mama had resented Papa for Mabel's death. Nara supposed everyone felt guilty for what happened that fateful day, what any one of them could have done differently in a split second of time. If she hadn't been playing around with Ella, Mabel would be here right now. If Papa hadn't let Mabel cut calves, she'd be here, but you can't replay time. All you can ever do is face forward and forgive.

Everyone swished through the crispy grass to gather around Mabel's grave. Jim stood in the background. His square face unreadable as always. She imagined in another century he might have burned sage, offered smoke like a prayer, whispered something to the wind, but instead, he took off his Stetson and placed it across his broad chest. The wind swooped in from the north, smoothing Nara's dress against her body, making her feel exposed, feminine. Jim's dark eyes roamed over her womanly form. During the workdays in her dungarees, stiff men's shirts, and boots, she could cover up her feelings and femininity, but in this flimsy dress, a powerful yearning came over her. But it was not to be.

Jim and her had hovered over the last cigarette in his pack the other night. In the dusky light they passed that white roll back and forth like the kisses they couldn't share. He told her he planned on going back to the reservation to raise bison. He looked her straight in the eye and said, "There's nothing out here for me. At least not anything I can ever have."

Nara had stood there, her heart pounding, body shivering with intensity from the emotions coursing through her. He was right, but it felt all wrong, and maybe if they just tried. She began to talk, but he put his dark finger over her lips and shook his head. "Your family would never allow it. I would be run out of town, and if you went with me, you'd lose all this." He held his hands wide. "They'd never take you back, and all you'd ever have is an old Indian who can't find work half the time."

She shook her head, pulled his finger from her trembling lips, but nothing came out. Jim had laid out the whole truth, and there wasn't one damn thing to be said about it. Her eyes burned and tears dripped down her shirt.

He grasped her wet face gently with both of his hands and kissed her fiercely on the lips. His eyes so close to hers, their lashes touched. The yearning in those dark orbs so perfectly matched her own. "Nara, I ache for you every day. I can't stay here for much longer. Please understand."

He broke the moment, their chance for love, and left her standing alone and untried. Her heart yearned to chase him, turn him around, and stay in his way until he changed his mind or crossed the line that she couldn't. But something powerful kept her rooted to the earth she was born to. She had knelt on that hard ground, forehead supplicating to the unyielding range. There in that soil she lost herself, surrendered the most god-awful sobs, soaking her father's hard-won land with the bitterness and despair born of generations of intolerance.

The same land that had consumed her sister. They stood around her grave now, hands clasped. Nara lowered her head and wiped her wet face. Nobody would ever know or understand her pain. Just Jim. Even now, he stood close enough that she could grasp him, if only she had the courage to let go of everything else.

Papa and Mama joined them, arm in arm. Mama pointed her finger where she wanted the roses, and John began to break up the soil, throwing in a shovelful of manure here and there. When he'd finished and patted the ground, Charles and Patrick hefted the tombstone to put Mabel's grave to rights. Opal walked over and wrenched that cross back and forth from the ground with just one good arm, and an intensity little seen from her. "Thank you, Mabel," she whispered.

Opal tossed that cross out into the grass and walked over to Nara. The girl had something to say. It was unnerving, those dark blue eyes gazing up, one forever changed. The trouble they'd seen in her short life stared back at Nara. "Mabel was your sister?"

Nara nodded.

"I know Mama misses her."

Nara wondered why words so often fail at these times. "Well, she's got you now. And I do, too."

Nara's raw heart felt hungry to love, and without thinking about it, she pulled Opal up into her arms for the first time ever and settled the girl on her hip. All that softness melting into her made Nara wonder why she hadn't done it before. A tiny arm came around her shoulders.

Opal looked her right in the eye. "Does that make us sisters?"

Nara hugged that bitty girl up tight. "I don't know what we are, but one thing is for sure, we're family."

CHAPTER 26

MOTHER NATURE HAS A WAY OF PICKING HER MOMENTS, FOR winter that year in Montana had been cruel. A blizzard had come through, taking with it some of their cattle, but even so, the family huddled together around the table for their meals and worked through butt-chapping wind to keep their animals alive till next spring. Papa tied that rope from the bunkhouse to the outhouse just like he promised. Setbacks in Montana never stopped anyone from living, rather, it stirred up the fight and the will to endure.

The rains began like a reprieve. The snow melted, and the creeks filled up with clean water. Sweet grass for the coming year greened up the hills. Nara opened the screen door and ventured out to the porch with Papa right behind her, his guitar in hand. Mama had driven the kids to Billings to see a picture show. They now sat on the steps, taking off their boots and putting them in that long muddy line. Everyone found a place on the porch to rest and enjoy the first warm day. Papa's gentle strumming and whispered words whirled all around them.

Let's pretend those clouds are islands in the sky
Let's pretend we're up there just you and I
Oh, let's pretend no one knew where to
find us in the blue, blue sky

Nobody ever came for Opal, and folks out West sure don't
take their marching orders from big shots in big cities. Out here
the law doesn't decide, the land does, and there's room for anybody with a good heart and an iron will. Folks minded their
own beeswax as Opal returned to school. She'd grown an ap-
petite for reading and had been pilfering cowboy stories from
the bunkhouse. So Mama drove her into Billings for some "ap-
propriate" reading material.

The Stewarts had settled into their place like the roots of a
resilient tree anchored firmly in the soil, a thing Papa always
had his hands on. He offered Ivar a good price for some acre-
age, so Papa could connect his ranch to an abandoned parcel to
the north. The money got Ivar through the winter with enough
spare to start up a horse farm, but most importantly, it healed
the breach between them. Folks around the county began to
hear talk about the mustangs Patrick began training. By and by,
they'd come to understand the boy had two solid boots on the
ground that worked hard every day. Whenever the weather allowed, he spent time gentling them. Ivar boasted that Patrick
had halter-broke three already. Word got around. They hoped to
sell a few come this summer when they were fully broke. Papa
wanted to know how Patrick managed it, because for the longest time folks thought they weren't worth anything, that they

couldn't be tamed. Patrick claimed even the ones who wouldn't ever accept a saddle could be bucking broncs at the rodeo. Every creature has a place. Patrick and Ivar never managed to capture that little blue roan, Huckleberry. It's still out there somewhere, running free.

Opal grew a whole inch over the winter. She'd never be a chatterbox, but her and Mama had been making some fancy new dishes, stinking the house up. One of them caught fire. Papa came into the kitchen, put it out, and asked what they were cooking. Mama said it was a flambé. Papa said it sounded more like a disease than food. Opal put her hand over her mouth and giggled at the joke. Papa gave her a few tickly rib pokes and got a few more giggles out of the tiny girl.

John moved around western Montana to paint the big mountains and rocky rivers in all three seasons of fall, winter, and spring. He returned home with many paintings and stayed for a bit, but when summer came, it was time to say goodbye. Papa wished him luck. They shook hands and Papa told him he would expect to see him again real soon. Mama cried, but her arms weren't empty or idle for long. Nara drove John to Billings to take the big train east. As the engine pulled her brother away to New York, she prayed he would find his place. She returned with one of those new, short haircuts. Mama nearly had a coronary. Papa grunted from behind his paper and said, "Quit your fussin', woman. She's always got a hat on anyway."

Jim had a friend on the reservation who had some land, and Papa helped Jim get a bison stock operation started there. On Jim's last night, Nara'd walked the shivering moonlight hoping to find those dark eyes, but she couldn't make the stolen moment happen, and the next morning, he putted away on that motor-bike, back to his own world. For weeks, she had drifted about in a melancholy state of mind, barely minding her chores.

Meanwhile, Charles got the best grades in the whole school and would be done with his education in June, and all while doing the work of two men. He hadn't beaten anyone up, though there were a few close calls at school. Charles patiently waited for Nara to come around and put him in charge as foreman. Papa told her this year she and Charles would go to auction alone. Papa was going to start taking it a little easier, so Nara made Charles foreman. Together, they spent many chilly nights with their heads together at the supper table long after it went dark, planning out the year before them. Charles figured a way to put in more irrigation pipes with water towers, so they could grow more hay. That meant they could winter more cattle and expand someday. He would be a fine cattleman, and when it came his time, Nara would gladly hand over the reins.

There existed no blood that bound them all together, and it was for certain they were a different kind of family. Different ages, temperaments, and backgrounds, but they wound together sure enough, each thread of the rope different. Some flexible and soft, a few tough and bristly, others unbreakable, but together they made one damn hard twist.

ACKNOWLEDGMENTS

IT GOES WITHOUT SAYING THAT ANY AUTHOR WHO HAS WORKED well on thirteen years crafting stories, selling themselves, and their books, feels a great deal of gratitude to those who supported them along the way. The trouble is *not* remembering them, it's finding the room on the page to fit everyone.

My family, all of them, in one way or another, are in this book, whether they supported me through the frustrating years, or read my shitty first drafts, and countless re-drafts of this novel. My father is a voice you'll hear in the novel. He especially helped me edit the man fights, guns, old cars, and trains. He is a great reader of historical fiction. He read for me and provided feedback on all the many iterations of this novel. Family members inspired characters in the book: Jessica, Justin, and Kendall, my children and angels. Some did a lot of both—Jessica, my eldest child to whom this book is dedicated and who is the basis for Nara, must have read every part of this book twice over, lent me advice on story, especially my ending, which we debated back and forth, but mostly she lent her ear and good readerly advice. Jessica read widely, and had cancer not taken her from us, I suspect she would have eventually burned the midnight oil, scribbling like her mother. Nara is named for my maternal grandmother, another strong female figure in my family. I know she is up there smiling. My aunts, Marilyn, Linda, and Sharon, and Uncle Jim all read for me, gave me feedback on titles, offered up dirty words Grandma used to say, horsey business, lyrics to my grandpa's old songs, and books on Montana and trains. I could never have written this book without them all. To Peter, who first encouraged me to write as a profession, thank you.

I have a wonderful bunch of writer friends and mentors who helped me so immeasurably, not by blowing sunshine, but by telling me the honest-to-goodness truth and placing a reassuring hand on my back when necessary. Weina Dai Randel, who dropped what she was doing more times than I can count to help me out, read my first chapter time and again when I had stage fright and just couldn't get it right. Rachel Bodner, Julie Rose, Erika Robuck, Carolyn Johnson, Cindy Vallar, Kristin Swenson, John Krasznekewicz, Rebecca Elkins, and Laura Vogel: I am profoundly in your debt for your helpful feedback. Kathy McGuire, my lovely artist friend, lent me her ear and was an inspiration for me when I needed to focus on major revisions—again. She showed me what fortitude really looks like. Alexis Gargagliano and Casey Fuetsch: amazing editors who helped guide me along with their red pens and able advice. Last but not least, Andrew Wille, a kind and encouraging mentor, editor, and friend who taught me how to TELL a story, not write one: Thank you so very much.

To my agent, Marly Rusoff, who found me at the most difficult time in my life, but never gave up on me. There are no words that cut it. I am so grateful and blessed to have crossed this kind woman's path. A force to be reckoned with in the literary world, but easily the warmest person you'll ever meet. And obviously the most patient.

To my lovely new editor, Lucia Macro, who is as lively and generous today as when I first met her at the Historical Novel Society in 2017. Asanté Simons for all her tireless efforts. I'm at least twenty lattes in your debt or will be by the time you've helped me usher this story into the world. I look forward to many years of working together with you both, publishing big-hearted stories that make readers cry, smile, and hope.

About the author

About the book

Insights,
Interviews
& More . . .

Meet Dianna Rostad

Jaden Photography

DIANNA ROSTAD was born and raised in the Pacific Northwest. Her parents and extended family come from the ranches of Montana and the farms of Arkansas. Dianna raised three kind human beings, and when they began to test their wings, she took to writing with a passion, completing Southern Methodist University's Writer's Path program in 2009. A favorite task of her creative endeavors is researching the people and places where her novels are set. She has traveled extensively to pursue the last artifacts of our shared history and has breathed life, truth, and hope into her novels. Now living in Florida, Dianna continues to write bighearted novels for wide audiences everywhere. ∽

Behind the Book

I read an article on CNN's website back in 2008 about the orphan train. I became so fascinated by this little-known adoption phenomena and decided it would make a riveting story. Since that time, I've been working on this project. When my father came to Texas for Christmas in 2010 and brought pictures of his parents' old ranches in Montana and of him there as a boy, I was delighted by all the family history and decided to set my book in Montana.

My father gave me a reading list of books by the likes of Larry Watson and Ivan Doig, both seasoned Montana writers he favored. Much of the characters, their lives, their voices, and the songs in this book have been lifted from pages of my family's history. My aunt Marilyn transcribed old lyrics from my grandpa Montana Bill's songs and other songs that were passed around in his time in Montana. I spent some time in the Billings area at the Yellowstone Historical Society and Yellowstone Museum researching what ranches looked like in 1925, the terrain, the animals. I sniffed the air, took pictures of local flora, climbed inside an old steam train. Read oral histories from the folks who lived there, indigenous and settlers. In the book, the story about Jim's brother being shot is sadly a true story.

The real passion to write about orphans must have come from my first "big girl job" as I often call it. I worked as a case manager for a Job Training Partnership Act (JTPA) program in Los Angeles after the riots there in the '90s. I had a caseload of youthful offenders, and it was my job to get them a job. Despite their circumstances, these young people were so open and reaching for the next rung on the ladder. They still had hope. Kids who've had to live by their wits on the streets will always have a special place in my heart.

It was often the case that predators of all kinds—wolves, coyotes, and grizzlies—were destroyed to protect stock without regard. Though I dramatize scenes of their destruction, it is not this author's opinion that they should be destroyed. Today, we understand better that these creatures are a valuable part of our ecosystem and should be protected as sentient beings.

The wild horses in this book were based on the Pryor Mountain mustangs that roamed the hills in the southeastern part of Montana. With all our many resources, I'm ashamed to say that the American mustang is as much at risk of destruction today as it was in 1925. They live with terrifying helicopter ►

roundups, separated from their bands, and live in crowded pens only to be destroyed or sold off. It's no way for a majestic creature to live. Just as Patrick portrays in my book, these animals can be gentled, and adoption is real and viable for these horses and burros. If you want further information, I recommend these sources:

- www.wildhorseeducation.org
- www.blm.gov/programs/wild-horse -and-burro
- www.americanwildhorsecampaign .org/
- *Unbranded* is a documentary film about four young men who adopt wild horses, gentle them, and then take them on an epic journey from the Mexican border to Canada to prove that mustangs are adoptable and viable animals.

The Children's Aid Society as portrayed in my book is still an operating social welfare institution. The contracts and postings in my book are paraphrased but come directly from old posts and artifacts. The way I portrayed the adoption is consistent with the way the Society operated and how children were adopted out with a little flair here and there. Their work helping children, first started by Charles Loring Brace, is still alive today. If at any time in my book I seem to disparage this Society, it was only for fictional effect. On balance, I believe they saved so many young people from the streets, and that they have done and still do so much good in this world.

You can read the full history of the Society here: www.childrensaidnyc.org /about/history-innovation. ᧞

Reading Group Guide

1. What do you think the wild horses represent or symbolize in the book?

2. At spring roundup, Opal is in harm's way and Charles steps in to protect her in the only way he knows how. When, if ever, is it okay to use violence as a form of punishment, protection, or justice?

3. Do you think Papa should have taken a stand against the people who slurred Patrick rather than encouraging him to hide his Irish lilt?

4. When Patrick prayed and made the sign of the cross against his chest, how different were the reactions of Mama and Papa Stewart to his Catholicism? Were they substantially different?

5. Charles protects Patrick from racist slurs at school by filling Billy's mouth with dirt and holding it closed. This is progress for Charles, but if he were your son, would you correct him, and if so, how?

6. Charles and Patrick go about things very differently and have unlike dispositions. How does it inform

the way they see and treat animals?
Their horses?

7. Nara's actions toward the kids are
   unmaternal at best. How does it
   contrast with her behavior toward
   the little horse caught on the fence?
   Did you think she'd ever make a
   good mother to the three orphans?

8. Were the children of this day and
   time better left in orphanages and
   asylums in New York or sent out on
   the train to the farms and ranches?
   Overall, do you think the orphan
   train was a better adoption program/
   foster care system than we have
   today? How would you compare
   them?

9. Nara tells her father that she wants
   Jim, their Cheyenne ranch hand, to
   be foreman. Papa says, "Ain't nobody
   gonna take orders from him." Was
   the racism in his reply representative
   of 1925 and the reality of that time?

10. Did Nara's unwillingness to admit
    that she was interested in Jim make
    you believe she was prejudiced?

11. Jim clearly tries to fit into the
    world beyond the reservation by
    how he dresses and cuts his hair,
    but ultimately, does it do him any ▶

good? If you were Jim, would you
have gone back to the reservation?

12. If it's the only way to raise livestock,
do you think it's okay to round up
wild mustangs and use them for
chicken feed to preserve forage for
stock?

13. Consider Opal's predicament at the
end of the book and the decision
made by Children's Aid. If that
happened today, what do you think
the response would be from our
social services?

14. How do you think the ranchers'
staunch individualism manifests
itself in our culture and politics
today? Why do you think it evolved
in our rural areas?

15. How do you feel the landscapes of
our world affect our social
interactions with others? The way we
interpret justice?

16. Do you think Mama Stewart was
happy in her marital/family role?
How does Nara's attitude about
women's roles play into her mother's
happiness in the story?

17. How does Nara's attitude toward
right and wrong differ from

Charles's? How do these two views converge in the book?

18. If Charles had been raised from birth by the Stewarts, how would he differ from the young man they encountered?

19. At the end of the novel, was justice served by the trooper? By what measurement or process can we effect justice in our world? ∾

Further Reading

40 Years' Gatherin's by Spike Van Cleve (1977)

Breaking Clean by Judy Blunt (2003)

Fourteen Cents & Seven Green Apples by Lee Rostad (1992)

Hard Twist: Western Ranch Women by Barbara Van Cleve (1995)

The Orphan Trains: Placing Out in America by Marilyn Irvin Holt (1992)

Orphan Trains: The Story of Charles Loring Brace and the Children He Saved and Failed by Stephen O'Connor (2001)

The Story of Five Montana Pioneer Families: Server, Getchell, Ross, Pokarney and Buzzetti, edited by Rickard A. Ross (2014)

Tracks of the Iron Horse by Ray Grensten (1984)

We Rode the Orphan Trains by Andrea Warren (2001)

When Montana and I Were Young by Margaret Bell (2002)